Seasons in MANANA

Delmer T. Cook
with Scott P. Cook

Legacy Book Press LLC
Camanche, Iowa

This book is dedicated to Coach Ray Snyder who didn't just teach us how to hit the cut-off man, but more importantly, how to comport yourself with grace and dignity in victory and defeat.

Table of Contents

Preface

It was some time in 1972 or 1973, probably right around my sixth-grade year. My brothers and I, along with some neighborhood pals, were playing baseball down at the Manana Baseball Field, located just down the grassy hill from the Manana Navy-Marine Housing area where we lived. It wasn't an official Little League practice or game—just a loosely organized sandlot scrimmage. Or we might have been simply just taking turns batting the ball around. Official Little League game or not, it was quietly understood by most of us that we were sharpening our skills for when the next season started. Now there are many skills to be sharpened when it comes to baseball, but by far the most fun to be had is when you work on your batting skills.

It was a typically gorgeous and sunny Hawaiian day. It could have been July, it could have been January. I was playing second base, or maybe center field, I can't remember. At the time I was feeling pretty good about myself because when I was at the plate to take my ten swings, I had not only launched one over the ball field fence, but over the Manana Housing Swimming Pool fence, just a few yards beyond! Everyone, including myself, apologized profusely to the lifeguard—after all, several young female pool patrons had screamed when the ball splashed into the pool waters. After giving us the expected 'Next time I won't give the ball back' lecture, the lifeguard finally tossed our ball back to us. I was a little chagrined... but far more thrilled at what I had accomplished with that mighty swing of the bat! For me, it was a new milestone.

I was *so* proud that I was now a member of the hit-it-in-the-pool-club that I could barely pay attention to my brother Eric's constant complaining about the "lousy cork bat" his friend Barry had convinced him to use. I think the bat was actually fiberglass – all we knew was that it was a short-lived early 70s experiment in futuristic baseball equipment. Supposedly our generation would come to love these new-fangled bats, but the fact is, we hated them. It seemed every time you connected with the ball, your hands and entire lower arm vibrated like you were being electrocuted. The attraction of these cork/fiberglass bats was that they were supposed to be indestructible—no cracking, no splitting. There was even a magazine ad for these bats showing a karate black belt weeping as his arm was in a sling, his hands heavily bandaged. Even *he* couldn't put a dent in the cork/fiberglass bat!

As for me, I had hit *my* over-the-pool-fence home run with my beloved dark blue *aluminum* bat. Yes, kids in the early seventies were gravitating slowly away from the old trusty wooden bats, to the new, neon-colored aluminum bats—though as my younger brother Kevin proved, these *could* be dented if you connected with a metal dugout pole.

All this to say, it was a pretty good afternoon of Hawaii baseball... until that guy showed up.

My buddy, Chuck Denno, happened to be lounging in the dugout. The Manana Field dugouts were truly old-school: a low, wavy, and rusted sheet-metal roof covered a long splinter-filled, green-painted wooden bench. A chain link fence that fronted your view of the ballfield made for a truly shadowy and cage-like atmosphere inside. But it helped keep you cool when you weren't on the field. Why Chuck wasn't out on the field playing at that juncture, I don't know—maybe he was waiting his turn at bat or he just felt like taking a break. In any event, he probably wished he hadn't chosen that particular moment to loiter in the dugout.

He seemed to appear out of nowhere: this long-haired, brown-skinned guy wearing beat-up clothes and clutching some kind of container in his hand. He was slightly built, in his late teens or early twenties, or at least I so ascertained from his wisp of a moustache and maybe whiskers. I didn't get the clearest look at him from my vantage point out in the field, he may have been Polynesian, maybe Asian-Filipino. But there was a vaguely out-of-it manner about him. He sauntered into the dugout and sat down a few feet from Chuck.

This didn't look good but we all kept playing, all the while keeping a wary eye on what this character might do. It didn't take long. After hunkering over the container in his hands, the odd young fellow straightened up and turned to Chuck. He seemed to say something to Chuck. I saw my good friend and schoolmate take in what the fellow had to say, then turn to face out towards the field. A few moments later, Chuck casually rose to his feet and walked past the strange character, out of the dugout and onto the field. Chuck quickened his steps as he approached me.

"What happened?!" I asked.

Chuck continued to act casual, but his tone was urgent. "We should get outta here."

I pressed him. "What did he say to you?"

Chuck repeated the two words the strange guy said to him. The first of those two words was, *You*. The second half of the salutation was a word I heard often at school. It was quite a non-complimentary slur that began with an F and (in Hawaii) usually ended with an A, rather than the more standard non-Hawaiian K or R consonant. But there was more.

"Oh yeah," added Chuck. "He's in there sniffing glue."

In many ways, that afternoon at the ballfield, that incident, encapsulated my Hawaii experience of 1971 to 1974. Not my baseball experience, mind you, but the overall experience. The good, the bad, the ugly. Hawaii was all of those things. And yet how do I look back on my childhood Hawaii years? Fondly. Quite fondly. To many people that may not make sense, but it's the truth.

Why is it that certain periods of one's life seem to have a special pull? Like a magnet, they seem to consistently draw thoughts in their direction. In his later years, my Grandpa Smiley seemed to always be talking about his youthful days living in the California Mojave Desert. Those memories seemed to make him happy—a place to which he could drift away, feel secure and peaceful. Was his fixation on that place and time purely random, or did those days hold some special key to his heart that we, his grandchildren, could never truly understand?

The older I become, the more I can identify with this phenomenon. In my case, that magnet has always been my boyhood days in Hawaii. For many years I've tried to analyze why that is. Yes, it was a happy time, but I had happy times before, and many happy times since. There were also unpleasant things about that period that are still vivid in my memory. True, Hawaii had several "paradise" qualities, but a true paradise-on-earth it was not. I've given up searching for answers. It is what it is. I imagine it's inevitable that when I am ninety years old I will be regaling my great-grandchildren with stories of "my days on the Islands." I apologize in advance.

In a sense I wonder if a book length story is even necessary to convey what it was like to be a kid in Hawaii during those magical years of 1971 to 1974. Truthfully, just listen to *Love's*

Theme by Barry White's Love Theme Unlimited Orchestra, and that will tell you just about all you need to know. This early-stage-of-disco instrumental came out in 1973 and was played constantly on island pop radio well into 1974. It's all there: the strings that conjure up the fragrant, sunny breeziness of the islands; the glory, optimism and energy of being young; the wah-wah guitar that speaks of the early 70s like no other pop instrumentation can, and most of all, the arching oh-so-very-Hawaiian guitar licks you hear in the intro. Yet underneath all the "happy" and "sunny" and "island paradise," there is just a hint of gravitas that seems to say, *"Don't relax too much—there are unseen dangers lurking in the shadows."*

For those who aren't all that into impressionistic paintings, however, I will be more specific. I mostly remember those Oahu years of 1971 to 1974 as an idyllic time of swimming in the ocean off white sand beaches, planning adventures (and telling ghost stories) in gloriously ramshackle neighborhood club houses and forts, playing sports in the streets with a myriad of friends. But most of all, baseball. Yes, baseball—the number one obsession harbored by my brothers and I during our Hawaiian sojourn; our national pastime in an island setting.

In so many ways, Hawaii is baseball and baseball is Hawaii. And that's not simply because that's where I learned to love the game. Baseball is big in Hawaii. Because of the warm weather, you can play it year-round, and innumerable island kids do. Hawaii Little League teams have made noise in several Little League World Series from the 1970s to present (four LLWS champions have come from Hawaii). Major League Baseball immortals like Babe Ruth, Lou Gehrig, Joe DiMaggio, and Barry Bonds all swung a bat there.

Oh, and ever heard of a guy named Alexander Joy Cartwright? He's only considered by many to be the Father of Baseball. Cartwright came up with the rules for the modern game and his New York Knickerbockers played the first recorded baseball contest. Shortly thereafter, Cartwright moved to Hawaii, continuing to promote the game there. Which means... baseball was big in Hawaii before 99 percent of the rest of America caught onto it! Hey, Cartwright is even buried in Honolulu!

The glories of playing baseball and otherwise indulging in all manner of island recreations notwithstanding, I still have to concede that my idyllic, vaguely *Lord of the Flies* existence was on a collision course with a darker world: that of the growing militant youth counter-culture of the time. Sure, there was still a significant and lingering element of Flower Power that hung in the pop culture atmosphere of the islands in the early 70s. Peace Sign jackets and jeans patches were everywhere, not to mention TV ads extolling the virtues of "Peace" and "Love." Hey, in elementary school we even sang, "I'd Like to Teach the World to Sing (in Perfect Harmony)," a song that also happened to be featured on a popularly running Coca Cola TV commercial, and that included lyrics extolling (you guessed it), Peace and Love. Still, by 1971, the era of Flower Power and Peace and Love had begun to morph into something darker: the Manson Family, the Yippies, the Weathermen (bomb-happy youth radicals), the Black Panthers... and the Symbionese Liberation Army. That's where my Hawaii experience took a chilling turn.

All I did was relay an interesting family anecdote to our babysitter, Cindy Medlock, that fateful night in 1973. We were engaged in the most innocent of activities: a Parker Brothers board game played on our family living room floor. Normally I wouldn't be so eager to share family secrets with a babysitter, but Cindy was different. We were good friends with her family, but more importantly, I had a crush on her. It was a crush that, to me at that age, resembled true love. Unrequited and out of reach love to be sure, but I was moonstruck nonetheless.

But Cindy didn't respond to my fascinating slice of family history the way I wanted her to and I felt pretty hurt. Insulted, in fact. We went back and forth about it briefly, but she finally dropped the subject (seeing how I was getting upset and throwing a minor tantrum). It shouldn't have been that big of a deal, but that seemingly innocuous bit of ancestral trivia I shared with her is what laid the groundwork for the horror to come.

Which is why my memories of our stay in Hawaii back in the early 1970s should actually be clouded in trauma. In no way should I remember those years fondly considering what I experienced that spring of 1974. For that memory alone I could be excused for altogether blocking those Hawaii memories of 1971 to 1974. Surprisingly, however, that is not the case. In spite of it all, I still retain quite fond memories of that time and place. It's not that I escaped that particular watershed experience with no lingering trauma. For years afterward, I had to contend with a growing sense of guilt that had I not been *so* enamored with Cindy Medlock, events would not have played out as they did. She would still be alive today. Married. A family. A happy and fulfilled senior-aged woman, still sharing holidays with family, loved ones. Thanks to the support of *my* family, not to mention years of counseling, I have been able to come to terms with it. Now, it is mostly the good times upon which I choose to linger.

My name is Alan Cook, and in the spring of 1974, I was having an All-Star season as a Little League baseball player. During the course of that baseball season my name was all over the newspapers in Hawaii. But one thing had nothing to do with the other.

Chapter 1
November 1973: I Should Never Have Mentioned It

This was destined to be a night that changed everything, though it didn't seem so at the time. Even as adults we rarely recognize when that seemingly insignificant word or action becomes the point where we actually cross the Rubicon and life is forever turned on its head. How much less so an elementary-age school kid?

We boys were spending the evening in the company of our babysitter, Cindy Medlock. I was about to turn twelve by then and in the weeks prior, I loudly insisted to my parents that I was way past the age where I needed a babysitter, even when they were gone on overnight trips. I could look after my obnoxious brothers by myself, and often did. However, John was sick and my folks wanted someone more adult there in case his temperature went up.

So when Mom announced they were talking to our good friends, the Medlocks, about Cindy coming over that particular evening, I kept my mouth shut. I was still besotted with Cindy Medlock. More than a kid crush—I considered it to be my first true awakening of romantic love. Of course she would never consider a kid like me as a romantic suitor. I was worldly enough even at that age to acknowledge this reality. But who knew—let three or four years go by, and perhaps Cindy would come around to what a highly-mature-for-my-years teen boy I would have become by then. Add to that the fact that I would *also* be a highly publicized high school baseball star by that time. How could Cindy Medlock NOT fall for me eventually, even with the age gap? By the way, how old would I have to be to legally marry Cindy? Sixteen? Seventeen? I wasn't sure. I did know a good many people got married in their teens (though looking back, the lion's share tended to be the women who owned up to being teens when they walked down the aisle).

For now, however, I was just happy to have an audience with this intoxicating teen princess. She had only grown more beautiful the last two years—long, shiny, raven black hair and dark eyelashes—the very picture of early 70s female desirability. Yes, the problem still existed. That I could tell, she was still dating the detestable Eddie Tangen. Surely, though, she couldn't possibly be enamored enough with this guy to stick with him long term.

Thank goodness Eddie would not be there when Cindy was to come over that evening. Mom assured me she would see to that. That was all I needed to hear. I would have Cindy to myself! Oh sure, my three brothers would also demand her attention, but they were too young and dumb and girl-hating to want Cindy's attention for extended periods—they would rather just fight amongst themselves and watch their favorite TV programs. Me, I would talk and joke with Cindy, show off my undeniable funny sense of humor. She would appreciate that.

Here's how it all went down that November evening in 1973. We boys and Cindy were sprawled out on the golden shag rug carpet of our living room floor, playing a board game called MASTERPIECE: THE ART AUCTION GAME. It was one of those early 70s board games that tried to compete with

Monopoly, only in this case you rolled the dice, moved your pegs, and then tried to buy or bid on rare works of art. Or something like that. All I know is, my youngest brother, John, was already in bed. My two younger brothers, Eric and Kevin, were busy battling to win and were focused primarily on that. Me, I was focused on talking to Cindy—and she was actually conversing with me as someone she *liked!* Then I told her about the real estate. I guess I was thinking along those lines because this board game had to do with objects of great value and wealthy people who could afford to own such objects. In any event, it occurred to me to tell Cindy about something Mom had shared with us boys a couple of weeks ago.

"You know what, Cindy? Our great-great grandparents owned most of downtown Los Angeles!"

Cindy looked at me with a disbelieving, bemused expression. "Nah uh, you're making that up."

I had her interest! No time to let up now: "No way! It's true. They told me!"

"Who told you that?"

"Mom did!"

Cindy still wasn't convinced. "How could they own all of downtown L.A.?"

I knew the answer—or at least thought I did. "They lived there when it was all just farm land! So they bought it all up and they grew orange trees."

Cindy had the most peculiar expression on her face, as if she wasn't sure whether to laugh or get angry. I was hoping she would try to "fight" with me, try to force me to admit I was lying. That's how teen romances get started—or so it seemed from watching TV. Then, she finally turned very serious. TOO serious. "You know, that land was actually stolen. It belongs to the Indians who lived there first."

I was crushed. The romantic moment was ruined, and what's more, I felt insulted. I lashed back. "It was not stolen!

The Indians weren't living there when my great-great grand-parents bought it. So they didn't steal anything!"

Cindy maintained her now schoolteacher-like demeanor. "Alan, that really doesn't matter. It's still stolen land. Maybe they didn't mean to do..."

I wasn't about to hear it. "My grandparents were good, honest people! You don't even know them!"

"There's a lot you don't know about, Alan. Eddie Tangen has studied this history and he could tell you...."

Eddie Tangen! She had actually stooped to bringing Eddie Tangen into the conversation! That's all I could stand and I couldn't stand anymore. I angrily shoved the pegs and playing cards, then leaped to my feet. "I don't want to play anymore."

Cindy lowered her head and turned quiet. It was if she realized she had gone too far. Finally, she apologized. "I'm sorry, Alan. I didn't mean to hurt your feelings. We just won't talk about it."

I plopped back to the floor and continued the game. I was still fuming over what Cindy Medlock had said. But hey, I still had a crush on her and wanted to be in her company. Nevertheless, the conversation was a little stilted for the rest of the evening until my parents came home.

I saw little of Cindy after that, but that was kind of okay. I remained somewhat miffed at her. Nevertheless, I continued believing somewhere down the road we'd patch things up and continue our "relationship," such as it was.

Chapter 2

Bizarre News: The Kidnapping of Heiress Patty Hearst

When Dad and Mom were taking in the evening news on TV, I was usually (and often seemed to be) sprawled out on the floor, reading a comic or a baseball magazine. True, I did momentarily come to life when the sports news came on, particularly when it involved Bill Walton of UCLA, the University of Hawaii Rainbows basketball team (who we followed on local TV), or anything having to do with *baseball,* whether it be Major League Baseball or news of our local Hawaii Islanders Minor League team.

But in February of 1974, Dad and Mom were transfixed by an ongoing and bizarre news story that was unfolding on the mainland, particularly Bay Area California where some of our relatives lived. It seemed a young heiress named Patricia Hearst had recently been kidnapped in Berkeley, California, by a band of radicals who used a multi-headed cobra emblem as their symbol. I could picture the University of Berkeley because my aunt and uncle had taken us to the campus only a month before we sailed to Hawaii—and let me tell you, long-haired radical "freaks" (mind you, that's what they called *themselves*) were everywhere!

On this particular night, Dad and Mom watched as the newscast played the latest tapes on which the kidnapped Hearst girl spoke to the world. I can still hear her drone in a dead-pan voice:

> "Mom, Dad, I'm okay. I had a few scrapes and stuff, but they washed me up and they are getting okay. I am not being starved or beaten or unnecessarily frightened. These people aren't just a bunch of nuts. They have been really honest with me, but are perfectly willing to die for what they believe in."

It was one of those really weird counter-culture crime stories you thought only existed on episodes of *Hawaii Five-O* or *Dragnet*. This story even got traction at Highlands Junior High School where I was now a student. I know, because we talked about it in Ms. Mansho's class. Every morning she had a list of Top Five Current Events Stories that we would briefly discuss before getting into the main lesson. The Patty Hearst kidnapping was frequently one of those Top Five stories.

Ms. Mansho addressed the class. "In review, why does this group call themselves the SLA? What does that stand for?"

One of the smart girls raised her hand. "It stands for Symbionese Liberation Army."

"That's right," said Ms. Mansho. "And what is this group demanding in addition to money?"

The same smart girl raised her hand. "They want food for the poor people."

"Correct," answered Ms. Mansho again. "They're demanding that the Hearst family provide free food for underprivileged people in the San Francisco Bay Area. So... what do you think about that? How does that make you feel?"

There was a pregnant pause of stone silence as we all mulled this over. Finally, the smart girl raised her hand again. Ms.

Mansho deliberately averted her eyes from the raised hand. "From someone we haven't heard from yet."

Another pause of silence, but finally, one of the other active participants in class—the boy who always wore large glasses and Aloha shirts—raised his hand. "I think it's really good to help poor people. But it's wrong to do it this way—kidnapping a girl and all that stuff. They should still go to jail."

Ms. Mansho solemnly nodded her head, clearly waiting for someone else to weigh in. Suddenly, a burst of enlightenment—I had something to contribute! You always waited for such rare opportunities (well, rare for me anyway) because Ms. Mansho counted participation in class discussion towards your grade. Ms. Mansho saw my raised hand and pointed towards me.

"How come the Hearst family has so much money?" I asked in my most why-is-this-so voice.

"That's an excellent question, Alan," said Ms. Mansho. She turned to the class. "Does anyone here know how the Hearst family made their fortune?"

You could have heard a pin drop. Even the smart girl didn't know, though she did take a faint stab at it: "Because they own so much land?"

Ms. Mansho decided to field the question herself: "Not so much from land. Patricia Hearst comes from one of the wealthiest families in the United States. Her grandfather was William Randolph Hearst who made his fortune in the newspaper industry. He created the nation's largest newspaper chain and for several years he dominated the media..."

Patty Hearst.

It was the first thing that leapt to mind that night Mr. and Mrs. Medlock came over to our house. Normally they arrived at our house wearing big how-are-ya smiles on their faces. Not on this night. Their faces said it all: something was wrong.

It wasn't so much Mr. Medlock, he could be grim and stone-faced when he wanted to be. But the distraught and teary-eyed expression on the face of Mrs. Medlock shook me to the core. Something bad had happened.

I hung back as I heard Dad, Mom, and the Medlocks converse in low tones. Even so, I could hear the sobs in Mrs. Medlock's voice. Dad turned to me. "Alan, you and the boys stay in your rooms for a while. We're going to talk out here."

I knew what that meant. Whatever the adults were going to talk about, it wasn't for us kids to hear. But in the days that followed, while my folks didn't divulge the details of what was discussed, there was no hiding the basic fact of what had happened. Cindy Medlock had disappeared. And I couldn't help but think about all those eerie news stories about Patty Hearst.

Chapter 3
Arrival in the Aloha State

"Aloha, Cook family! Welcome to Hawaii!"

We had just entered the Aloha Tower terminal as arriving passengers and this was the   greeting we received that sunny morning in March of 1971. As per Hawaiian custom, our necks were graced with plumeria flower leis. A pretty standard, conventional island greeting for arriving mainlanders. Oh, and by the way, we Cooks had already been prepped, prior to arrival, as to what the term, *Aloha*, meant. It was (and is) a term used in greeting, as well as a term to wish you a fond farewell. We learned that on the passenger ship we took over to the islands in the form of a tourist film that initiated visitors as to what to expect once they arrived in Paradise. One segment from that film showed several islanders saying "Alo-ha!" into the camera.

Only our traditional Hawaiian greeting didn't come courtesy of lovely island maidens, but rather from a couple of grizzled Marines in uniform. That alone should have been a portent of what was to come—that the Cook family was about to begin a vastly new and decidedly peculiar chapter in our lives.

Even the way our family was transported to the Islands was rather unorthodox, especially for a young officer military family. Sure, ocean liner voyages from the mainland to Hawaii were the norm, say, in the 1930s and 1940s, whether you were traveling there as a tourist or to relocate. By 1971, however, most mainlanders traveled to Hawaii by jet plane, though a minority of mainland tourists might indulge in an ocean liner voyage as part of their Hawaiian vacation. The fact is, it was *not* standard U.S. military procedure to splurge for the cost (not to mention the added transport time of several days) to relocate rank and file servicemen and servicewomen, as *well* as their spouses and children, from the mainland to their new duty stations in Hawaii via week-long ocean liner voyages. But that's exactly what happened in our case—and when I say "our" case, I am referring to my U.S Navy chaplain father, my mother, and we four Cook boys. It wasn't a mistake, but rather a quirk of the non-standard middle-of-the-year deployment schedule that pulled my father from his previous duty station in Millington, Tennessee, to his new duty station on Oahu. In short, given the odd circumstances of Dad's middle-of-the-year transfer (to cover another chaplain's sudden departure), Navy authorities made concessions for us simply to sail to the islands aboard the *U.S.S. President Wilson*, rather than fly us over.

A seven-day-long voyage across the Pacific, at first blush, seems to give one a warped, distorted perspective as to how distant the Hawaiian Islands lie from the United States mainland. Then again, maybe such a lengthy ocean crossing is the *truest* reflection of how isolated a destination, indeed, is Hawaii. In fact, I read somewhere that Hawaii is the most remote point of civilization on the face of the earth! I still find that hard to believe, simply because there is so *much* civilization to be found on the Hawaiian Islands (on Oahu especially). Sure, majestic, volcanic-shaped mountains, swaying palm trees, and lush jungle-like forests abound, but so do cities with skyscrapers, expansive suburban home tracts, as well as several U.S. military bases.

Moving into Momalani: A Four Month Holding Tank

Fortunately, the U.S. Navy had a home set aside for us upon our arrival in Hawaii. It was a rental house located in a sub-urban tract of Pearl City known as Momalani. Laid out on the side of a very steep hill, this house was to be our four-month holding tank until a unit was freed up in the nearby military housing community. Our modest one-story Momalani home was about halfway up the hill, sandwiched between two simi-lar houses. The homes were terraced in such a way that as we stood in our tiny backyard, we could almost take a running leap and land on the roof of the house next door. This made for a breathtaking view of Pearl Harbor in the distance be-low. On clear days, the Honolulu skyline was visible, with the shadowy form of Diamond Head crater just beyond. From our vantage point it seemed like the harbors and beaches of Oa-hu's leeward side were a vast stage and we were living on the high balcony of an enormous amphitheater formed by the sur-rounding green hills and mountains. It was a beautiful sight, the kind that tourists from the mainland pay good money to visit and see.

Momalani. The Ali-Frazier Super Fight. For me, the two go hand in hand. Popularly known as 'The Fight of the Century' this March of 1971 bout pitted undefeated heavyweight box-ing champion, Joe Frazier, against undefeated *former* heavy-weight champion, Mohammad Ali. No I didn't actually *see* the fight. You had to shell out big bucks to see it at venues show-ing the fight on special closed-circuit TV. Still, even as a kid, you couldn't get away from the pre-fight hoopla. The bout ac-tually took place just before we sailed out from San Francisco to Honolulu. But even for several weeks after the fight, it was still everywhere you looked. It seemed every newspaper and magazine I encountered featured huge color pictures of the fight, the centerpiece shot always being that of Ali on the canvas with Frazier walking away from him. I just assumed Ali had been knocked out cold and counted out. Only later would I learn Ali had actually gotten back to his feet and finished the fight after that devastating knockdown.

Heavyweight boxing notwithstanding, Momalani would witness the birth of my greatest pre-high school sports obsession. One that would dominate my passions for the duration of our Hawaii sojourn. And for my brothers and I, the house at Momanlani would serve as our very first, but quite unorthodox, Field of Dreams. But that's getting ahead of our story.

That First (But Somewhat Humiliating) Sunday at Camp Smith

Camp Smith. It was the very reason we were sent to Hawaii in the first place. A relatively small military installation located in the wooded green hills overlooking the outskirts of Honolulu, Camp Smith was a U.S. Marine base of some importance. This was the headquarters for the entire United States military effort in the Pacific. Back then the steep terraces of the base terrain were covered with mostly 1930s and 1940s period concrete and wooden plank structures that originally were part of a large, sprawling hospital facility. During the early 1940s many casualties of the war with Japan were treated and convalesced there. This was to be Dad's duty station, the place where he would do his chaplain ministerial work.

Perched on the highest terrace level of Camp Smith was Dad's office and the chapel facility. Of course, Dad's chapel would be *our* chapel as well. This would be where we would attend Sunday Protestant Chapel services. Now there are actually striking, even spectacular-looking, U.S. military chapels that exist. The Cadet Chapel at the United States Air Force Academy, with its awesome seventeen 150-foot-high church spires leaps to mind. Well, the Camp Smith Chapel was the *anti*-Cadet Chapel. A simple wood-plank structure on the outside (though, yes, at least crowned with a simple cross), the interior featured a low, level ceiling with two large ceiling fans serving as church "air conditioners." At least the altar platform added a little color: the back walls were shellacked wood plank and centered by a small stain glass window with cross design.

Just as had been our weekly custom at our previous duty station in Tennessee, when Sunday morning dawned, we boys were given one last motherly inspection before being prodded into our white '68 Dodge van for the twenty-minute drive to chapel. During those years, there were no back seat belts to impede our movements. All four of us, including one and a-half year old John, bounced around on the back bench seat like popcorn in a kettle. Besides catching our little brother whenever a bump in the road sent him airborne (I got him! I got him!), there were several interesting sights to entertain us along the way.

Our route took us past the new Pearl Ridge shopping center, a modern edifice overlooking a field of rice paddies still worked by barefoot Chinese laborers wearing traditional straw hats. It was as if a scene from the 19th century was transported forward in time and dropped in the middle of modern-day Hawaii. Further ahead the highway curved towards Pearl Harbor where we could see the gleaming white Arizona Memorial and the towers of modern-day naval ships moored beyond.

Turning left towards the misty green hills which led to Camp Smith, we viewed a large construction site on our right. An entire subdivision of pre-World War II wooden houses was being demolished (years later we learned that singer/actress, Bette Midler, grew up in that particular housing tract). Over three years, Sunday by Sunday, we monitored the progress of this mammoth project. First, the land was cleared of all vegetation and a giant hole was excavated. Then, over several months, huge reddish girders were slowly erected around the hole, like the ribs of a giant dinosaur being unearthed. We were watching the slow creation of Aloha Stadium, the new home for the island's minor league baseball team, the Hawaii Islanders.

After passing the soon-to-be-condemned housing tract (and eventual Aloha Stadium site), we eventually turned left onto a narrow winding street heading up the steep mountain to the base. The base's location high in the Aiea hills, offered a breathtaking view of Pearl Harbor, the International Airport, and, down below in the distance, Honolulu. On the lower section, at the edge of its athletic field, stood a forty-foot white cross which, when illuminated at night, could be seen for miles, even by ships offshore. It served as a famous Oahu landmark for years until the mid-1980s when a separation of church and state lawsuit got it removed.

After my father was saluted by the gate guard, we were waved through and wound our way up to the base Chapel, perched on the highest terrace level of Camp Smith. This humble building housed Dad's office as well as the chapel where he would serve as Protestant Chaplain. Catholic services were held in the same small chapel.

The Chapel building was connected to the Sunday School building next door by a long covered walkway. These covered walkways, with sides open to the air except for a low wooden fence way, ran between the major buildings on base, serving as a protection from the weather when patients were being wheeled about in earlier days. By the early 70s, the sounds of gurneys and wheelchairs being pushed across the wooden board walkways had been replaced by the loud clanking of children running towards Sunday School classes.

Almost as soon as Mom and we boys walked into the Chapel foyer that Sunday in 1971, I sensed something was amiss. Granted, we were the family of the new Protestant Chaplain and that alone set us apart from everyone else. Even so, it seemed like we were garnering a little too much attention.

"Why is everyone staring at us?" I asked Mom in low tones.

Mom tried to be reassuring. "They've all been expecting us, that's all."

I wasn't convinced. "But they're all *really* staring!"

And they really were. Okay, it wasn't so bad with the adults. They were looking at us, sure, but those looks were accompanied by smiles. Then again, when you're a kid, adults often tend to smile at you. It was the stares from kids our own age that bothered me. They were looking at my brothers and I like we had two heads. I couldn't wait to get inside and take our seats... so I could stare at the floor and hope it would swallow me up. Naturally, it didn't help matters when the Chapel assistant, from the pulpit lectern, insisted that Mom and we boys stand up during the service so we could be recognized and welcomed!

During the course of the service, I did happen to glance around—particularly at the other kids. I was starting to "get" why they were all staring at us funny. It was like the oft-sung line from the educational TV show, *Sesame Street*: "One of these things, is not like the other... one of these things just doesn't belong!" We resembled that remark. You see, that morning Mom had dressed us four boys in normal Tennessee church outfits: little sports coats, white button up shirts, and bow ties.

After the service, during meet-and-greet time, a veteran Chapel lady spelled it out for Mom and us boys. In fact, she laughed aloud as she set Mom straight: "No one wears a suit and tie to church in Hawaii. You boys are probably pretty happy to hear that." We were, but we would have been a lot happier hearing that sooner! It was a valuable first week lesson: Dressing up in the islands simply meant wearing shoes instead of flip flops.

From that Sunday on, our normal Sunday morning attire would be flowery or paisley design Aloha shirts. I never wore a tie to church again until we moved back to the mainland.

Chapter 4
Education of a Haole

Obviously every kid is enrolled at school to get an academic education. But as we all know, there's plenty of education that takes place outside the confines of Reading, 'Riting and 'Rithmatic. Especially for "haoles" who have just relocated to Hawaii from the mainland. For me, school was in session before school actually got around to being in session. My first homeroom morning roll call, as a matter of fact.

One by one, Ms. Nakamura called out the names according to the class seating chart: "Sese Lafaele?"

"Ya."

"Andrew Miachi?"

"He'ya."

Then, she got to my name: "Alan Cook?"

"Yes, Ma'am."

According to the *Guinness Book of World Records*, those two words elicited the loudest sustained laugh ever recorded on the island of Oahu. As I quickly found out, the southern manners, pounded into me during two years of Tennessee public schooling, didn't quite carry over to the islands. Then again, excuse me—I was only two months removed from Millington Elementary in the cotton country near Memphis, Tennessee!

Further education from the textbook entitled, *Vital Life Lessons for Transplanted Haoles*, came later that first week of attending Highlands Elementary in Pearl City. My brothers and I were heading home from school one afternoon, just about to start up the hill to our Momalani house. Just as we were about to cross the street, a local boy rode up on his bike and came to a stop next to me. He put the following question to me, and he wasn't smiling when he said it. "Eh, you like beef'um?"

I wasn't sure what to make of this. This boy clearly didn't have any meat products in his hand so I just kinda stared back, baffled. An older boy noticed what was happening and quickly stepped in. The boy who had queried me about "beef" turned and went on his way—the older boy may have threatened him, I can't recall. What I do remember, quite clearly, is that the older boy then turned to me and said, "He's asking if you want to fight. So whenever someone asks if you want to 'beef,' always say no." That all important lesson I never forgot, for as long as we lived on the islands.

That instance differed slightly from another head-scratching interaction I experienced my first week or two of school in Hawaii. In this particular instance, a boy in my class approached me with the following query: "Why is your face look like an ass?" As with the previous request as to whether I would like "beef'um," here too I was at a loss to verbally construct an adequate response that would satisfy the needs of both parties.

When we Cooks first arrived from the mainland in early April of 1971, I soon discovered that the brochures on Hawaii had left out a few crucial details. The lush splendor of the green mountains, pristine beaches, beautiful waterfalls, swaying palm trees, and enchanting flowers were all there, as advertised. Yet so were the contrasting sights of Oahu's urban jungle: high rise apartment buildings and hotels, urban high-ways jammed with traffic, and fairly large swaths of an economically struggling local populace crammed into rundown, low-income housing. Somehow all these were missing from the glossy photos. I also discovered that actual native Hawaiians were hard to find on the island—their numbers were shrinking every day. Instead, the locals were primarily a mixture of Caucasian, Chinese, Japanese, Samoan, Filipino, and a variety of other Polynesian islanders. No one wore grass skirts or lived in thatched huts. And no one was dancing the hula down at the local park. Anyone wishing to see such iconography had to pay for the experience at one of the hotel tourist shows or visit the Polynesian Cultural on the windward side of Oahu (over the mountain range from Honolulu). Away from the tourist spots, the average islander worked, played, and pursued interests very similar to what I'd experienced on the mainland. That's not to say there weren't differences—take school for instance.

In 1971, Hawaii public education reflected the more liberal, informal culture of the islands, just as Tennessee's schools reflected the more conservative and traditional values of the Deep South. In my Tennessee elementary school, instruction was heavy on the three "Rs," teachers were addressed as "Ma'am," and corporal punishment was the discipline of choice. Prayer and Bible stories started every school day. While Black and White children did socialize with each other at school, they were rarely together in cliques. Neither side seemed to question this arrangement. Hawaii, as a left-leaning state, embraced the newer, more progressive educational philosophies emerging from the 1960s. Hawaii and Tennessee both shared statehood and there the similarities seemed to end.

As a "military brat," I considered my new environment just another problem to work through. Already a salty veteran of six elementary schools, my specialty was adapting to new environments. I quickly evaluated my surroundings for ways to blend in. Changing my look was the first order of business. After observing how my fourth-grade classmates looked and dressed, it was clear that I would need what the fashion magazines now call an extreme makeover. Most of my peers were naturally dark-skinned or tan and either of Asian or Polynesian descent. I soon realized that being Caucasian and sporting the whitest thighs in school was not going to work for me. However, it was going to take a while for the sun to reintroduce itself to my legs and torso.

Although most of my classmates were pretty accepting of me, there were others who made it clear that they weren't terribly fond of "haoles." I soon learned that the word "haole" was not Hawaiian for "pale one who is much admired." It originally meant "newcomer" in the native language. However, by 1971 the word had evolved into a derogatory term reserved exclusively for Caucasians, loosely translated as "watch your back at recess." So began my education as a new minority student.

If I couldn't change my skin color, I was determined to at least dress the part of an island boy. Most students came to school in tee-shirts or bright flowered Aloha shirts, shorts, and flip flops--even barefoot. I didn't do barefoot. My feet lacked the calloused underside, toughened by years of walking without shoes. Sandals, or "flip-flops" as they were sometimes called, were the island's most popular footwear. They lived up to their name on my feet, constantly flipping and flopping off every time I tried to hurry or run. I never mastered the skill of pinching the rubber thongs between the first two toes to keep the stupid things on. Eventually, I went back to the comfort of shoes. Like my white thighs, this didn't endear me to the local kids either.

Learning Island Pidgin

Changing how I spoke was another tall order. My classmates all talked in a strange island dialect called Pidgin English, a mixture of Hawaiian, English, and Creole-sounding slang, spoken with a thick island accent. For instance, "I'm pow" means "I'm finished." Here's something you might overhear in a Hawaiian schoolyard: "Johnny wan cry because Stevie went hit him wit da stick dat stay dere. Stevie da kine loco." Translation: "Johnny is crying because Stevie hit him with that stick that's right there. Stevie is crazy." And of course, we've already discussed the all-pervasive, "You like beef'um?"

I was much too inexperienced to speak Pidgin convincingly, or even to understand it at first. However, I eventually learned a few phrases such as "shakka bruddah," the Hawaiian equivalent of "take it easy man" or simply, "All right!" That popular phrase was accompanied by a hand gesture where the pinky and thumb were extended while the wrist was shaken quickly back and forth. I knew that was cool because I'd seen Jack Lord use it on the hit television show *Hawaii Five-o*. Jack was the epitome of island sophistication, and he somehow pulled it off while not only being a haole, but a haole wearing a suit and tie on the beach!

School Curriculum: Hawaiian Style

One welcome change was that schoolwork in Hawaii was easy compared to Tennessee. I partially credit this to the progressive educational philosophy that Hawaii embraced in its public school curriculum. Objective academic standards were de-emphasized in favor of life application, student-set goals, and increasing the fun factor. The philosophy seems to have been based on the belief that children are born with an innate thirst for knowledge. From this perspective, traditional teaching methods had suppressed that natural desire by forcing kids to memorize obscure facts that had little relationship to their daily lives. Schools simply needed to unleash a child's natural affinity for learning. Now, I was no expert in educational philosophy, but I did know my peers. If they had a natural affinity, it was for goofing off, not pursuing knowledge. But no one asked me.

So what did this mean in the classroom? Instead of learning important Civil War leaders and dates, we would discuss what it felt like to be a slave and how that applied to our own interpersonal relationships. In Music class we danced under strobe lights to the classical music of Grand Funk Railroad instead of learning about wind and string instruments. Not all classes followed this pattern, but many did.

To be fair, there were pure motives behind some of this new thinking. Educators were desperately trying to compete with a popular culture that was capturing young people's attention and convincing many that what they learned in school was irrelevant. However, the path from outstanding idea to outstanding execution is fraught with stumbling blocks. In my school, these stumbling blocks were short, prone to mischief, and numbered about thirty per class. To illustrate this clash of educational theory and living breathing fourth-graders, let's walk through a typical day at Highlands Elementary School in 1971.

My first morning class was Hawaiian History, a subject I found fascinating. Where else in the country can a kid study a state history that involves kings, queens, battles with spears, wooden idols, and volcanoes? As *my* idol Greg Brady would say, "Far out!" The only part that made me uncomfortable was when the discussion turned to the English explorers, whalers, and missionaries of the late 1700s and early 1800s. Apparently, these visitors often lacked appropriate sensitivity to island culture and, whether intentionally or unintentionally, didn't always treat the Hawaiians very well. Cultural misunderstandings abounded. As our teacher recounted these tales of Haole maltreatment of the natives, I would glance around the room, my paranoid mind conjuring up a sea of disapproving faces staring back at me. I fought the urge to spring to my feet and start sputtering apologies on behalf of all haloes for our forefathers' abominable behavior.

Captain Cook was credited as the first white explorer to visit the Hawaiian Islands. Since we shared the same last name, I was always asked if we were related in any way. However, knowing that Captain Cook was first treated like a god, then subsequently stabbed to death by enraged Hawaiian warriors, I vehemently denied any connection. In fact, I said our family came from a long line of land lubbers. I even got seasick taking a bath. Luckily, few of my classmates ever learned that both my dad and uncle were Navy men.

History was followed by Health class, where we were warned incessantly about the evils of drugs. We would receive these moral lessons under the watchful, yet glazed-over eyes of the Beatles, Jimi Hendrix, and other acid rock icons, whose posters adorned our school and cafeteria walls. Even at nine years of age, I knew there was a mixed message in there somewhere. Hawaii schools, like other school systems during that period, were walking a tightrope. On one hand, they attempted to encourage good citizenship and positive life choices. Yet, at the same time they were trying to be hip by eagerly embracing the images of popular culture, a culture which often undermined the very lessons the schools were teaching.

Cafeteria Sweat Shops

By noon, we were all exhausted by the constant unleashing of our thirst to learn. It really worked up an appetite. Lunch time in Hawaii schools had its own unique flavor. For example, the traditional cafeteria lunch ladies were augmented by students who were drafted each day to work the serving line and wash the dirty trays. All the students were required to perform cafeteria duty at least a couple times a year. In fact, because of budget cuts that year, teachers and students were also enlisted to stay after school to sweep and mop their classroom floors. While learning had been unleashed at Highlands Elementary in 1971, lawyers and child labor laws were apparently still restrained. The only compensation these modern Oliver Twists received for working the cafeteria line was missing two hours of class and receiving a free lunch. For most kids, that was a fair trade.

The meals we ate in the school cafeteria had a South Pacific flavor just like everything else in Hawaii. Besides the typical pizza slice or corndog served in every school from sea to shining sea, most Highland Elementary menus included oriental noodles, rice (often wrapped in seaweed), pineapple, and other island food. When I say pineapple, I mean the good stuff, chilled and fresh from the fields only a few miles up the coast. You could buy a whole pineapple for a quarter at the local grocery so there was no need to skimp. The rice was not as tasty, normally served with an ice cream scoop, plopping down on your tray like a small white ball held together by Elmer's Glue. All these delicacies were wolfed down amid that special school cafeteria ambiance—a mixture of ear-splitting noise and the smell of spilled sour milk drying on the concrete floor.

Of course, much goes on in a school cafeteria besides eating. As soon as the trays were cleared, we boys would break out our old worksheets and fold them into little footballs. Then, we would amuse ourselves by taking turns flicking them through the air, trying to split the goal posts formed by your buddies' forefingers (uprights) and thumbs (cross bar). The less sports-minded kids would be opening packets of ketchup, placing them carefully under the chair leg of an absent classmate, then laughing uproariously when the kid sat back down and sent the red goo spurting all over the legs of nearby diners. If caught, these mischief-makers would be sentenced to an extra hour of unleashing their thirst for learning after school.

In short, my island re-education came in several forms. I had to adjust to a new school environment and a new kind of school curriculum. I had to learn a new way to converse verbally with school mates and neighborhood kids. I had to adapt to new ways of navigating social interactions with island peers. Hey, I even had to learn to dress differently! Oftentimes these lessons were mildly to highly painful. Up until this point, it all took place in the classroom, on the recess playgrounds, or in the neighborhood streets. But another kind of education was soon about to take place. This one, however, would take place on a ball field. Painful lessons? On a ball field? You better believe it.

But it would lead to *really* good things.

Chapter 5
I Have Discovered...
Baseball!

After lunch on Monday, Wednesday, and Friday, Highlands Elementary afforded me yet another opportunity to take control of my own education, this time courtesy of Activity Period. On those days, I (and everyone else) was allowed to select enriching experiences from either Art, Music, or Physical Education (P.E.). You could select something different each day, so our enrichment tended to be haphazard as we floated in and out of these subjects based on our daily whims.

Although I loved to draw, school art seemed to consist mainly of "crafty" things such as making ceramic ash trays or cardboard Christmas tree ornaments. I could not seem to channel my inner Martha Stewart, so after a few Art sessions, I decided to switch to P.E. My buddy Dennis was an athlete and convinced me to go because they were starting a unit on softball. I was not really interested in sports (except for some basketball) and hardly knew the basic rules of softball. The only time I'd ever played ball at all was a year earlier when I tried out for Little League baseball in Tennessee. I was cut. Yes, that's right—back then they actually sent kids home who did not have the right stuff needed to compete in the highly skilled world of Little League! That may give you a clue to how uncoordinated I was.

I hoped that this softball unit in P.E. would sharpen my skills enough to make me, if not Little League material, at least not the butt of schoolyard jokes. However, if you've spent any time in American public schools, you'll know that Physical Education classes frequently major on the physical and minor on the education. At that time I hardly knew a backstop from a shortstop (one has a lower fence right?) and could have benefited from some basic softball instruction. At first, I learned only from my buddy Dennis. He showed me where to go when I was told to play a position in the field. He discreetly pushed me to the right spot when someone yelled, "Hey, kid, take left field!" I had to learn how to "tag up" and the difference between "taking a base" and "covering a base." I was amazed how much there was to know about this game! But what truly mortified me was that everyone else seemed to have this bat and ball game down pat! Everyone except me.

"Hey, kid, you're on deck!"

I turned to the boy who shouted impatiently at me. I was still standing cluelessly on the sidelines, and this boy's directive only enhanced my cluelessness as to what I was missing. Thank goodness for Dennis. He sidled up to me and whispered, "That means grab a bat and go stand over there, 'cause after that guy hits, you're up to bat."

I nodded in a way as if to say, *'Of course!'* Well, the boy ahead of me whacked the ball far out onto the field on the first pitch, and in no time, had reached third base. I heard Dennis' voice again. "Alan, you're up! Just keep your eye on the ball. Swing level."

As I walked to the plate, I mulled over what it meant to "swing level." Did that mean do a half swing and bring my swing to a halt when my arms extended out into a plane level with, say, my hips? I didn't know. Trembling, I approached the plate, and trying to ignore the catcalls—most of which seemed to reference how "muff" (i.e, athletically incompetent) I looked—I got into what I felt approximated a batter's crouch. The unsympathetic-looking teacher lofted the ball underhand in my direction. I swung and missed. By a lot. The jeers rose up in cacophony.

"Just keep your eye on it!" yelled Dennis from the sidelines. Yes, that was the key! I would keep my eye on the ball. REAL-LY carefully.

The ball was lofted my way again. I swung and missed. Again, by a lot. And the third pitch yielded the same result. No matter my keeping an eye on the ball or whatever a level swing was, it seemed next to impossible to hit this arcing, rising-then-falling white sphere. A torrent of verbal abuse came my way—or so it seemed. But one phrase now rang out above all the others: "Strike out! Strike out! He struck out...!"

I looked over at Dennis and he sadly waved me in. I had struck out. I had disgraced myself in front of God and what seemed like the entire male population of Highlands Elementary. But my teacher, Ms. Inoue, was not going to let me off that easy. "No, no," she said. "We need to teach you how to bat."

How humiliating! And it was even worse when she dropped her glove and walked towards me. Then, taking a position directly behind me, Ms. Inoue reached over my shoulders and held the bat with me. I heard her whispering something about my stance and how to swing, but I was so embarrassed that nothing was penetrating at all. I could sense all the other boys staring at me as my face and neck turned bright red. I felt utterly emasculated and just wanted that teacher to get away from me. When she finally did back away, my skill and emotional levels were as low as ever. And you know what? When she allowed me a few more pitches—I *still* missed every one. Finally, she let me skulk away with my tail tucked between my legs.

It was a long walk back to the dugout and (except for my sympathetic friend, Dennis) an icy reception awaited me. It was hard being a new kid. But being a new haole kid who couldn't play ball was a whole 'nother level of social ignominy. I took care of this issue with a classic response—avoidance. I vowed never to pick P.E. for Activity Period again.

Let's face it. After my ultra-humiliating softball experience in P.E, I doubt anyone would have blamed me if I never went near a ball diamond for the remainder of my days. But then, a funny thing happened. By late spring, memories of my Physical Education catastrophe faded as I was caught up in my classmates' excitement over the beginning of Little League baseball season. Oh, and just a quick note for the uninitiated, the main ways *baseball* differs from *softball* are the following: the smaller, harder ball and the overhand pitching.

Baseball was the most popular sport in Hawaii and it wasn't hard to figure out why. Hawaii's year-round tropical climate made it a perfect setting for outdoor sports. The Islands' large Japanese population further promoted the game's popularity since it was the favorite professional sport of their homeland.

Unlike football and basketball, which give competitive advantages to larger athletes, baseball skills are not necessarily tied to physical size, affording smaller Asian players the ability to compete alongside their taller or heavier counterparts. The Hawaiian kids not only loved the game of baseball but were very good at it. In fact, that very summer, a team from nearby Wahiwa went all the way to the final eight of the Little League World Series in Williamsport, Pennsylvania. Their picture was in the paper and they became local celebrities. Although my initial baseball-related experiences in Hawaii were less than pleasurable and rewarding, it was hard not to get swept up in the excitement. Being a part of a team, wearing a cool baseball uniform and winning the admiration of my peers suddenly seemed very appealing.

Then came that fateful Saturday. Dad took my brothers and I up to the Highlands Elementary and Junior High ball fields to watch my pal, Dennis, play in an actual real, live Little League baseball game! I was mesmerized. For the first time in my life, I thrilled to the electricity of a cheering baseball crowd, was struck by how cool the players looked in their uniforms, saw dirt flying on a head first slide, heard the pop of a fastball hitting the catcher's mitt, and gazed in awe as a majestic home run cleared the outfield fence. As for Dennis, he waved to us as he walked up to the plate to bat, but he struck out. Even with that great swing of his, he was still overmatched by the heat-throwing pitcher on the other team. This only reinforced to me that these Little Leaguers were top of the line athletes! Apparently you had to be to even *make* a squad! From that afternoon on, I was hooked.

School was almost over and three months of freedom lay before me. It would not go to waste. I made a vow to start learning everything I could about baseball. Then I was going to practice every day until I was good enough to make a Little League team next season. Then I would finally be able to walk onto the field at Highlands Elementary with confidence and with my head held high.

Chapter 6
Our Backyard Field of Dreams, Field of Nightmares

I must reiterate: We Cook boys didn't land in Hawaii with baseball on the brain. In fact, when we first moved to Hawaii, it's not like we were athletes, or even sports-minded. Only eighteen months earlier, I didn't know a bunt from a base on balls and was quite content in my ignorance. Except for just starting to discover a little bit about basketball when we lived in Tennessee, sports in general played almost no part in my life. Instead, my spare time revolved around normal nine-year old pursuits such as reading, drawing, riding bikes, building forts, and researching the life of Abraham Lincoln. Okay, maybe I wasn't totally normal.

Yet here we were, our time on the islands now having run just a little over two months, and now this dramatic change had taken place. Now my brothers and I were willing to risk life and limb to engage in our new sports obsession of baseball. Sure, there was a nearby park, but it was a long hike down the hill. That meant the easiest and most convenient place to regularly ply our "trade," was... the backyard of our Momalani house.

While our home surroundings boasted impressive views of Pearl Harbor, our immediate environment was not so spectacular when it came to baseball training. The front of our house was almost entirely cement driveway which emptied into a two-vehicle carport and fronted by a steep street wherein errant balls tended to roll down from here to eternity. The sides of the house had thin rectangular patches of grass that hardly qualified as lawn. The backyard was not much bigger.

We started out by playing catch mostly in the backyard. This soon proved to be a mistake, not to mention the catalyst that thrust us Cook boys deep into the throes of a harrowing and ongoing drama. You see, throwing length-wise meant one party was throwing directly towards our lower neighbor's backyard. Despite our most diligent efforts to be careful, a throw would inevitably get past the receiver and the ball would go bounding into the yard next door. This was a problem. A *big* problem, and one that culminated on a fateful day in May of 1971.

"Who's gonna go get it?" asked Kevin, innocently. His voice broke the silence as we three Cook brothers (John was too young to join us) stood at the edge of our lawn, staring down into the neighboring yard. There, right in the center of that lovingly-manicured and watered plot of radiant green grass lay... our one and only baseball.

Of course I knew full well what Kevin wanted me to say in reply to his question: *Well, as the oldest brother, there's no question that I should be the one to go fetch the baseball.*

Nothing doing.

Anyway, it wasn't that simple. You see, when you're engaged in a game of throw-the-ball-around (i.e, Catch) and the ball winds up in the neighboring yard, then it's either the fault of the thrower or the catcher. If the throw is reasonable and catchable, then it's the fault of the catcher for allowing the ball to sail out of the throw-around boundary. Therefore, the catcher is obligated to go fetch the ball.

On the other hand, if the thrower throws wildly and the catcher has little to no chance of snaring the ball, then it's up to the thrower to go after the wayward baseball. In our particular case, I was the catcher, but Kevin had thrown the ball way too far to the side. From there, it sailed over the top of the wooden slat boundary fence and bounced down the short hill into the neighboring yard. In other words... it was Kevin's responsibility to get the ball. I tried to make that clear to Kevin.

"You threw it wild. You should go get it."

Kevin went to his first line of defense. "But what if I get caught?"

Not only was that a pretty good defense, he did have good reason to be afraid. As did I. You see, the owner of that yard was a middle–aged Japanese fellow with the build of a professional wrestler. This stern-face man cultivated his small piece of land as if it was a modern-day Garden of Eden. The entire yard was beautifully landscaped complete with oriental gardens, little fountains, and precisely trimmed bushes. It was his pride and joy and we Cook boys were viewed as potential destroyers of his man-made paradise. From the time we took to throwing around the horsehide, our intimidating neighbor made it very clear he was not thrilled that us boys would be using the open patch of grass right next to and just above his as our own personal Field of Dreams.

This particular neighbor never really introduced himself, never gave a friendly wave, and only spoke to us when he was barking or scolding. Such as the morning I accidently aimed the hose too high during my plant–watering duties and sprayed his bay window below. His harangues were normally a mix of English and Japanese so it was never exactly clear what he was trying to say, only that he was not happy. We didn't even know his name, so we just referred to him as the "Mean Guy Next Door," or "MG" for short.

Little wonder our hearts froze in our chests that afternoon as we helplessly watched the ball sail over the fence, only to come to a bouncing and rolling halt in MG's yard. We knew that we had gambled... and lost. And one of us would have to gamble again if we were to have any hope of getting our one and only baseball back.

Now Eric chimed in. "Alan, you're the fastest. You could grab it real quick and get outta there."

I glared at Eric. He *would* throw the 'you're the oldest and the fastest' line at me. I still wasn't convinced I should go. But there the ball sat, just a tantalizing sixty feet away, in plain view of us and MG's rear windows. So near but yet so far. The birds were singing, a soft breeze was blowing, but we could sense evil lurking somewhere over that fence. We had no doubt MG was watching from some hidden spot, waiting for his prey to take a step onto the sacred grounds. Entering would be pure suicide. But enter we must. Did I mention it was our only baseball?

As in any military operation, I had to decide who would be assigned point for this mission. "Are you sure neither one of you wants to volunteer?" I asked. I still hoped one of my brothers would step forward. Being littler, MG might go easier on them if they were caught. To put a little more pressure on my younger brothers, I uttered a truth neither of them could deny: "I went last time. Remember?"

Still no volunteers stepped forward. Precious minutes were being wasted and we were getting nowhere. I still thought Kevin was at fault, but finally, as squad leader, I just didn't have the heart to send the rookie in there. He was young and had his whole life ahead of him. No, it must be me. So the three of us went into a quick huddle.

I spoke in low tones. "Here's what we'll do. I'll go, but you guys pretend like you're going inside the house—but you'll stop behind that corner and keep watch. Then, I'll hop over the fence and go grab the ball. I'll crouch really low so he can't see me out the window."

Kevin and Eric were excited by this plan. I could tell by the now-fiery confidence in their eyes that they saw my strategy as foolproof. "Yeah!" said Eric. "I don't think he knows the ball is out there. I don't even think he's home! He hasn't come out at all."

I added my fail-safe addendum. "Just to make sure, I'm not gonna come back the way I came. I'm gonna run down the hill through the other yards, then cut back over to the street. THEN I'll come back to the house with the baseball."

"All right!" said Kevin, chomping at the bit for the daring mission to get underway. Still, I wasn't done. I needed some added protection.

I waved my hands with emphatic force. "Now listen. If you guys see him coming out, yell, 'Tennessee!'"

Kevin crinkled his nose. "Tennessee?"

I gritted my teeth impatiently. "He won't know what you're talking about. Come on! Go! Get over behind the house!" My brothers dutifully did as they were told. Meanwhile, I took a deep breath and made ready to leap into action while the coast was still clear.

Taking cautious steps to the edge of our yard, I glanced at the drawn curtains of MG's back windows for any signs of peeping eyes. All appeared calm—there was no sign that the wayward ball's presence had been discovered. The house and the surrounding bushes were quiet. *Almost too quiet*, I thought. With trembling hands I slowly climbed over the slat fence and dropped down onto the edge of the yard. After a quick side to side glance, I scurried over to the ball and bent down to pick it up.

Just as my fingers curled around the seams, I felt a strong hand grab me by the shoulder followed by the ball being ripped from my grasp. In our debriefing later that afternoon, the only explanation we could come up with was that he must have either parachuted from the roof or supernaturally risen through the grass from the underworld below. My heart leapt to my throat and whether it needed it or not, I proceeded to water his lawn and my own pants. Turning around, I was confronted with my neighbor's enraged face, contorted in a most hideous fashion with Japanese words and spittle spewing from his twisted mouth.

There was the weak sound of Eric's voice in the distance: "Tennessee..." That was all. I could only assume my brothers had bailed on me, fleeing for the safety of our house. Me, I was in the clutches of the enemy. I was terrified.

MG released his grip on my shoulder but continued haranguing me, now using some English which included words like "call the police," "trespassing," and "keeping ball." In a rare moment of courage, I grabbed the ball back (okay, maybe he just slammed the ball back in my hand, I can't quite recall), sprang to my feet, and sped down the embankment to the far yard, not slowing down until I was at the last house at the bottom of our hill.

For days afterwards I had nightmares where MG was chasing me with a huge sword, slashing and smashing objects behind me as I ran, a ball cradled in my arms like a fullback making for the goal line. Still, it was going to take more than scary nightmares to keep me away from my beloved baseball.

I know the movie *Field of Dreams*, when enrapturing on the magic of baseball, pinpoints, "the thrill of the grass." Up to a point, I agree: a lovingly manicured carpet of deep green grass, coupled with a golden dirt diamond and base paths, is indeed a thing of beauty—whether plopped within an Iowa cornfield or nestled on a flat, palm tree-studded acreage next to a beach on Oahu. However, I would add to that, the *thrill of the white ball.* Yes, that almost glowing white sphere with the red-stitch seams (especially the new ones just broken out of the box) can be mesmerizing like nothing else in this world. It can whistle from the mound to the plate like it was shot out of a cannon or evade contact with a batter's bat by looping around it or sharply dropping below the swing in circus-like fashion. That same white sphere can also be sent soaring majestically into the blue sky when the bat makes solid contact.

No, it would take more than a scary next-door neighbor to dissuade us Cook boys away from our new obsession. Still, we agreed it was time to take our game to the next level. Namely, a proper ball field.

Chapter 7

Landing Amongst the Marines

It was move-in day and the huge box truck was parked in front of our new Birch Circle home. As the movers busily rolled or hauled our furniture out of the cargo bed, Dad and we boys were likewise busy moving boxes, cases, and containers into the quasi-garage carport. We happened to be wrestling with a particularly heavy metal trunk. In the midst of our grunting, a husky, tough looking Marine noticed our struggle and came sauntering over. "Can I give you all a hand there?" he asked.

Dad looked up through sweaty GI issue glasses and smiled. "Sure. Thanks!"

With that, we boys parted like the Red Sea as the tough-looking Marine took over, grabbing the end we three boys had been battling to raise airborne. The two adult males grimaced as they hauled the trunk into the garage, finally plopping it down in an appropriate out-of-the way spot. Dad grunted, "Right here is good."

As the weighty foot-locker was dropped to the concrete surface, the Marine drew a heavy breath and raised himself upright. "Whew! God-damned heavy son of a bitch, huh?"

Dad came around the tool case, extending his hand. "Chaplain Darren Cook."

The Marine shook Dad's hand but lowered his head in embarrassment. "Y'know, I heard there was a Navy chaplain comin' in and there I go with the French. I do apologize, Reverend."

Dad was used to such apologies. He simply chuckled and pointed skyward. "Might wanna square it with him first."

"I hear ya, chaplain, sir. Me and my big mouth. Gunny Thornton. I live two houses down that way."

"Say, Gunny, do you and your family have a church home?"

"Uh.. no, chaplain, can't say that we do."

Dad had him where he wanted him. "Well consider this an invite to Protestant Chapel at Camp Smith. We'd love to have you and your family join us on Sunday."

"Well, I appreciate the invitation, chaplain sir..."

"Services start at eleven. Have any kids, Gunny?"

"Three, Chaplain."

Dad nodded and smiled wider. "We have Sunday School for them. Starts at nine."

The Gunny nervously dabbed his forehead. "Gettin' earlier and earlier."

Dad wasn't having it. "Hey, I know for a fact you Marines are used to getting up way before that!"

Gunny Thorton shook his head, trying to look for a way out. "You don't know *this* Marine, chaplain."

It was August of 1971, and at the tender age of nine, I had joined the Marines. Actually, our whole family had. This had nothing to do with sweeping patriotic fervor or even a shortage of able-bodied recruits for Vietnam. Chaplain Cook's name had finally reached the top of the military housing waiting list and Dad was offered a house in the Manana Navy/Marine housing tract located near the peninsula that jutted out towards Pearl Harbor. Granted, Manana was mostly an enclave for U.S. Marines and their families, but there were also a handful of Navy families, like us, who lived among them. Though located a mere three miles from our former house, Manana, as were soon to find out, was a whole different world from Momalani.

As for the helpful but salty-tongued new neighbor, Gunny Thornton, it wasn't the first time I'd witnessed this phenomenon: a tough-as-nails military guy suddenly turning sheepish around my dad. But it always amazed me when it did happen. And for the record, Gunny Thorton and his family did end up attending chapel. In fact they became one of our most faithful attendees over the next three years!

What was Manana like? It was a typical middle-class American neighborhood. Two hundred families comprised of wives, assorted kids, dogs, cats, and fathers, Oh, and those fathers all happened to be trained killers. Although none of us looked forward to the stress of another move, we were thrilled with the improved living situation awaiting us in Manana. The new house would offer us neighbors who shared our military lifestyle. Our new housing area would also offer us innumerable recreation opportunities unavailable in Momilani, as well as a substantial decrease in our cost of living. In short, we entered into the welcoming embrace of our new landlord, the U.S. Government.

For the next three years our family lived, slept, ate, played, worked, and grew in a world surrounded by United States Marine Corps personnel. My dad was anxious to move to Manana because he wanted to be closer to the people he ministered to. As a chaplain, developing personal relationships was crucial. A Marine was more likely to consider attending church, ask for prayer, or seek out counseling if he already knew and was comfortable with the chaplain. My father found Marines more open and relaxed around their homes than at the office where his chaplain's uniform, military rank, or the proximity of co-workers could often squelch personal conversation.

In our previous home at Momilani, we were isolated from other military families and Dad's ability to develop rapport with people outside of work was somewhat hindered. Manana changed all that. Not only did my father meet and develop bonds with neighborhood families, but his accessibility also helped diffuse several domestic disputes. I can remember instances when the doorbell rang at night, a neighbor turning up at our door asking for Dad to come over to either intervene or counsel someone in crisis.

Relationships were important to my mother as well. Because of the unique lifestyle shared by military spouses, friendships tended to be forged earlier and more easily than those of women in a civilian community. In Momilani we seemed to be looked upon as outsiders and most of our neighbors hardly acknowledged our presence. In the civilian world you have time to combat that attitude by slowly ingratiating yourself over several years. The military doesn't give families that luxury because a typical military assignment only lasts two to three years.

Because they share a similar lifestyle, military wives immediately empathize with newcomer concerns: frustrations with trying to decorate another boxy government house, anxiety about children adjusting to new schools, the pressure of shouldering all parental duties while dad is overseas, the trials of being uprooted for the fifth time in nine years. We hoped for that type of welcome in Manana and we weren't disappointed. By the end of our first week, we had been visited by more neighbors and had met more people than our entire four months at Momilani. In a sense, even as clichéd as it sounds, the military is indeed like a family.

Then... We Met the Medlocks

The day I met Cindy Medlock was one of those thunderbolt moments you have in life, and you never forget it. It happened shortly after we moved into our Birch Circle house in Manana. I'm assuming it took place on a Saturday morning because my brothers and I were lounging on the gold-colored shag rug of our living room (it's amazing how much time one spends on the floor as a kid), transfixed by the latest episode of *Scooby-Doo* on our black-and-white TV set. The doorbell rang and Mom went to answer it. We hardly looked up as we heard Mom exchanging pleasantries with a woman who had dropped by to welcome us. This wasn't unusual and hardly reason enough to abandon our cartoon program.

I did happen to glance over. I spotted a woman with thick, shortly-cropped mustard-blonde hair. She was holding a pan of brownies. From my vantage point in the living room, the woman appeared to be in her mid to late thirties or so, much like so many other military officer wives who lived in Manana. I heard the woman say something akin to, "We saw you all move in last week and we wanted to welcome you to the neighborhood!"

Mom, ever gracious when receiving guests, welcomed the woman into our house. "How thoughtful! Do come in!" This was followed by the expected call: "Boys!"

That was our cue to get up, come to the door, and greet the company. And that's when I first saw her. Not the woman holding the pan of brownies, but her teenage daughter. I was immediately struck by the beauty of this princess-like female. Right away I assumed she was a young woman—perhaps college age. In actuality she was only sixteen at the time. Cindy was shorter than her mother, only about five foot-one or so. She was petite but with striking, chiseled facial features framed by thick, cascading raven-colored hair. In retrospect I would say she somewhat resembled a cross between Marlo Thomas of the hit TV sitcom, *That Girl,* and Olivia Hussey in the 1968 cinematic treatment of *Romeo and Juliet.* On this particular morning, she was wearing a paisley print blouse and a miniskirt tied at the waist with a thick, orange sash. And from that moment, I was smitten with her. Yes, it happened that quickly.

One by one, Mom introduced each of us boys and each of us politely said 'Hi.' Then it was our neighbor's turn. The woman holding the pan of brownies spoke. "Hello boys. I'm Darla Medlock, and this is my daughter, Cindy." In a somewhat bashful, demure manner, Cindy smiled and offered a hello back.

A few moments later we were all seated in the living room. Naturally we boys sat politely by, fulfilling our duty to be present and attentive when we had visitors (at least until we were dismissed). Naturally the television set was turned off. Retreating to our back hallway bedroom to continue our cartoon watching was out of the question. That's because, well, our house boasted only one television. Darla Medlock looked us boys over and smiled widely. "Four boys!"

Mom nodded. "Yes. They can be a handful at times."

Darla shook her head. "They're all so handsome!"

Mom thanked Mrs. Medlock for the kind words, then had each of us announce our ages. Of course as the oldest, I went first: "I'm Alan. I'm in fifth grade at Pearl City Elementary." Now it was my brother's turn.

"I'm Eric. I'm nine."

Then Kevin spoke up. "I'm Kevin and seven." It was a rhyme Kevin was fond of repeating that year. Then, Kevin nudged little John and whispered, "Say your name!"

John didn't hesitate. "John!"

Cindy made eyes at little John. "Ohhhh, he's so adorable!" I wondered if Cindy thought as much of me. Right.

Darla had a mischievous grin on her face. "You know, Cindy does babysitting." Cindy rolled her eyes, then nodded bashfully.

Mom's eyes lit up. "Is that right? Well. I just might give you a call some time."

Darla leaned her shoulder into Cindy's. "You see? It never hurts to ask."

A short time later, Mrs. Medlock and the lovely Cindy stood to leave. I knew enough to rise to my feet also. It couldn't hurt for Cindy to see that I was a mature young man. Mom thanked them again for the visit and the brownies. Before walking out the front door, however, Darla turned to us all. "Just so you know—our family has a little musical group we've put together. We're doing a small neighborhood concert today at our house. It's at two o'clock and you all are certainly invited. It's free!"

Mom nodded. "We just might do that."

After the Medlock women left, I made a minor show of not being wholly enthusiastic about going to the neighborhood show, but I agreed to go anyway. In truth, I wouldn't have missed it.

We arrived a little late. The concert was already underway when we walked up to the Medlock family carport. Their family band, as I was to learn, was called Island Blue and on this sunny Hawaiian afternoon they were performing before a fairly large neighborhood crowd of mostly pre-teen kids and their mothers. A fair number of teenage and middle-school boys were also in the audience, but I could only assume they were there to ogle the stunning and wholly alluring Cindy Medlock. Even at my age I could surmise as much.

The crowd sat on folding chairs while Island Blue performed on a low "stage" towards the back of the garage port. Island Blue was very much the picture of an early 70s family pop band, a la the Cowsills, the Osmonds, or The Partridge Family. The band consisted of Darla and Cindy Medlock on piano and electric organ respectively. On drums was fourteen-year-old Brent, a virtual Donny Osmond clone with a thick head of hair that came down over his eyebrows. Each member of the band took turns on lead vocals, but mostly their voices blended.

The number that affected me most was their rendition of "Love (Can Make You Happy)" which had been a recent soft rock hit for the band, Mercy. Up to that point in my life I had never heard harmonies as lovely as this. What's more, I could not take my eyes off Cindy.

Then I saw him. Sitting on a stool towards the back of the stage, a sullen-looking teenage guy. He was strumming an electric guitar player. This, I was later to learn, was Eddie Tangen. His hair was long, dark brunette, and flowed down in Jim Morrison-like swirls around a face that seemed to be perpetually scowling, pouting. He wore a football shirt and cut-off jeans. I disliked him immediately. I could only hope he was, somehow, a member of the Medlock family and not a boyfriend of Cindy's.

Then came the awful moment. At a certain point in the concert, it seemed to me that Cindy and Eddie were making eyes at each other. I still hoped he was just a family member—an older brother who Darla Medlock had forgotten to mention earlier. To be sure, I whispered over to Mom. "Who is that guy in the back? Is he one of their family?"

Mom shook her head and whispered back, "No. I think he's just a friend of theirs."

When the concert was over and people were heading home, Mom and a few other families lingered on the front lawn to congratulate Mrs. Medlock. When it came Mom's turn, Darla profusely thanked us all for coming. She also introduced us to her teenaged son, Brent. While I assumed Brent would be a cocky teen idol type, he actually came across as polite and gracious.

Then, just as we were about to head for home, my head happened to swivel back in the direction of the Medlock family carport. A horrible sight greeted my eyes. I spotted Cindy and Eddie. They had found a quiet, private place towards the back of the garage port. Eddie was holding Cindy in his arms. Then, they kissed.

It was a sickening kick to my stomach. I turned and stormed home ahead of Mom and my brothers.

My unhappy exit from the concert venue notwithstanding, our family became good friends with the Medlocks over the next two years. They became regular attendees at Camp Smith Chapel. Well, at least Mrs. Medlock, Cindy, and Brent attended regularly. Mister Medlock, a rather intimidating U.S. Marines officer, came only sporadically—and during Pro Football season, almost never. Still, Cindy eventually helped out as an assistant in Kevin's Sunday School class (and don't think I wasn't jealous). What's more, the Medlock family band would, on occasion, perform special music during chapel services, including at one point, a rendition of the currently popular Carpenter's hit, "Top of the World" (with lyrics tweaked to portray *God* looking down on creation).

As it turned out, Island Blue were minor local celebrities, playing regular gigs at schools, business functions, small clubs, weddings. That didn't matter to me so much. What did have me walking on clouds were those times when Cindy would filter over to our house, sometimes to accompany her mother, but other times to be our babysitter when Dad and Mom went out for the evening. Mind you, I would never tell any of my buddies that I had a babysitter, but I was willing to submit to such guy humiliation just to bask in Cindy's company. Now I wasn't stupid—I knew she didn't see me as romantic material. Not at my age. But she did seem to enjoy my sense of humor and would laugh at most of my jokes. In my mind, that was a promising start. At this stage in life, I considered it a victory that she would even show me any attention at all. How many other boys my age got to rub elbows (okay, not literally) with such a fully-realized female vision of loveliness?

Chapter 8
Baseball Education Continues for the Cook Boys

"You have to be *good* to hit Major League pitching!"

No, my new pal, Doug, wasn't talking about the necessary skill level one needed to make it in the pros. He was talking about Little League here in Hawaii, the top rung being designated as, "Major League." In Hawaii, "Major League" Little League was primarily the 9- to 12-year-olds. The baseball league just below that was "Minor League" and these were mainly 8- to 10-year-olds, though an 11-year-old still working on basic skills might still play in the Minors. At the lowest rung, the beginners were the boys in T-Ball League (mainly 6- to 7-year-olds).

What's more, Doug was mainly referring to the *Pearl City* Major League pitchers who threw with such jaw-dropping speed. I figured Doug should know because he played in the Pearl City Minor League the year before and that, in my mind, was impressive enough. Manana and the nearby Navy Peninsula Housing Area had their own combined Little League, but it was smaller and less high-powered than the Pearl City Little League. Sure, Doug was prone to exaggeration, but not by much. Keep in mind, the Pearl City Major/Little League

All Stars would place third in the *world* that coming baseball season! Still, Doug stretched the truth maybe a wee bit.

"How fast do they pitch?" I asked with wide-eyed wonder.

Doug leaned towards me, his expression growing even more intense. "When they start their wind-up, you better start swinging your bat right then! It's too late when they let go of the ball—BOOM! It's already gone past you!"

I still was not quite convinced. I wanted a visual. Unfortunately, there was no Pearl City Major League pitcher present with us as we stood in the open grass field behind a row of Manana houses. So Doug decided to show me himself. We already had a ball and our ball mitts handy. We also had a catcher. No, not me—I wanted to watch the pitch, not catch it. The catcher would be the chain-link fence.

So as I stood off to the side, Doug walked a few paces back from the fence and stopped. He figured he was about pitching distance. Then, he went into his windup and threw a hard one. It was a pretty impressive fast ball for a 9-year-old, but then he may not have been at the official pitcher's mound distance from the fence. After the ball slammed into the fence, then dropped to the ground, Doug turned to me and bellowed: "And that's their *slowest* pitch!"

I tried not to look impressed, but the fact was, I was dazzled. And intimidated. That was one fast looking pitch. But that was, as Doug had intimated, just a warm up pitch. I was now seriously beginning to wonder if I could really handle bonafide Major (Little) League fast balls. Or would I swing and whiff at air while the crowd watching from the bleachers roared with laughter and Ringling Brothers circus music played in the background?

No, it couldn't be. Little Leaguers couldn't be that good. My friend Doug was surely just blowing smoke. Then (as so often happened in Manana where kids and teenagers were always roaming about), a tall, long-haired blonde teen boy wandered over. He was bored and probably just decided to check out what we were doing, maybe get in on a little ball playing himself. Doug knew the guy.

"Travis!" yelled Doug as the teen boy came sauntering over. "Let's see you pitch one!"

The teen seemed sleepy, not quite taking in this abrupt request. "Pitch one? To who?"

Doug pointed dramatically towards the chain-link fence. "Throw at the fence. Your fastball!"

The teen still looked baffled. "Why?"

Now Doug pointed at me. "Show him how fast they throw in Major League!"

The tall blonde, athletic teen took the baseball in his hand but hesitated. "Uh... I don't think I can throw it that fast."

That was it! I was dead! If this big, tall teen couldn't throw it as fast as the local Little League supermen, what chance would I have trying even *trying* to get a hit! Well, the teen reared back and threw a pretty impressive fast ball. It crashed hard into the fence. Doug turned to me again, the same look of angry intensity on his face.

"That's more like how fast they throw in Major League!"

It was only years later that it dawned on me: that tall athletic teenager got tripped up on the terminology. He thought my knucklehead friend was asking him to throw as hard a PRO-FESSIONAL Major League Baseball players! Oh well.

It didn't take long for my newfound passion for baseball to rub off on my brothers, though granted, John, at age two, was probably a bit too young to truly appreciate the National Pastime. Dad, meanwhile, sensing our now rapidly expanding interest in the game, decided to take us boys up to Camp Smith to watch the evening men's softball games. This was a Camp Smith Marine league and was strictly fast pitch. One Marine pitcher in particular had a sharp, robot-like, three-part wind-up that culminated in a whipsaw fastball that befuddled virtually every batter he faced. I remember him as a hardened, grey-haired fifty-something leatherneck sergeant with a mean crew cut beneath his red ball cap. In retrospect he was probably 31 years old or something like that

What *really* made an impression on me as I watched those grown men play the bat and ball game was the awesome sight of a ball being hit high into the air. *Any* ball being hit high into the air! Sure, any soaring flyball to the outfield was a sight to behold, but I was also turned on even by infield popups or towering foul balls that soared in the wrong direction over the backstop. This awe-inspiring skill, to smack a pitched ball and send it soaring heavenward, was a skill I *desperately* wanted to master!

Apparently Dad had noticed how locked in my brothers and I were to those Camp Smith softball games, because in a matter of a couple of weeks, he had joined the league himself! The night we went to watch him play for the first time, I was nervous. How would Dad do against these seasoned mercenary Marine ball players who hit towering flyballs and threw flaming fastballs? Soon enough we would find out, for in the second inning, Dad, decked out in his official uniform of a white T-shirt, blue jeans, and blue ball cap, stepped up to the plate, took a couple of practice cuts, and then crouched in a batter's stance. This was a nerve-wracking moment: Would he strike out in front of everybody? Barely get his bat off his shoulders as the pitch whistled past him and landed with a thud into the catcher's mitt?

Happily, after missing the first pitch, he connected for a line drive out to left field—falling between the fielders sufficiently enough for him to reach second base for a double. As play got ready to resume, one of the Marines on the opposing team hollered out to him, "Chaplain! Thou shalt not steal!"

Unhappily, Dad's Camp Smith softball career was cut short two games later. He was playing first base when an overzealous Marine, running out a single, tromped over Dad's leg with his metal cleats and fractured it.

Hitting the Ball High!

It was driving me mad. One glaring shortcoming in my game was dampening my spirits and shaking my confidence as a ball player. It all came to a head one night when I opened one of our family's 1950s Children Lit Classics books and read an entry about the great home run hitter, Babe Ruth. Paragraph after paragraph detailed Ruth's baseball exploits, how he sent towering home run after towering home run into the outfield stadium seats. I couldn't take it anymore—I slammed the book down on my bed and stormed out to the living room where Dad was watching TV.

I had to know. "Dad, how can I hit the ball high in the air?" There. I finally put it out in the open. Yeah, I was getting better and better at making solid contact with the ball when my brothers and I did batting practice. Nevertheless, no matter how many times I stepped up to bat, I continually hit only grounders and line drives. Never had I hit so much as even a pop up! Why?! Babe Ruth surely never had this problem.

Dad thought for a moment. "Well, I think... if you swing slightly upward, the ball will hit your bat and go upwards."

It made perfect sense! I had never deliberately tried to swing upwards. I couldn't wait to test out this theory. That Saturday I had my chance. Dad took us to a nearby park on the outskirts of Honolulu where he pitched us batting practice. He threw. I swung—making sure to swing slightly upward when I connected. It worked! I looked on in wonder and delight as the handiwork of my hands produced a ball that sailed gloriously skyward into the blue! It didn't fly terribly far, but that didn't matter. My bat hit the ball and up, up, up it went!

I would go on to hit countless more towering fly balls, but I never felt more like Babe Ruth than I did that afternoon.

I can speak for myself and my brothers. From that summer on, we were hooked—or should I say, even *more* hooked! And as our baseball knowledge and skill level slowly increased, so did our confidence and baseball interest. It was a wonderfully vicious cycle that would propel us happily through the next three years.

The Major League Baseball Game of the Week

But what about the BIG Leaguers? The *professional*, grown-up baseball players? What was it like to watch *these* masters ply their trade? Unfortunately, we could not find that out in Hawaii—there was no Major League Baseball team on the islands (though there *was* the Islanders, a Triple A Minor League team). There was, however, a way to actually watch Pro Major Leage Baseball. It was called the Major League Baseball Game of the Week, and it was broadcast on TV every Tuesday around 6 PM or so.

Once we learned about the Major League Baseball Game of the Week, I could hardly wait to feast my eyes upon it. Up until this time, I always wondered how fast a real, live big league pitcher could throw. What I kept hearing from kids at school and in the neighborhood was that big league pitchers could throw so fast that you couldn't even *see* the ball! Actually, we also heard that some of the local *Little* League pitchers could ALSO throw so fast you couldn't see the ball (but that's another story).

When this momentous television event finally arrived, we Cook boys planted ourselves in front of our massive black and white (and rented) television set. We were determined not to blink. We would take in every moment of baseball action, study every nuance of the players. At last, be still my beating heart, it came on!

A few things stood out to me watching that first Major League Baseball game on TV. The first and foremost surprise was that the pitcher's mound was only *three feet away* from the batter's box at home plate! Of course it wasn't—it was actually 60 feet and 6 inches away from the plate, but the TV camera lens gave the illusion that the pitcher could almost reach out and pat the batter on the head! And yet even with that intense "closeness," the pitched ball still seemed to float startlingly slow towards the plate. Dad assured us that this too was a mirage—a trick of the TV camera lens. If you were actually a batter standing at the plate, that pitch would be zipping towards you at the speed of light!

There was only one home run that game, a mild home run output even for back then. More incredibly, that home run didn't even leave the playing field! Yes, the first Major League home run I ever witnessed was a bizarre and super rare inside-the-park home run—a long fly ball that landed in an awkward corner of left field and kept being bobbled by the outfielder until he finally managed to corral the dastardly bouncing horsehide and heave it towards home plate. Too late. The batter had made it all the way around the bases and had touched home plate. After watching that game, I came away with the erroneous impression that ALL home runs were accomplished this way!

It was all too much to take: all these glorious visuals of green (at least in my *mind* they were green) infields and outfields, smooth dirt diamonds, lined base paths, backstops, soaring fly balls, zipping fast pitches, a white ball thumping from leather mitt to leather mitt, a stadium packed with cheering fans. And the players too, what a sight! Every player was decked out in impressive uniforms, confident, athletic, highly skilled.

I wanted to be part of all that. I *really* wanted to be part of all that.

Trading Baseball Cards at School

In time I would have my own baseball card collection, but in the spring of 1971 I was still learning the difference between a home run (where the hit ball sailed *over* the outfield fence) and a ground-rule double (where the hit ball *bounced* over the outfield fence). That didn't stop me from trying to be one of the in-the-know baseball guys in my home room class at school. The fact is, I kind of enjoyed looking in on these periodic (but under the table, i.e., out of eyeshot of the teacher) duels known as baseball card trading.

Needless to say, baseball cards appealed to me instantly. Back then, quite unlike today, it was the allure of 3-D baseball cards that was of particular interest to myself and my baseball card-loving classmates. One reason for this is that the 3-D cards, which you either had to send off for in mail-order catalogues or collect one at a time from cereal boxes, featured only star or superstar players. But the main reason, of course, is that their colorful, multi-layer 3-D look was just so cool to look at!

Naturally, the excitement of the other boys in my class over baseball cards rubbed off on me. Though I could not participate (I had no card collection of my own at that early juncture), I enjoyed being one of the observers. For instance there was that morning where Sese and Scott Patrick squared off in the back of Room 14, my fourth-grade homeroom.

The last ten to fifteen minutes of each home room was designated, more or less, as free time to converse, read books or magazines, play board games—just as long as we didn't get too loud and rowdy. That was when Sese and Scott Patrick would go at it like two heavyweight champion prizefighters. These two guys, by far, had the best baseball cards of anyone in the class—maybe in the entire school! But on this morning, Sese was determined to pry away a 1970 Topps Vida Blue baseball card away from Scott Patrick.

From what I gathered from the "baseball gang" talk going around the room, Vida Blue was a hot commodity in the late spring of 1971. A superstar pitcher for the Oakland Athletics, Vida Blue was like superman. He was winning every game he pitched and he was striking out *everybody*! And he was just starting out. He might become the greatest pitcher who ever lived at this rate!

"Do you know why they call him Vida Blue?" one classmate with really bad breath asked me one morning.

I shook my head. "Why?"

"Because he throws so fast all you see is a blue streak going past you!"

"Wow!" And I meant it. Hey, I had no reason to doubt this information. How was I to know that Blue was actually just his last name? Anyway, the duel began: Sese and Scott squared off on the carpet floor next to the cubby holes. We all huddled around them. We gasped in awe as Scott Patrick pulled out his Vida Blue card and held it up.

"What'll you give me for it?" asked Scott with a smirk on his face.

Sese pulled out another card which drew a chorus of 'whoas!' from the admiring onlookers: a 1970 3-D Johnny Bench card. I had already heard of Johnny Bench. He was last year's Most Valuable Player, a terror at the plate who smacked home runs left and right, driving all the runners home too. Like Vida Blue, he was also young, also just start-ing his career. And at this rate, he might become greater than Babe Ruth! "You like?" asked Sese, confident that he had Scott's attention.

Scott's expression turned serious. "Yeah, I want that one."

"Trade then!" exclaimed Sese. But Scott shook his head.

"For Vida Blue I want two cards," said Scott.

Sese was not happy. "I give you Bench and a muff playa'!" Everybody laughed at this. But Sese was serious.

"I want the Johnny Bench 3-D and your regular Brooks Robinson."

Sese practically leaped to his feet. "Brook… No way! You _suffa_'!"

What Sese was telling Scott, in effect, was that he wanted Scott to "suffer." Not so much physically, but in an emotional sense. "Suffa'" was Hawaiian pidgin slang for "go home and hang your head in disgrace because you're not getting anything close to what you want." Or something to that effect. In short, Sese had made it clear to Scott that as a baseball card trade, his demand for superstar Johnny Bench *and* superstar Brooks Robinson… was a dog that wouldn't hunt.

After much haggling, and with all us observers watching with bated breath, Sese and Scott finally came to a mutually satisfying agreement. Sese would get his coveted Vida Blue card, while Scott would walk away with a Johnny Bench 3-D card as well as a 1970 Topps Jim Palmer card. Palmer, by the way, was a star pitcher at this time—not yet a superstar. I had seen him in a recent shaving commercial where the voice-over insisted, "Jim Palmer. He plays hard. Jim Palmer. He *throws* hard…!"

Clearly, baseball was starting to take over my brain.

Chapter 9
The Wonderful and Bizarre World of LEE'S

This must have been sometime in 1972. My brothers and I were walking down the sidewalk towards one of Manana's open grass spaces to (what else) play a little baseball. Our walking route took us past the Medlock house, and as we made our approach, we happened upon Mrs. Medlock and Brent unloading some paper sacks from the car. Brent looked up and waved in greeting. "Gonna throw the ball around some?"

After we all voiced our assent, I made my contribution to the friendly small talk. So I asked the obvious, "Were you all shopping at the base Exchange?"

Brent shook his head as he gathered up three bags in his arms. "No. We were just getting some stuff at Lee's."

Lee's! My eyes lit up when I heard this. "Do they have a new Top 30 chart?"

Brett grinned. "Yep. They put up a new one."

"What number is 'Crocodile Rock'?!" I asked eagerly. It was my new favorite song. I *had* to know what number it was now rated!

"I think it was like number five or something."

I was a little disappointed to hear this. "I thought it would be number one already."

"It probably will," said Brent in a reassuring voice. "Maybe the next chart."

Lately I had become obsessed as to how high my favorite pop songs were "rated." I didn't realize that pop songs weren't "rated" the way Olympic judges held up number cards to numerically reward points for a particular high dive. I had yet to learn that a pop song's placement on the charts was calculated by a mixture of radio airplay and store sales of the 45-vinyl record. What I did know was that currently, the song "I'm Stone in Love with You" was the number one rated song. Just to clarify for you pop musicologists (*wait a minute, that song was never number one on the Billboard charts!*): I only later realized that this Top 30 chart at Lee's only reflected popularity in Hawaii. Still, I couldn't quite figure out why "Stone in Love with You" was still ahead of the super zappy, super catchy "Crocodile Rock." "Stone in Love" was a pleasant enough song, sung by a woman with a quite peculiar tonal quality. Only later did I find out why this woman sounded so odd—it was because the singer was actually a *guy*, singing in falsetto. Nevertheless, there was clearly an unseen panel of music experts who placed votes every week to rate the best songs, and "Stone in Love with You" continued to get the highest rating. As it turned out, however, Brent was more excited about something *else* he had seen at Lee's that day. "Next time you guys are at Lee's, check out their new table tennis game!"

"Where in the store is it?" I asked, my curiosity piqued. We Cooks happened to love table tennis—or Ping Pong if you preferred to call it that.

"You'll find it," grinned Brent. "Just look for the crowds."

Eric chimed in. "They let you play it in the store?"

"Yeah," replied Brent. "But you don't play it on a table!" With that, Brent zoomed up the walk to his house and disappeared inside the front door with his armload of bags. He ignored our pleas for more information. No problem. We would be making a trip to Lee's ourselves that night. Dad and Mom had promised.

A night out at Lee's Department Store. It was a regular highlight of our Pearl City existence. An evening at Lee's usually began with a stop at the red-and-brown brick McDonalds, which shared a large front parking lot with Lee's. "Dining in" at this particular McDonalds was actually a soothing experience: the eating area was a framed roof, open-air-sided patio that overlooked the main avenue which bisected downtown Pearl City. What's more, our one-dollar allowance money always afforded us boys a dream dinner comprised of a regular hamburger, small fries, and a chocolate milkshake (augmented at times by the once-yearly green Shamrock Shake).

After indulging in the McDonald's experience, we would make our way across the crowded parking lot to Lee's Department Store. It was *the* place to shop in Pearl City—kind of like a Walmart in that it had everything, save for a grocery section. I'm sure in some ways, Dad and Mom wished that Lee's didn't *quite* have everything, namely their post card racks. Oh sure, there were the usual postcards adorned with scenes such as Diamond Head crater or Waikiki Beach or Paradise Park or coastal Hawaiian sunsets. No problem there. But it was those *other* postcards that tended to leap out at you: namely, the lovely but quite topless island maidens who smiled happily at you from the metal postcard racks, not at all hidden from the eyes of little (or just basically, underage and curious) ones. I suspect Dad and Mom didn't make an overt fuss over these erotic postcards for fear that this would only draw our attention to them more.

That night, however, we boys weren't looking for the postcards. Almost immediately upon entering the store, we saw the "crowd" Brent had told us would certainly be there. We hurried over to see what was going on.

There it was—just as Brent had said. Like the rest of the gathered gawkers, we Cook boys stared, transfixed at what we were seeing. The crowd of people were huddle around and just behind two teenaged Asian boys who were engaged in their contest. They were playing table tennis all right, but it was being played on a TV screen, affixed to a high display shelf! Their "paddles" were actually on the TV screen and the two players used hand levers to maneuver their televised "paddles" up or down. A tiny moving white square represented the "ball" and the paddles had to be moved up or down to intercept the slowly-moving electronic square "ball" and, making contact, would result in "hitting" the ball back to your opponent.

This was incredible! This was amazing! This was... futuristic! This was a game the Jetsons (TV cartoon family who lived in the distant jet-age future), if they actually existed in real life, would play in their home! And who knew—by the time we reached adulthood, we might *all* be playing games like this on our home television sets! What a concept! And Lee's was leading the way.

Chapter 10
A Clash of Two Worlds

Music Hour at Pearl City Elementary—October of 1971. On this particular day and this particular Music Hour, our Singing class joined forces with the Ukelele class. I think we were practicing for a school musical presentation, though I don't recall it ever coming off. In any event, we repeatedly practiced what was to be our showcase number—a pop music anthem du jour. It was a very "now" song that, apparently, the fourth-grade teachers had deemed important enough for all of us to present as a unified musical statement. So, while most of us sang (reading the purple-colored lettering off the mimeographed song lyric sheets), the ukelele players strummed the rhythm. I must say, as our harmonies soared out the cranked-open upper wall windows, the words and the music turned the grounds of Pearl City Elementary into one gigantic Love-In:

I'd like to build the world a home
And furnish it with love
Grow apple trees and honey bees
And snow-white turtle doves

I'd like to teach the world to sing
In perfect harmony
I'd like to hold it in my arms
And keep it company

If you had grown up during that time, those lyrics might pique your memory as familiar, and for good reason. This song was not only a recent pop hit by a group called the New Seekers, but it was also used in an oft-played Coca-Cola TV commercial. In this bucolic ad, beautiful young people held hands and belted out this song, though with slightly-tweaked lyrics to extol the virtues of Coca-Cola as being consistent with the sentiments of world peace and love. Should there be any doubt about this, the next verse, which I sang through my tears (or maybe it was the teachers who listened to it through *their* tears) drove the point home:

I'd like to see the world for once
All standing hand in hand
And hear them echo through the hills
For peace throughout the land

All this to say that...well, Peace and Love was all over the place in Hawaii back in the early 1970s, particularly in the years of 1971 and 1972 (after which, well, Kung Fu kinda started to take over). That aforementioned song we had to sing in Music Hour is Exhibit A. But it was more than just singing "I'd Like to Teach the World to Sing." And it wasn't just Hawaii, it was nationwide. On TV, you still had the episodic comedy-drama *Love American Style* on the air. When the intro theme song came on, the harmonies of the Cowsills rang out:

Love love LOOOOVE

Love American Style
Truer than the Red White and Blue-ue-ue-ue!

Love American Style
That's me and you
And on a star-spangled night my love
You can lay your head on my shoulder

Likewise, the Partridge Family in *their TV* show theme song promised:

A whole lotta lovin' is what we'll be bringin'
We'll make you happy!

Even TV commercials were trying to bulldoze young people with the message of Peace and Love. I recall one particular soft drink TV commercial song proclaiming the following about its product:

Ginger Ale
Tastes like lo-ove
Canada Dry
Ginger Ale!

Hey, you didn't even need to switch on the TV. All you had to do was walk around the neighborhood and you'd see upper elementary school-age through high school age young people walking around wearing Peace symbol and LOVE cloth patches sewn onto their blue jeans and jackets (yes, jackets were worn in Hawaii for the "look," not for necessity). These patches were advertised for sale in all the comic books at the time. You get the picture. Peace, Love, Togetherness, Brotherhood, Harmony—this was the direction towards which right-thinking adults/parents/educators/Madison Avenue were trying to steer young people at the dawn of the 1970s.

Flower Power may have run its course in the previous decade, but... well, come to think of it, big, colorful flowers were *also* everywhere at the dawn of the 70s, just mostly on posters and as clothes patterns, rather than worn in your hair. Hawaii had a big advantage over every other state in the Union when it came to flowers—they grew here big, colorful, and year-round. Oh, and Hawaiians wore flowers in their hair *centuries* before Scott McKenzie sang the admonition to do this in the 1967 hit, "San Francisco (Be Sure to Wear Flowers in Your Hair)."

There was only one hitch when it came to the Peace and Love indoctrination of us Cook boys. We were military kids. Not that peace, love, and brotherhood couldn't be a part of a military upbringing, it's just that these sentiments, as expressed in current popular culture, often seemed to be coupled with a subtle, veiled contempt for military culture. Sure, we Cooks were a Navy family, but we lived amongst a culture of One-Two-Three-Four, I love the Marine Corps, and this seemed quite out of step with the current cultural ethos of peace, love, and brotherhood. In short, as a kid growing up in Hawaii during the early 1970s, I most definitely straddled two worlds.

Actually, the early 70s Hawaii clash of worlds went beyond the basic conflict twixt Peace and Love versus Semper Fi. To live on the island of Oahu from 1971 to 1974 was to exist in juxtaposition to two different *eras*: one that existed in black and white, the other in vibrant, living color. In one era, men with smoothed-shaved faces wore short hair and went about— even on the islands—wearing coat and ties, wide-brimmed hats. In the other era, men with thick moustaches and sideburns wore their hair either long or thick and tousled, while walking around in T-shirts and cut-off jeans. One era was big band, the other era was electric rock, pop, and soul. There's no mystery: I'm talking about fully living in the early 1970s, yet, weirdly, the era of World War II still seemed to linger all about us.

There's good reason for that. One, at the time our family arrived on Oahu, the islands were only 29 years removed from the Japanese attack on Pearl Harbor. Oh, and where did that take place? Well, consider where we were living: Pearl City.

That kinda tells you how close in proximity we lived to where it all took place. Yes, the Day of Infamy at Pearl Harbor took place virtually in our backyard.

Now to us boys, indeed to any kids our age, thirty years ago might as well have been the Ice Age. It was a time we couldn't relate to as it took place *decades* (almost three) before our birth. To an adult? Thirty years is a vivid, fairly recent memory that one can almost reach out and touch. As for those aforementioned adults, in 1971, well, many of them hadn't even attained grey hair yet. They were everywhere and they remembered Pearl Harbor and World War II. Vividly. Take my fifth-grade teacher, for instance. Ms. Asato was an Asian-American woman who grew up not far from Pearl City. She was in her mid-thirties or so, yet she could share to our class her personal memory of that morning when Japanese fighter planes flew in low over the Oahu landscape. One of those Japanese fighter planes even took a shot at her brother who (foolishly) stood in the field near their house, taunting the Japanese gunners with a broom stick! Thank goodness they missed him!

Then there were the visual reminders of that Pacific War, and they were abundant on the island of Oahu. Several military bases dotted the island and on most of these bases 1930s to 1940s style barracks, airfields, air hangars, shipyards, and officer's clubs were virtually everywhere you looked. The Camp Smith Chapel and adjoining Sunday School building, bright yellow World War II period plank board structures, were also tangible holdovers from that era.

Even in the mountains above Camp Smith there were reminders of those traumatic war years. Our family often hiked the Aiea Loop Trail, a wooded path that wound through a jungle-like landscape of pine and palm trees with thick, vine-covered slopes. But at one particular bend in the trail was a sight which brought most hikers to a dead stop. Just a few feet below the trail, entangled in a heavy growth of dark green brush and vines, was the wreckage of a World War II fighter plane. Clearly it had crashed into the mountainside and was left there to rust. We boys actually climbed down onto the wreckage to examine it up close, though I was nervous I might find the charred remains of some long-dead fighter pilot. Luckily, there were no such gruesome remains. Of course many kids at my school knew of this wreckage and the popular story went like this: It was the crash site of a Japanese fighter plane that went down in the mountains above Honolulu (long before there was an Aiea Loop Trail) on that fateful morning of December 7, 1941. In actuality, as I would later learn, the old wreckage was that of a U.S. fighter plane that had crashed during training exercises in 1944.

Pearl Harbor and Ford Island

Speaking of Pearl Harbor, it was actually one of my favorite military places to visit on the island. It was then, and still is, a bustling U.S. Navy port with everything from aircraft carriers to submarines moving in and then out again to sea. Of course it is famous for the Japanese attack on Dec 7, 1941. Since 1961, the centerpiece of Pearl Harbor was, and is, the U.S.S. Arizona Memorial. I had never lived so close to such a historic spot. When we visited the Memorial in 1971, there was no elaborate visitor's center, no IMAX theater, and no expansive gift shop like there is today. There was just a barren dock with a single ticket booth and a small canvas-covered waiting area for the boat that ferried people to and from the Memorial. On the boat ride out to the white, concave-roofed structure that straddles the ship wreckage, I was struck by the other visitors in our group. They were almost all Japanese. As I stared at them, I wondered how they felt about the war and the attack specifically. Were they proud? Embarrassed? How would I feel if I visited Hiroshima?

Even as a boy I could sense that the memorial was a very hallowed place. As visitors gathered around the displays, the only sounds were low whispers, cameras clicking, and waves lapping up against the rusted hull of the ship. It was a little spooky to imagine that the remains of several hundred servicemen were still trapped just a few feet below us.

From the vantage point of the Memorial, one has a good view of Ford Island which is situated right in the middle of Pearl Harbor. Several battleships were anchored around Ford Island that morning of December 7th. The little island once boasted a long runway in the center, surrounded on its outer edges by a traffic control tower, some officer houses, enlisted dorms, a small dispensary, and various hangers to house the aircraft it serviced. A small dock area was used for boats that would ferry people, supplies, and vehicles back and forth to the main base at Pearl Harbor.

Back in 1971, only military and their guests were allowed on Ford Island. It remained fairly isolated until just recently when the *USS Missouri* was tied up alongside the island and a bridge was built to the mainland. Now tour buses are allowed to drive people onto Ford Island, but just to the dock where resides the *Missouri,* the site of the formal Japanese surrender at the end of the war.

Back then, Ford Island looked pretty much the same as it did the morning of the attack. Almost every structure from World War II was still standing, although many were now abandoned or used for storage. Some buildings, like the Dispensary, still bore the evidence of strafing bullet hole marks left by low-flying Japanese attack planes. The air control tower still stood, silently standing watch over the runway, which had been abandoned years before and now had grass growing up through its many cracks. The hangers were locked up, but with a boost I could still peer through the grimy windows and imagine what they must have looked like when they were filled with airplanes.

On the other side of Ford Island, near the water, was a row of large bungalows, homes to some very fortunate senior Naval officers and their families. In 1971 there were around twenty of these government-owned officer quarters on the island, making for quite an exclusive little community. Many of the yards had enormous banyan trees which seemed big enough on which to build a Swiss Family-like tree house within the branches. There were colorful flowers everywhere, lush gardens, and a view out of the living room windows of the water, just fifty yards away.

Passing by these windows on a daily basis were ships of every kind. In the evenings, the residents were treated to a red sun setting over the water and the chirping of exotic birds. Paradise. And all free, courtesy of the United States Government. Did I mention that you should never feel sorry for military kids? The one hardship for the inhabitants was waiting on a ferry for every errand from grocery shopping to going to school. Even that inconvenience is now a thing of the past since the Navy built the bridge about ten years ago.

But the most fascinating aspect of living in some of these homes was what else could be seen from the living room window. Right off the edge of the island, directly adjacent to one of the streets, was the rusting hulk of a ship turned over on its side. Much of its superstructure was missing, but it was still recognizable as a World War II battleship. It was the final resting place of the *U.S.S. Utah*, also sunk on December 7, 1941. While thousands of people visit the *Arizona* on the other side of the island every year, few know the *Utah* memorial even exists. In the intervening years a small dock, flag, and plaque have been erected to commemorate this ship's sacrifice. Even today, if you were to visit the site, you would probably be the only one there.

Chapter 11
Little League Rookies

The phone call came the evening of March 25, 1972. "Hi. This is Mr. Synder. I'm the coach for the Cardinals."

I didn't hear these earth-shaking words myself. My heart probably wouldn't have been able to take it. But we pestered Mom to give us a full recounting of the conversation—word for word. Still, it's not like she had to tell us the nature of the phone call. We could tell she was talking to a coach. That's all we needed to know... we had made the team! Or at least one of us had. Was it only just one of us?

We stammered out our demand almost in unison, "What did he say, Mom?! What did he say?!"

A lot had happened in the previous year (or very nearly a year) leading up to this moment. We had moved from Tennessee to Hawaii via ocean liner; moved into a tract house in a Pearl City suburb for four months; started attending a new chapel at a Marine base just above Honolulu; finished the 1970-71 school year at Highlands Elementary; moved to Manana Navy/Marine Housing in the summer of 1971; began attending a new school (Pearl City Elementary) in the fall of 1971. Oh, and we Cook boys had become absolutely baseball *batty*.

In the several months leading up to that momentous phone call, my brothers and I had been so anxious to play on a real-live baseball team with uniforms that, well, we made up our own team. We knew we could do this because I'd checked out a fiction book from the library about some kids who created their own neighborhood kid's baseball team and somehow ended up taking on the local little league champions in a big game. They beat the champs, of course. So my brothers and I—since we had yet to connect with a local Little League—created *our* version of a Little League team: the Stingers. We even made official uniforms by coloring the name and team colors on three old white T-shirts. We tried to round up some neighborhood kids, but sadly, the Stingers never got off the ground. We Cook boys were the only ones who consistently showed up for practice. That was all in the distant past now. The day we boys had been anticipating for nearly a full year had finally arrived. We would find out once and for all... if we had made the team!

Prior to that, however, we had to take part in that nerve-wracking rite of passage known as LITTLE LEAGUE TRYOUTS. My brothers had never been through a little league tryout. I had—and it had turned out badly. Why I went out for the local little league baseball team in Tennessee, I'll never know. I didn't play baseball back then. I didn't practice baseball back then. I didn't follow baseball back then. Some friends of mine were going to try out for the baseball team, though, and I felt I could go along with that. I was cut. How humiliating. All through the tryouts I had regaled my younger brothers with stories about how I would be playing in big games with lots of people in the stands watching and cheering. Nearly two years later, I was determined that *this* time, things would be different.

On the designated morning, Dad drove us three older boys over to Franklin Field (just across the street from the waters of Pearl Harbor). We were signed in with the other hopefuls and given a number to wear for quick identification. Then we were divided up into groups according to age. As I waited in my gaggle of baseball-mitted ten- and eleven-year-olds, I was somewhat intimidated to hear the confident talk of other boys who had played before and knew the drill. They were veterans and wanted to make sure everyone knew it. There were other boys like me who were new and pretty much didn't say anything, all the while eyeing everyone else and silently assessing the competition. It didn't help my nerves to see the coaches standing on the sidelines, their eyes concealed by sunglasses, clipboards in hand, and waiting for their opportunity to pass judgment on my skills as a baseball player. Or more to the point, waiting for the opportunity to make my fondest dreams come true. Or...to crush my dreams, and my spirit, forever.

The first part of my tryout consisted of fielding five balls, three ground balls and two fly balls, then throwing the ball to a designated base. After that I would be directed to don a batting helmet, step into the batter's box, and take five swings at pitches thrown by one of the coaches. I was heartily relieved to complete the fielding portion without error and solidly hit four of the five pitches thrown to me. Eric did well also, but there was a twinge of jealousy when I learned he had hit all five of his pitches, one more than me. As we drove home, all of us were very satisfied with how we had performed. No one had choked or embarrassed themselves in front of the other boys. That was a goal almost as important as getting picked high in the draft.

Finally, Mom got to the important part of the phone conversation. She smiled at Eric and I. "He said you both were picked to play on the Cardinals."

How can I even convey how over the moon Eric and I were at the news? To complete the day's victory, we received another phone call later that evening. Seven-year-old Kevin had been selected to play on the Braves in the Manana Navy-Marine Tee-Ball League. For the uninitiated, Tee-Ball is where youngsters (still working on their rudimentary baseball skills) hit the ball off a tee stand rather than stand at the plate and swing at pitches.

The Big White Blob

Our first Cardinals practice began with Coach Snyder gathering the team together on Franklin Field #1 (right next to Franklin Field #2). Standing chest deep in a sea of giant baseball caps and leather ball mitts, he began by sharing his coaching philosophy. To me, Coach Snyder had the commanding presence of a General 'Stormin" Norman Schwarzkopf, and I hung on his every word.

"Winning is good," he started. "Everybody likes to win. But wins and losses aren't going to be our primary focus."

I was surprised to hear this. Yet somehow, I found this beginning to be somewhat comforting. Immediately, the pressure was off. Mr. Snyder continued. "The main thing is, I want to see you all improve as ballplayers. Learn to play the game right. I was watching each of you while you were warming up." By this he meant he studied us while we were throwing the ball around, while we were each trying to look like we were already stars. Coach Snyder went on.

"From what I saw, there's plenty of room for improvement. For everybody." This worried me a little. I felt I was one of the more impressive throwers out there, but apparently Coach Snyder had already found me wanting.

Although Coach Snyder spoke in a calm, kind manner, he had an aura that said this man was not to be trifled with. I had no intention of getting on his bad side and eagerly drank up every word like the last glass of water in the Sahara Desert. For one thing, his manner may have been calm and kind, but his body was tank-thick and he had the stoic no-nonsense expression of a powerful Indian chief. He continued. "When I say play the game right, I mean backing each other up and being gentlemen in victory and defeat. I don't tolerate taunting the other team or hot-dogging on this team." I wasn't sure what hot-dogging was and hoped I wouldn't accidentally commit that sin.

After a year of trying to teach myself the fundamentals, I was thrilled to finally have my own baseball coach. Coach Snyder drew his opening address to a conclusion. "Finally, when I'm talking, all moving around and noise will cease. I want every eyeball on me." It was a subtle message directed at a couple boys who already were goofing off near the perimeter of our little circle. Sensing the sternness in his voice, they stopped immediately. Taking no chances myself, I immediately fixed my eyes on the coach's head in a laser-like stare of such intensity that it would have given even Charles Manson cold chills. Coach Snyder shot me a quizzical glance as if to say, "You look a little *too* motivated for my taste."

Having regained our undivided attention, Coach Snyder began to discuss the practice schedule. It was pretty simple to remember. Every weekday when there was not a game on the schedule, we would be practicing. The prospect of daily workouts was exciting to me, but I could see from the expression on my teammates' faces they were not as enthused. It was dawning on everyone that this wasn't your average "we're all just going to have fun" coach. This was no cheerleader coach with a silly grin, clapping his hands and telling us, "great job," as we booted the ball all over the field. No, school was in session and our performance would be graded.

A boy named Frank raised his hand. "Coach, when we come for practice, how do we know which field we're on?" Frank asked this because Franklin Field was actually made up of four fields: two playing fields and two large practice fields.

This question didn't phase Coach Snyder. "Don't worry about which field to meet on," said Mr. Snyder. "I'm easy to find. Just look for the big white blob. That will be me."

We all laughed, but that description proved to be accurate. From a distance, that's what he looked like. Although his skin was very tan, most of it was usually covered by something white: white hair, white ball cap, white shirt, and white shorts. Mrs. Snyder must have been a whiz with the bleach considering how much dirt gets kicked up around a baseball field.

The blob adjective was descriptive of the man's stocky body which consisted of thick muscular arms and legs centered around a prodigious belly. As they say in the interior decorating business, the belly was the focal point. It was a belly that had been affectionately nurtured during 23 years of Naval Service and had been his companion through white-knuckle storms, enemy encounters in Korea, and numerous cruises to exotic ports. Such a stomach was a badge of honor among Navy Chief Petty Officers, the crusty upper echelon of the Navy Enlisted ranks. These respected elders were given the professional courtesy of a blind eye when it came to nuisances such as military weight standards. It was a symbol that said, *"After all I've achieved in the Service, my feet have earned the right for some home-grown shade."*

Mr. Winston

Standing behind Mr. Snyder, nodding in solemn agreement at every pearl of wisdom he uttered, were the two assistant coaches—Mr. Tighe and Mr. Winston. Coach Snyder insisted that we always address these assistants as "Mister." Besides their shared title and deep respect for Coach Snyder, there wasn't much else the assistants had in common.

The older of the two was Coach Tighe, a young single sailor who was all of twenty-three years old. To us he was the epitome of masculinity with his strong jaw, flat stomach, and a mischievous twinkle in his eye that attracted the ladies. He had an easy air of confidence about him that young boys admire and aspire to. As a very eligible bachelor, Coach Tighe was sacrificing some serious Waikiki girl-watching time each week to work with us. This was primarily because of his devotion to David Detry, our second baseman. David's family had kind of adopted Mr. Tighe as another son a couple years earlier. David and all the Detry kids worshipped him. In the end, Mr. Tighe couldn't resist the boy's repeated requests for him to help coach the Cardinals.

On the other hand, it was highly doubtful *anyone* had pleaded with Mr. Winston to help coach their team. He had volunteered his services throughout the league but had no takers until Coach Snyder offered him a job with the Cardinals. Although somewhat intimidated by our other assistant, Mr. Winston was anxious to be seen as an equal. That was a tall order. Mr. Winston was the anti-Mr. Tighe. As graceful and handsome as Mr. Tighe was, Mr. Winston was just as awkward and plain.

If Mr. Snyder resembled a white blob from a distance, Mr. Winston resembled a tall ostrich wearing a baseball cap. The bird-like effect began with his small head swiveling upon a very long neck. His head was topped by light blond hair closely-cropped and away from the ears, probably at the insistence of his Navy father. Matching the thin top covering, Mr. Winston cultivated a forlorn garden of chin stubble below, a self-conscious attempt to appear older. Below those lonely hairs, centered halfway down his long neck, was an Adam's apple that gave the impression he had swallowed an egg but couldn't quite get it down.

The rest of Winston's body was long and skinny, covered in the torso by his unique fashion statement—a gargantuan bowling shirt. The shirt was intended to make him look thicker around the middle but just accentuated his skinniness with pipe stem arms that dangled out from the large sleeves. He looked like a guy who Puberty was punishing for some unknown offense. I found out years later that there was a reason for that—he was actually *going* through puberty. "Mr. Winston" was only fifteen years old!

Although we grew quite fond of the guy, Mr. Winston could also be very annoying. He was constantly telling us about great things he had done that we knew he didn't, great people he'd met that we knew he had not, and unbelievable experiences he'd had that were just that, unbelievable. All this thinly veiled bluster made him the constant target of our jokes. Most of these jabs were whispered behind his back, but some were bold enough to say them to his face. Under normal circumstances, such disrespect would have invited a beating from a kid four years older. But even we could tell that this was a guy you could push without fear of physical harm. Although he sometimes muttered some empty threats and turned red as a beet when teased, Mr. Winston was a pretty good sport. He realized that underneath it all, we really did like him. And he in turn liked us.

Looking back, I'm sure that if ten- and eleven-year-old kids found it so easy to make fun of him, his life in high school must have been pretty rough. High school culture has never been kind to the Mr. Winstons of the world. I imagined that every morning when the bell rang to start first period, it was actually ringing the start of an all-day round of boxing for our illustrious assistant coach. A round of boxing where he was always on the defensive, covering up against a torrent of jabs, hooks, and right crosses both verbal and physical. Mr. Winston had not been blessed with many tools to engage in these types of battles, save one. God had given him the ability to hold his chin up and never let an opponent know he was hurt. He wrapped himself in a blanket of false bravado that hid each

bruise and tried to convince the world that every swing directed his way had missed.

Once we were making fun of his baseball glove, which was
obviously very old and way too small for someone his size—
over six feet tall. I'm guessing that his parents, for whatever
reason, had refused to buy him a decent one and he was forced
to use a ball mitt from his elementary school days. Unfortunately, we were too young and stupid at the time to realize the
real embarrassment this caused him. "Mr. Winston," laughed
David Detry, "that little ol' glove was old when Babe Ruth was
playing!" We all laughed as Mr. Winston shot David an indignant glare. We weren't done. This time it was Joe Kossler who
jumped in.

Joe pointed at the old, tiny glove. "That glove is so small you
should be picking cotton with it!" We all weren't sure what that
meant but it sounded funny, so we all laughed aloud again.
Now Mr. Winston shot Joe an indignant glare. He was ready to
fight back now and he wasn't going to give us the satisfaction.

Mr. Winston craned his necked towards all of us and jabbed
his miniscule glove in our direction. "You guys think you know
ball gloves, but you don't!" Now, he pounded his trusty old
leather mitt. "This is your classic pitcher's glove! Sandy Kofax
uses a glove like this!"

A chorus of catcalls and expressions of rabid disbelief rang
out from us boys—we *knew* Sandy Kofax never pitched with a
glove like that. Mr. Winston wasn't rattled by our skepticism,
and he went on: "Pitchers need a small glove. It cuts down
on the wind resistance. Listen, when you go into that wind-
up, you want *both* arms movin' fast. 'Cause the batter'll smack
that ball right back at you. You gotta snag it and throw! First
base, maybe home plate where the runner's tryin' to score!
You can't do that with those big ol' new modern gloves."

We still weren't convinced and we rained down more mockery upon him. But Mr. Winston wasn't done. He continued to

mount his defense with a Barney Fife-as-coach voice: "Look at that giant webbing on those gloves you guys play with! They just swallow the ball up. By the time you dig it out of there, that base runner's already at first base laughin' at you!" Mr. Winston leaned in and with a stern eye, he rested his case: "Not me. I'll take my Sandy K special any day of the week. No ball gets stuck in *my* glove! With this, snag and fire, snag and fire! Wouldn't trade this glove for anything." It was classic Mr. Winston. By the time he was through we were almost ashamed of our expensive gloves.

But all that bravado takes energy—a lot of energy for an awkward teenager. Sometimes when Mr. Winston came to practice, we could tell that he had exhausted a good supply of it that day at school. The bell had finally sounded and our fighter was trudging back to his corner a weary man. I think that's what Coach Snyder saw almost immediately and we never did. Here was a fighter who needed a good corner man. Someone to give him confidence between rounds. Someone to offer him a cool drink and reassure him that he was doing great. Someone to, if only for a couple hours on a baseball field, stop the bleeding. So, on those bad days, at the start of practice, Coach Snyder would be waiting in Mr. Winston's corner, towel thrown over the shoulder, a stool in hand, ready with some words of encouragement.

"How you doing today, Champ?"

"I'm feeling a little tired, Coach. They stung me a few times out there today."

"Naw, you're fine. They hardly touched you. Besides, tomorrow is your round. I can feel it."

"I don't know sir. Today in P.E. we were dressing out and..."

The Corner Man delivers sharp slaps on the back. "Hey, you know what. I'd like you to pitch batting practice this afternoon. These kids need to see what some real heat looks like. They're a little cocky after we beat the Giants so bad. But those Pirates this Saturday are going to be a different ball game. Hank Buchanan can really throw. I need you to get the guys ready for that speed. Give'm a wakeup call."

"Well, I haven't pitched in a while. I'm wild sometimes..."

"Don't worry about it. It'll sharpen their reflexes. Hey, after we're done today, you, me and Mr. Tighe need to figure out how we're going to pitch some of these Pirate batters. Can you stay a little late?"

"Sure Coach—if you need me. Matter of fact, I got some ideas how we can handle those guys..."

And so it went. Soon Mr. Winston would be back to his lovable, obnoxious self, strutting around the field, barking out instructions like a drill sergeant, whipping the troops into shape. Mr. Snyder just stood back and let him go. We could never understand why. As I gathered my things after practice, I would see him standing with the other two coaches, arms folded exactly as theirs were, laughing uproariously at some private coach's joke Mr. Tighe was telling. I would shake my head and think, "What a goofball!"

But I had missed it. I couldn't see the wonderful thing happening right in front of me. Couldn't see an old silver-haired coach saving a young man's life, one baseball practice at a time. It was so subtle. There were no long counseling sessions. No rousing speeches about "when the going gets tough, the tough get going." All Coach Snyder did was give Mr. Winston the opportunity to be called "Mister" and then treated him like one—every day. It's the kind of therapy for which people pay thousands of dollars for a fifty minute session. Mr. Winston received his therapy for free and never knew he was getting it. A lucky guy. I've never been very good at Math, but I do know one thing. There's not a 1:1 ratio of Mr. Winstons to Coach Snyders, and that's as they say, "a very sad statistic."

Chapter 12
Standoff Between Eddie Tangen... And Cory Beetle

Of course I was aware of Eddie Tangen. He was Cindy Medlock's boyfriend, and that alone was enough for me to dislike him intensely, never mind the added detraction of his surly personality (or so it came across to me in our brief encounters). I doubt, however, that he took much notice of me in those first two years. Eventually though, I did come to fall across his radar. Not because of anything I personally had said or done to him, but because I was often in the company of...Cory Beetle.

Cory Beetle was a member of my close circle of friends in Manana. He was a scrawny, somewhat loud-mouthed little guy with a burr haircut, a face full of freckles, and a God-given talent for making people want to strangle him. I think his annoying behavior was actually a pre-emptive tactic, meant to defend himself from the barrage of teasing he endured about his last name and small size. Because he could be so infuriating, I would sometimes wonder how we ever became friends in the first place. We couldn't have been more different. I was rather quiet and studious, always concerned that my behavior didn't upset the teacher. Cory was loud and unstudious, always concerned that he wasn't upsetting the teacher enough.

In reality, we hadn't just become friends; Cory had almost demanded it. He, without invitation, had attached himself to me and my circle of buddies. Like a tick, he had bit into us and could not be dislodged. We made several unsuccessful attempts to tactfully ditch him, but finally, in exhaustion, we accepted our fate. Despite his lowering our group's "cool" factor by several points, Cory was actually a funny guy to have around, and engendered our begrudging respect because unlike us, he never, ever, gave in to fate. He may have been a pest, but he was our pest. However, attaching yourself to Cory Beetle could also be hazardous to your health.

Why is it that the Cory Beetles of the world so often choose for their practical joke or mocking targets, a guy who is older, meaner, and infinitely capable of pummeling him to a pulp? In this instance, it was none other than Eddie Tangen who Cory Beetle had chosen to "torment." Maybe Cory just wanted to be "cool" like Eddie Tangen, and by being regularly obnoxious to him, perhaps, in Cory's mind, Eddie would playfully punch him on the shoulder and say, "Hey, you're all right, kid. Wanna be in our gang?"

And this is the way Cory intended to accomplish this: Every time he would spot Eddie Tangen around the neighborhood— and Eddie would usually be in the company of the long-haired teens of Manana—Cory would yell out in a sing-song voice:
"Kai-ser
The Pizza Pie
Man!"
When we asked Cory why he taunted Eddie Tangen with such lyrics, Cory informed us that he'd learned that Eddie's middle name was Kaiser. It made sense to us. Kinda. The only problem was, a group of us kids, and Cory was a regular part of our group, would walk together to school every morning. As we started off marching down the main avenue of Manana, we would inevitably pass a group of teens, huddling together, of-

ten smoking cigarettes, and waiting for their high school bus to arrive. Cindy Medlock was usually amongst that group (though not one of the smokers). But, naturally, so was Eddie Tangen.

Before the "incidents" started, this group of high schoolers hardly took notice of us. Occasionally Cindy might look up and our eyes would meet. At that point I would wave and smile. She would usually smile and wave back. For me, that was the perfect start to any school day. I wish I could say she was always looking out for me to walk by, but that wasn't the case. Eddie Tangen demanded too much of her attention.

It was towards the latter part of the 1972 school year, however, when Cory Beetle first started doing it. As our group walked past the high schoolers, gathered on the opposite side of the street, Cory would sing out in a loud voice:
"Kai-ser
The Pizza Pie
Man!"
Where did the song come from? A TV commercial? One kid at school said it was from a soul record put out by a football player named Rosie Grier, but none of us could verify that. All we knew was, Cory Beetle got a huge kick out of singing those three lines every time he spotted Eddie Tangen.

For a full week or more, as our group of school walkers passed the teen group, Cory would make sure Eddie saw him and then sing out his song:
"Kai-ser
The Pizza Pie
Man!"
At first Eddie just glowered at Cory and retorted with something like, "Get outta here, punk." As the days went by and Cory's singing continued, Eddie's threats grew stronger: "Come over here, punk, I'll kick your ass!" At that our group would walk faster—none of us, other than Cory Beetle, *dared* make eye contact with the teens, much less Eddie Tangen. Pretty

soon, it got to the point where even Cory was aware of the risk he was taking—so after he would yell out his 'pizza man' song, he would break into a run. So did the rest of us. Once safely out of the boundaries of Manana Housing, however, Cory would inevitably break into loud cackles.

How did this make the rest of our group feel? Mortified. We all made our own threats to Cory: "You better cut it out, Cory, or he's gonna beat you silly!" Cory would just laugh. I think our threats and warnings just encouraged him. Worse, however, is that Cory was making me look really bad in front of Cindy. What must she think of me that I willfully hung out with a knucklehead like Cory Beetle? I began to contemplate taking a different walking route to school—one where I wouldn't cross path with Cory Beetle.

It all came to a head soon enough. One morning, our group passed the huddled teens as usual. But this time, Eddie wasn't with them. Cory had no one to sing his song to. So we marched on and finally turned left to cut across the small grass plot and from there, down the hill towards King Street. As we moved onto the grass plot, we all suddenly froze. There stood Eddie Tangen. He was waiting for us. My legs turned to jelly—I knew I was dead.

I wasn't the one Eddie was after, however. Completely ignoring me, Eddie stormed right up to Cory Beetle and lifted the yelping miscreant up into the air by his shirt.

"You got something to say now?" demanded Eddie. Cory could only gape back in terror. With that, Eddie hurled Cory to the ground, then pounced on him. There were two quick flashes of arms and fists—Eddie's that is. Then, breathing heavier, Eddie slowly got to his feet and began walking away. Cory was still laid out on the grass, moaning. Blood poured out of his nose. Gail, one of the girls in our school walking group, angrily turned to Eddie and shouted, "You didn't have to do that! He's really hurt!"

Eddie half turned to us and exclaimed back, "Good! I hope he dies!"

Cory continued with us to school, only now he was quiet, teary-eyed, subdued. We all felt bad for him, but we knew something like this was inevitable. "Maybe you'll learn your lesson now, Cory," said David, another one of our gang.

Cory's response was in character. "Shut up!"

The next day our school walking group, as usual, filed down the main avenue of Manana in the early morning hours. As usual, we came upon the group of teens who huddled together, smoked, played rock and pop music on their transistor radios. Eddie was with them this time and he was waiting for us. He turned to us with a wicked smile. "Not so cocky this morning, are ya, punk?" It was clear Eddie was addressing Cory. We all ignored Eddie and the other teens who laughed. Out of the corner of my eye, I could see Cindy tugging at Eddie's shirt sleeve, urging him to leave us alone. It was a horrible moment.

What was Cory's response? Well, it looked like he had finally learned his lesson. He didn't answer Eddie. In fact, he didn't even look over at the group of teens. His head was hung in disgrace. He slunk by the group of teens like a dog with his tail between his legs. Eddie yelled one final taunt at Cory, but we just urged him to keep going.

Once we reached the edge of the grass clearing, I patted Cory on the shoulder. "That's the way to keep your cool, Cory," I said. "You were the bigger person." Suddenly, Cory whipped around and darted past me, back in the direction of the Manana street. He paused at the edge of the grass and shouted in his loudest voice: "Hey, Eddie...!"

Then, you guessed it. In his loudest, most obnoxious voice, Cory sang out:

"Kai-ser

The Pizza Pie

Man!"

And with that, we all (Cory included) took off running at full speed.

Chapter 13

Baseball School Is in Session (And We Bring the Pain!)

Those pre-season practices were planned to precision by Coach Snyder. Everything we did from the time we walked on the field had a purpose. Either separate or in combination, our work was designed to improve our skills, mental focus, knowledge, fitness, teamwork, or prevent injury. Coach Snyder believed that "having fun" was the byproduct of achieving the above list, not the end goal. It started with simple things. When we arrived for practice, we were to pair up on our own and begin playing catch. To avoid straining our arms, we were told to begin throwing at a close distance, then slowly move back as our arm muscles warmed up. Then, came the part we dreaded: exercises!

Coach had us all spread out in three lines facing him and then turned us over to Mr. Tighe. We began with some jumping jacks and stretches, which weren't too bad. Then came those six dreaded words: "On your backs for leg lifts!"

At this point, Coach Snyder took over. Leg lifts called for a harsh, uncaring demeanor that Mr. Tighe frankly didn't have the stomach for. Before leg lifts had entered my life, I had been little acquainted with extended stretches of physical pain, other than a few trips to the dentist in Millington. Okay, that and my two front teeth getting knocked out when I tried to jump through the chain uprights of a swing set (also in Millington), but all in all, my life had been fairly pain-free. Until now.

We dropped to our backs with a groan, arms at our sides, eyes staring up at the clouds floating by. Then Coach would give a chirpy, "Up!" At that command we were to lift both legs together about six inches off the ground and hold them in that position. If you have never had the pleasure of trying this, it very soon brings a rather uncomfortable tightness to your stomach muscles and slowly sets the back of your legs on fire.

As we held this position, the coaches would wander amongst the grunting and groaning players looking for cheaters. These were rascals who watched the coach and as soon as he turned his head for a second, let their legs down to catch a second or two of relief. Or, they would sneakily take their fists and slide them under their thighs thus providing two undetected pedestals to rest their tired legs upon. These criminals were almost always caught and then the whole team was punished by having to do an extra leg lift. But we were not through with "Up!" The next command was 'Out!" At those words you spread your legs out—ten boys doing their imitation of a woman in labor. Then, a few agonizing beats later came, "In!" But "In" only brought minimal relief—your legs are still being held airborne!

When our legs were vibrating uncontrollably in a last-ditch attempt to keep them raised above ground level, Coach Snyder would *finally* say, "Down!" With a collective thud, our legs would gratefully succumb to gravity and smash down on the grass. At that time there arose all around the sounds of moans, sighs, and other noises of thankful relief. The bad news was that was simply run-through number one! A typical session called for *ten* sets of these tortuous leg lifts.

I'm not sure how leg lifts helped us become better players, but it sure made us tougher. For the first time in my life I realized that I could push myself through physical pain. Another realization (somewhat unrelated) was that Mr. Winston needed a good swift kick in the pants. He seemed to get distinct pleasure in walking around and measuring to make sure our feet were off the ground the required six inches.

When we were done exercising, the final item on the fitness agenda was to run one lap around the Franklin Field complex, a distance of about half a mile. One of my friends, Jeremy Simmons, was always complaining that he couldn't do this because of his asthma. Coach Snyder, being the sensitive Navy Chief Petty Officer he was, replied with a compassionate, "Get running!" Jeremy reluctantly took off but when he was across the field and moving behind the snack shack, he would stop to catch his breath, supposedly undetected by prying eyes. After about 30 seconds, he would appear on the other side, somehow thinking that he had fooled the coaches. I guess they were supposed to believe that it took him 35 seconds to cross behind a building ten feet wide. When he arrived back, the stunt usually earned him extra jumping jacks.

Phase Two: Actually Playing Baseball

Now that we were exhausted, it was time to begin playing baseball. Almost immediately Coach Snyder decided I was going to play centerfield. This crushed me. My heart had been set on first base. I wanted to be part of the infield where most of the action was. My feelings of being put on the "B" team were only reinforced when he divided up infielders and outfielders for separate drills. He and Mr. Tighe would hit balls to the infielders and guess who would hit balls to the outfielders? That's right, Wonderboy Winston.

As I trotted out beyond second base with my fellow outfielders, I could feel a very bad attitude coming on. This group had all the bad players! There was Frankie who didn't take anything serious. Joe, a suspect fielder. David, whose glasses were so thick, I wasn't sure if he could see his baseball glove, much less a ball coming at him. Even my nine-year-old brother Eric was living it up with the infield group, albeit as a back-up second baseman.

Mr. Winston carried a bag of balls and a bat with him to the outfield and started hitting us fly balls from about 150 feet away. He was having some difficulty throwing the ball up with one hand, quickly grabbing the bat with both and hitting the ball out to us. Some of his tosses dropped back to the ground, untouched as he whiffed. Other times, he took a mighty swing, but miss-hit the ball so it just dribbled out a few feet in front of him. When this happened, he would holler at us. "Okay, you guys, let's see some hustle. You need to run in on these ground balls. Every ball isn't going to come right to you!"

After several practices in what I considered "the low reading group," I finally gathered up enough courage to confront Coach Snyder. "Coach, can I switch to first base? I think I'm better playing there."

Coach Snyder's reply was calm and soft-spoken—but firm. "Son, a baseball team needs its strongest fielders up the middle. That means second base, shortstop, and center field. They get hit the most balls. In the outfield, I need someone fast, with a strong arm to back up the left and right fielder in case they misplay a ball."

This wasn't the answer I wanted, but it made me feel a little better about my assigned position. Besides, Coach would be proven right. I spent that first season chasing down balls my teammates sometimes let get by them. I threw out several runners, a skill that would have been wasted at first base which rarely required a throw longer than sixty feet.

After we practiced a while in separate outfield and infield groups, Mr. Snyder brought us together to work on what he called "situations." The Gospel according to Snyder said that a good ball player is thinking ahead at all times. For instance, as a centerfielder, I needed to know before every pitch what the balls and strikes count was on the batter, which bases had runners on them, and how many outs there were. All that information would help me anticipate where to throw the ball if it came to me.

Nothing infuriated Coach more than an outfielder grabbing a ball, then freezing as he tried to think what to do with it. This hesitation could give an alert base runner time to score or at least advance a base or two. No, you needed to know where you were going to throw it before the ball came to you. In fact, he wanted all of us on every pitch to be repeating in our heads, *"If it comes to me on the ground, I'll throw to base X. If I catch it in the air, I'll throw it to base Y."* Unfortunately, my quirky friend Jeremy Simmons, alertly patrolling right field would be thinking, *"Jeremiah was a bull frog, was a good friend of mine. I never understood a single word he said but...* (whizzzz)...*oh man what was that?!!"* (It's the ball Jeremy).

All these reactions are not instinctual for your average fourth, fifth, or sixth grader. So, Mr. Snyder spent hours going over these situations again and again until our reactions were automatic. When all nine players moved as one unit, it was a beautiful sight and one that gave us much satisfaction.

Batting practice was a different story. In over a hundred years no one has figured out a way to make this activity a thing of beauty. It was, and still is, like a visit to the DMV for renewing your driver's license—an hour of waiting with nothing to do, culminating in ten minutes of excitement when it's your turn at the head of the line! Mr. Snyder or Mr. Tighe normally pitched, feeding us balls at half-speed, allowing us two bunts followed by ten swings, running the last one out. If our star, Bill McMillan, was hitting, we outfielders paid close attention. He could hit them pretty deep, and no one wanted to get nailed by a line drive.

If it rained, we still practiced. Coach just used the puddles and mud to his advantage by having sliding practice. The mush made it more fun for us and prevented injuries from legs being skinned up on the normally hard dirt surface. Our confidence grew as our abilities did. We were getting very anxious to show what the Cardinals could do in actual competition.

Pitching

I had expected to get better once I was on a real baseball team. What I did not expect was something that happened one afternoon before practice. Coach Snyder called me over and said that he'd been impressed with the strength and accuracy of my arm. Would I be interested in pitching? My mouth said "yes" but my brain was telling me this was a step too far. Even in my limited experience, I knew that there was a lot of pressure on pitchers. Every play began with a pitch and games were won and lost on how well the pitcher performed.

Although I was proud of my arm strength, I had no idea how to properly handle myself on a pitcher's mound. Throwing a ball hard and low from the outfield to home plate isn't too difficult when you are on level ground and can take two or three steps to get momentum. Trying to get the same effect throwing from a mound of uneven dirt, keeping one foot on a half-buried rubber slab with a batter leaning closely into the area you are aiming at is quite another. The few times I tried it, the mechanics of it all felt very awkward. Besides, I had no idea how to throw any pitches besides a fastball. Coach Snyder could see the doubt in my eyes but reassured me he would teach me everything I needed to know. I was only ten years old and he said I had three seasons left in Little League, so there was plenty of time for improvement.

Coach Snyder started my education by helping me find a wind-up. The first ones I modeled for him were those I had stolen from watching major league pitchers on television. Unfortunately, many of these pro wind-ups involved arms thrown way over heads, twisting turns of the torso, and high leg kicks, all intended to prepare the body for releasing a ball with maximum velocity towards a small white plate sixty feet and six inches away. After a few seconds of my Rockettes routine (one, two, three, kick!) Coach Snyder stood up from behind our portable home plate and walked out to the mound.

"Alan, you're not Vida Blue and you're not Juan Marichal. Those guys are pros and spend years learning how to control all those sweeping body movements. You can't handle that right now. It seems like after all the kicks and turns in your wind-up, you're almost too dizzy to see where the throw is supposed to go! We need to work on a very simple wind-up that keeps your eye on the target (catcher's mitt), builds some momentum, but doesn't throw you off balance as you release the ball."

So, it was back to the drawing board. Soon we had settled on a very simple motion that I thought was a little dorky but got the job done. Instead of throwing my arms up behind my head, I simply brought them to my chest almost like a boy cradling a young chick in protection. From there it was a simple straight forward stride to the plate, following through down across my chest and below my knees. After about fifteen minutes of repetition, it began to feel like second nature and the ball began popping into Coach's catcher's mitt without him having to move it hardly at all.

That "thud" of a speeding horsehide ball hitting the padded leather of the catcher's mitt becomes almost addictive. It is an experience right up there with other sensory delights such as the "crack" of a wooden bat when a ball is struck on the sweet spot, the smell of a new leather baseball glove, and the sight of a pristine baseball field with its white chalked lines, dark green mowed grass, and red dirt infield raked to smooth perfection. These and many other small pleasures are what make young boys sleep with their baseball gloves and old men in Florida spend hours of each Spring sitting in hard wooden seats at some ballpark. I was no exception. Once I struck out my first batter, I was hooked. From then on, no matter how frustrating the experience oftentimes became, I still wanted to pitch. Even now I miss the "high" of winding up, the ball whizzing out of my left hand like it was shot out of a cata-pult, seeing the batter swing and miss, hearing the thud of the catcher's mitt, and watching an umpire stand and yell, "You're out!" It still gives me goose bumps.

Before we knew it, the first scrimmage game was upon us. We couldn't wait. In just three short weeks, Coach Snyder had molded this motley group of bubble gum chewers into a lean mean baseball machine. Or so we thought. It was time to show what we could do against a real opponent with all our fans (well okay, moms, dads, and siblings under duress) filling the stands. Looking at the schedule, I almost pitied the Dodgers—our first victim.

Chapter 14
The Medlocks: Trouble in Paradise?

Though it was Cindy Medlock who tended to fill my romantic thoughts and dreams, it was actually Brent Medlock with whom we Cook boys bonded the most. He would come over on several occasions to play Catch or Pickle with me and my brothers. To my surprise, he was actually a pretty good baseball player. I had expected him to be some kind of pretty boy songbird who would probably be a "muff" at sports. But that wasn't the case.

"See if you can catch my drop ball," he would say. Then, he would proceed to execute a perfectly credible, and tricky, drop ball pitch. Many times I actually had trouble catching it! Brent could also throw a not-too-shabby knuckle ball, a pitch I could not master at that time to save my life. We Cook boys agreed amongst ourselves that Brent would probably do pretty good in Pony League (the league for 13- to 15-year-olds) if he had gone out for it. The fact is, as talented a singer and musician as Brent was, we boys judged him far more on his baseball ability. That's just kind of where our minds were at that point in time.

Brent also had his own catch phrase. He would use it whenever one of us made a good play or said something he agreed with. For instance, when we were all throwing the ball around, Eric might throw a pitch to Brent and then ask, "Was that good fast ball?"

Brent's inevitable response would be, "It was all right. Outta sight!" This would set Eric and Kevin off, especially Kevin. "You always say that! What does that mean?!" Kevin would stomp his feet in frustration, just to drive the point home. Brent would just laugh.

In hindsight, maybe Brent didn't mind hanging out with a bunch of bratty younger kids because (largely unbeknownst to us boys at the time) things were not always harmonious at home. Only later would we discover that all was not peace and harmony within the Medlock house. The key point of conflict appeared to be Cindy Medlock's romantic infatuation with n'er do well, Eddie Tangen. At least that's how Eddie came across to us boys, not that we knew him personally. Still, I was blissfully unaware of any Medlock family troubles until that week Dad and Mom took an anniversary trip to the Big Island. We boys stayed home, though Cindy and various adult friends would check in on us from time to time. During that week, Mr. and Mrs. Medlock were good enough to give Eric, Kevin, and I regular rides to baseball practice.

One day, as we three boys arrived at the Medlock house for our ride to ball practice, we were startled to hear loud arguing coming from the house. Mr. Medlock's deep, growly voice boomed out several angry words, but the ones that stood out to me were, "Because that guy's a punk! He's a bum!"

This was followed by tearful protestations from a voice that I recognized as Cindy's. "He is *not* a bum...!" Now the voice of Mrs. Medlock, echoed from the house but I couldn't tell what she was saying or whom she was addressing. All I could tell was that Mrs. Medlock sounded awfully upset, maybe even crying. It seemed to me like she was trying to smooth things over between her husband and her daughter.

As for us Cook boys, we just stood there, outside the front door. Frozen. Completely unsure of what to do. Finally, Brent emerged from the house, smiling sheepishly at us. "Some messed up family, huh?"

We didn't know how to answer this. I just kind of laughed nervously, as if I was used to such blow-ups. A moment later, Mr. Medlock emerged from the house, fiddling with his car keys. He looked up, saw us Cook boys standing in his driveway. He looked a little embarrassed that we might have heard the ruckus. He proceeded to unlock his car door and then ours. As he did so he growled, "My daughter and her damned boyfriend are about to drive me up the goddamned wall!"

Needless to say it was a pretty quiet ride to practice. For the most part, anyway. Finally, though, Mr. Medlock decided to confront the elephant in the room: "Have you guys seen how good those Oakland A's are doin' lately? They just might be in the World Series!"

A topic I could relate to! I brightened up. "They have great pitchers! Vida Blue, Jim Hunter, Blue Moon Odom, Kenny Holtzman..." The conversation flowed more easily from there. Even so I was more than a little chagrined to have witnessed even those few moments of the Medlock family disturbance. Up until that point I had always assumed the Medlocks were the kind of family that always held the winning hand. Unlike other families, they just seemed to float above it all. I wouldn't be that naïve again. That day I learned that lurking beneath even the most ideal of family facades, there is often trouble in paradise.

Chapter 15

Season One:
"There be Pirates..."

There was some serious posing going on. One person blocking another, elbows being thrown as each maneuvered for a more prominent place up front. Everyone was turning from side to side, viewing their figure from every angle. It was vanity on parade and I was disgusted. How was I going to see what my uniform looked like with Eric and Kevin hogging the mirror? On the morning of our first scrimmage game I was donning the green and white of the Little League Cardinals uniform for the first time. Next to Batman's cape and cowl, I couldn't conceive of a cooler outfit than my baseball uniform. I especially liked the look of my cap pulled down with the bill shading my eyes. It made me feel like an old gunfighter staring steely-eyed from underneath his cowboy hat.

Every boy in some way yearns for two things—affiliation with a respected group and admiration for some masculine-related ability. For me, baseball provided both. From the cleats, to the stirrup socks, to the cotton button up shirt with "Cardinals" stitched across the chest, to me each uniform piece said, "I am a skilled athlete, one of the chosen few to be part of an elite male club (yes, male, because females were not yet allowed to suit up for Little League baseball)." I would have worn that uniform to school every day if my mom had let me. Kevin and Eric felt the same way. So, there we were, vying for mirror time to check out our batting stances, scrutinize our pitching motions, and fine-tune the angle of our baseball caps. Looking this good, how could we not succeed?

Our confidence reflected that of our team as we approached the first exhibition game against the Dodgers. We had a great head coach—Mr. Snyder. We had a great assistant coach, Mr. Tighe. We had Mr. Winston. Uh, did I mention we had a great head coach? The year before, the Cardinals had won the league championship and we saw no reason why that success would not continue this season. It was true we had lost the two dominating players from last year's team, one being Mr. Snyder's oldest son. Both of them were now over the age limit. If asked about our prospects, I would reply that we had made up for our losses by adding other potentially dominant players like...well...I didn't have time to discuss details at this point.

At any rate, we had already scouted the Dodgers and were unimpressed. Our extensive analysis came courtesy of the one lap that took our team around the Dodgers' practice field the previous week. Eric had seen the pitcher who would be taking the mound against us in today's scrimmage: a small black kid named Roy. As Eric jogged past the Dodgers practice field, he observed Roy throwing from the mound. Eric came back to us and reported confidently, "He isn't that fast! We can hit him! Easy!" Case closed.

The scrimmage began at 5:30, just late enough so many of the military dads could make it home from work and watch. I was a little nervous since this was my first time playing in front of fans, even if it was just a small group of parents. There were also a few kids watching, but it would be a stretch to call them fans. The one hour of televised cartoons was over for the day and their moms had forced them to play outside until supper. It was either watch us play or dig holes in the dirt. In a very close decision, our game had edged out dirt. Clearly the one thing I did not have to worry about was my concentration being broken by rabid autograph-seekers. What a relief.

As I took my place in center field for the start of the first inning, I ran through the checklist of items Mr. Snyder had taught me. At each pitch I needed to be leaning forward, up on my toes, ready to dart quickly in either direction to field the ball. If a ball did come my way, it was very important to quickly throw it back to the infield, hitting the cut-off man. For a fly ball hit deep over my head, I should turn and run towards the outfield fence, looking over my shoulder to find the path of the ball. My job was also to back them up my teammates in case the ball escaped their lightening quick reflexes. Not surprisingly, the ball eluded my teammates on a regular basis.

As I went through my mental checklist, I glanced at our left-fielder, Jeremy Simmons, to see if he was also in review mode. It was difficult to tell since he was standing with his baseball glove over his face, apparently enjoying the aroma of new-glove leather. I mentally put him down for a "no" on the skill reviewing. I looked to my left at our right-fielder, Frankie Anderson. He was running around in circles, apparently locked in mortal combat with a mosquito, using his glove as a swatter and yelling, "Die, die, you scourge of mankind!" It was comforting to see my teammates so focused on the task at hand.

In the midst of contemplating the shameful mental state of the Cardinal outfield, I heard a familiar high-pitched voice. It was Mr. Winston yelling at us from the dug-out. "Hey you knuckleheads, look alive. Game on!" Ah, the cool, dignified guidance of our coaching staff. Sure enough, Bill McMillan was delivering the first pitch to the Dodger lead-off man. I jumped into a cat-like posture ready to defend my centerfield territory.

The first couple of batters were easily dispatched. One hit a weak ground ball to the shortstop and the next guy struck out on four pitches. "Two outs!" I yelled to Jeremy and Frankie. As leader of the outfield, it was my job to keep them abreast of important facts, and in the case of Jeremy, remind him what planet he was on. For some reason, Jeremy often talked to himself, engaging in fantasy role play, totally unconcerned that a baseball game was going on in which he was a key participant. "Jeremy, there are two outs. You are not Kon-Bar the Dragon Slayer. You are an eleven-year-old boy playing in a Little League baseball game." While I was slowly coaxing my left-fielder back towards the light of reality, I heard the crack of the bat. The next hitter had smashed a low line drive up the middle that was now bouncing towards me at an alarming rate.

My training automatically kicked in. Just as Mr. Snyder had preached, I charged the ball ("Play the ball, don't let it play you!"). When the hurtling sphere was about fifteen feet away, I dropped to my knee and turned sideways to block the ball. I placed my glove firmly on the grass between my legs (Get your glove down so the ball can't skip underneath it!). Now in text-book position I watched as the ball made one final hop. I stared intently as it flew right towards me (Look the ball into the glove!) but bounding a little higher than I had calculated. I was in perfect position—to be hit right in the mouth. BAM!

Waves of stinging pain flowed over me as I flashed back to visions of that metal swing-set seat descending from the sky. I cried out, fell backwards on the ground, and began rolling around while clutching my burning mouth. I tasted blood. All I could think was "Did I break another real tooth or just my false-teeth flipper?" As my fumbling fingers discovered that teeth and flipper were still intact, relief turned to embarrassment. I couldn't believe it. The first play of my baseball career was letting a ground ball hit me in the mouth. I could hear people yelling in the distance. Where was the ball? Where was my back up?

Just then Kon-Bar the Dragon Slayer showed up. Out of breath and disoriented by being so abruptly summoned from his medieval world, Jeremy nevertheless remembered his training. He grabbed the baseball still lying behind me, wound up, and let loose a throw intended for the cut-off man. He hit the cut-off man all right. Unfortunately, it was the man in cut-off jeans eating a snow cone over by the concession stand. Needless to say, the batter scored an easy inside-the park home run.

I finally sat up as Coach Snyder called time out with his two assistants following close behind, running out to make sure I was all right. The Cardinal coaching staff performed a cursory oral examination, consulted, and quickly reached the traditional coach's medical diagnosis: "He'll live." With that they hustled back to the dugout and the contest continued with a living, but very embarrassed, centerfielder.

The game went downhill from there. It turns out the Dodgers were a little better than we thought. Maybe we should have run a couple more "scouting" laps around their practice field the week before. They were not intimidated by our previous year's championship and their pitcher Roy turned out to be very accurate and *very* fast. When Eric had "scouted" him, Roy was apparently throwing half speed so he wouldn't wear his arm out before pitching against us. When the score got to be 8-0, it was my task to inform Eric that a vote had been taken and he had been relieved of his duties as lead scout. The memory that stayed with me to this day was how much it stung to the see the Dodgers' coaching staff jumping with delight at each run (all theirs) scored and then punctuating the added insult to injury by hollering a loud, raucous, "Let's go, let's go, let's GO!!"

Finally, after six very long innings, the game came to a merciful end. At the plate, I had only managed to ground out and strike out. The hardest hit I got was to my own mouth. We lost 10-0 and gained a new sense of humility. Thank goodness it was only a practice game, but to experience such a shellacking right out of the gate still stung.

As we all sat, utterly dejected, in the dugout, Mr. Snyder calmly stood before us in the dugout and calmly said, "Now you know what it's like to lose."

Now the games count

As the real season began, it became apparent that the four league teams fell into distinct levels of ability. At the bottom of the talent pile was the hapless Giants. They had three decent players and ten other guys who owned a glove, a live pulse, and not much else. Hitting ground balls to their defense was like playing croquet, as ball after ball bounced through human wickets. One of my friends, Robby, was their star pitcher and hitter. I felt sorry for him. At the middle ability level was our team and the Dodgers. Despite the result of that first scrimmage, our two teams turned out to be evenly matched. They had Roy, but our star, Bill McMillan, was his equal in both hitting and pitching. At the top of the talent heap was the Pirates.

If the Pirates rode the big ship, the rest of us were packed into rowboats trying desperately to avoid their booming cannons. The Pirates had somehow ended up with a treasure trove of talent including the Manana Navy-Marine Little League Goliath, Hank Buchanan. After about six games, the standings reflected these talent levels. The Pirates were undefeated at 6-0, we and the Dodgers were both 3-3, and the Giants were 1-5. It looked like we were destined to fight it out for the privilege of proclaiming at season's end. "We're number Two! We're number Two!"

As the games progressed, so did my hitting ability. Much of that success was simply learning to focus better. That mental discipline began even before I stepped in the batter's box. While standing in the on-deck circle waiting to hit, I learned to watch the pitcher warming up and study his motion. Where did he release the ball? Low? High? How fast was he? Did he put spin on the ball? Did he tip off his curve by winding up differently than when he threw the fastball? Getting the flow and rhythm of pitcher's motion was crucial to good hitting.

With only 44 feet between the pitcher and the batter's box, there is little time to react. Stepping into the batter's box, my first job was tuning out a myriad of distractions. First, there was a large umpire hovering so close behind me he could wipe his nose on my shoulder. Below him was the chattering catcher trying to annoy or distract me by calling out what pitch was coming (of course he lied) or yelling at me to "Swing!" right before the ball arrived. Then there were the cheers from our dug-out, the catcalls of the opposing dugout, and the kid crying behind the backstop because his mom wouldn't buy him another hot dog.

Once that white blur was on its way, I had about a quarter of a second to decide whether to swing at it, let it go by, or duck. That decision is made even more difficult by pitches that rise, sink, or curve in another direction as they fly towards the plate. There's a reason the great Ted Williams said hitting was the single most difficult thing to do in sport.

Earning My B.A.

Achieving success as a hitter was crucial to reaching my goal of becoming a major league baseball player. I measured that success by the most hallowed statistic in baseball—the batting average (B.A.). It's a simple statistic that's derived by dividing the number of clean hits by the number of at-bats. Walks don't count in the equations, and if you reach base because a fielder made an error, that counts just like an out. My batting average was everything to me. It was my report card of athletic success. When it was high, I was too. When it sank, my spirits went with it.

Baseball, unlike any other sport, is built on a foundation of statistics. Debates about who is better than so-and-so are always argued in accumulated totals, percentages, and a variety of other numerical comparisons. Statistics take on a life of their own and become almost famous in themselves. For instance, ask any baseball fan the significance of the numbers 1941, 56, and 406. He will immediately tell you that 56 is the number of consecutive games that Joe DiMaggio hit safely in. He set that record in 1941 and it still stands today. That same year, Ted Williams hit .406, the last year a major league baseball player hit over .400. Ask the same guy the significance of 1776 or 1812 and you may get a blank faraway look. However, when it comes to numbers, every baseball fan is an expert historian.

Certain numbers are key dividing lines in assessing skill. A player with a .300 batting average is considered a very good hitter, although that only denotes three hits out of ten tries. A .400 batting average is the mark of a great hitter, one who is elevated to superstar status. I desperately wanted to have a respectable batting average. My self-esteem was so wrapped up in that number that I teetered on the edge of dishonesty to inflate it, something I never would have done in other areas of my life. Clearly, I needed professional counseling.

Mind you, there were semi-ethical ways to pad your batting average—and I succumbed to the temptation. My favorite loophole was the "too hot to handle" rule. Basically "too hot to handle" meant that some balls, although flubbed by the fielder (and a fielder "error" meant you did NOT get credit for a "hit"), should be counted as official hits anyway because they were struck so hard that it was unreasonable to expect the fielder to make a play. I considered most of my batted balls that went by or through a fielder's glove to fall in that category. "Too hot to handle" saved my batting average and each night when I said my prayers, I thanked God for its inventor.

I had one little problem—the official scorers. These were volunteers, normally moms with little training and absolutely no understanding of "too hot to handle." Many times I stood on first base, mentally giving myself a hit, but knowing Mrs. Jones up in the scorer's booth was writing down a big fat "E-5" (error on the third baseman) instead.

With that kind of scoring expertise, I was not shocked to learn at the end of the season that the league had me down for a .324 average while by my calculations it should have been .355. I never acknowledged the lower number. Twenty years later when I selected my lock combination in Officer's Training School it was 3-5-5-0. A state of denial can last a long time.

Once the season was over, I made myself a nuisance by asking every other boy I knew what their batting average was. Once I yelled that question over the swimming pool fence to my friend Robby. He was a little irritated since I had interrupted him just as he was about to jump off the diving board. However, he paused long enough to say that the league had him down for a .340 average. I told him that couldn't be right. He snorted back, "Why Alan, just because its higher than yours?" Ouch—the truth hurts.

Chapter 16
Grooving to Island Pop & Digging Island TV

I didn't know the kid personally, but I knew him as one of my fellow fifth graders at Pearl City Elementary that school year of 1971-72. Outwardly he was unremarkable in appearance—a fairly average Polynesian boy with short hair and fond of aloha shirts with matching shorts. But then, in the midst of one of our school assemblies, he stepped up to the microphone and in front of the entire student body he belted out the first line of the song:

> *Jeremiah was a bullfrog!*
> *Was a good friend of mine!*

Here, my memory is faulty because I don't know if the teachers insisted he alter the next two lines for the sake of appropriateness, but I have a feeling he just plowed through with the original lyrics:

> *I never understood a single word he said*
> *But I helped him drink his wine*
> *And he always had some mighty fine wine*

Yes, a good many of you know the song: Three Dog Night's 1971 smash hit, "Joy to the World." It's actually not surprising this boy wanted to sing it at the school assembly/show, because that year it seemed *all* my classmates were belting out this song! And I don't think it's because they appreciated the song's rhythmic chord progressions or its message of harmony and joy for all creatures—I strongly suspect they just got a kick out of belting out, *Jeremiah was a bullfrog*! The point I'm trying to make is this: Before moving to Hawaii, pop music (which could also be broken down into rock, blues, or soul) wasn't part of my universe. But during those island years of '71 to '74, my brothers and I, especially me, couldn't help but be swept along into the world of Top 40/pop music.

Over those years, I found myself spending more and more time with my little black transistor radio pressed to the side of my head. I listened to a few stations, but KKUA was my favorite. Like today's morning shows, the evening radio shows of that era featured several DJs who incorporated skits and bigger-than-life personas into their core job of playing 45's. I specifically remember a nasally DJ named The Real Neal Steele, and also a Dr. J, whose show consisted almost entirely of kooky characters (all him I'm sure) supposedly calling in or busting into the studio. During this period, I began what became a multi-year ritual, lasting until I graduated from high school.

Every night I would lie in bed with the radio on my chest, listening to music until I fell asleep. On Saturdays, that meant tuning into my favorite radio program, *Casey Kasem's Top 40 Countdown*. The call-in song dedications were sometimes sappy, but I enjoyed Kasem's background trivia about the singers and other fun facts. Although his voice had a soothing familiarity to it, I didn't learn why until years later—turns out Casey was also the voice of Shaggy on the *Scooby Doo* cartoons!

One of the things I enjoyed most about popular music back then was the variety of styles, all played on the same radio stations. This was well before radio was chopped into thin slices of oldies, soft rock, hip hop, R&B, heavy metal, progressive rock, alt-rock, and other categories which prevent listeners from sampling different types of music today. Though I'm leaping ahead a tad bit, on a February night in 1974, I could hear back to back on KKUA a diverse range of songs such as "The Way We Were" (Barbra Streisand—easy listening), "Top of the World" (Carpenters—soft rock), "Rocky Mountain High" (John Denver—country-pop), "Bennie and the Jets" (Elton John—pop), "Dancing Machine" (the Jacksons—disco), "Papa was a Rolling Stone" (Temptations - R&B), "Brown Sugar" (Rolling Stones—blues-rock), and "The Candy Man" (Sammy Davis Junior—show tunes).

There were also tunes that were huge hits in the Islands, but not so much anywhere else. That the radio stations on Oahu would regularly play the Young Rascals' *My Hawaii* on a regular basis should come as no surprise. But other almost exclusively-Hawaii pop hits of the time included some organ-rock instrumental that always seemed to accompany surf film footage; the smooth Karen Carpenter-like sound of Liz Damon's Orient Express singing, "Me Japanese Boy"; and lastly, the all-pervasive (in Hawaii) upbeat pop anthem of the Newbeats,' "Groovin' (Out on Life)." For anyone who truly wants to time-travel back to early 70s Hawaii, I highly recommend seeking out these lost tracks.

Island Television

Naturally, television was a big part of life in that era of 1971 to 1974—after all, I was a pretty normal American TV-happy kid of the period. And for those three years, like a lot of kids across the entire United States, we tried to always catch such popular sitcoms like *The Partridge Family* and *The Brady Bunch* on a weekly basis. In fact, the Brady Bunch paid a visit to Hawaii while we were there—they filmed a three-part episode and aired it, all during 1972 when we Cooks, of course, we're just a few miles away! More on that later.

But there were also a few shows that were unique to our island situation, and we took them in (for all three years in living black and white) often enough for them to be seared into memory. After all, what early 70s Hawaii kid DIDN'T immerse themselves, virtually on a daily basis, with *Checkers and Pogo*?

Checkers and Pogo

Carrying on in the tradition of the *Howdy Doody* and *Bozo the Clown* programs of the 1950s, *The Checkers and Pogo Show* was a televised studio program with skits and games performed before a live studio audience of kids. Supposedly the whole thing took place inside a blimp-sized hot air balloon called The Albatross (shown as a little model suspended by wires in front of a blue screen). The live mayhem in the studio was broken up by frequent sponsor plugs and a variety of cartoons, including one of the early Japanese anime programs (which I hated) called *Princess Knight*. The cartoon was about a princess who was always showing up her chauvinistic male adversaries with superior sword-fighting skills. Of course, that alone made it abhorrent to any boy under the age of thirteen. This cartoon was a Japanese product and very popular in Hawaii.

Our favorite parts of C&P were the live skits involving Checkers, a large man with a checkered bowling shirt and thick, black-framed glasses, and his impish sidekick, Pogo, a smaller man with a goatee who always wore suspenders and a little Peter Pan hat. Every weekday Pogo was either messing up some important project of Mr. Checkers' or they both were being double-crossed by Super Spy. Super Spy somewhat resembled Cheech of Cheech and Chong and always hyped himself up by singing his own theme song to the tune of Jesus Christ Superstar: *Su-per Spy, Su-per Spy... Oh, what a spy, what a spy am I!* Some of the storylines were so convoluted they would have made a Soap Opera writer blush. In what sometimes seemed like a mini-series, additional characters would make guest appearances in these skits, adding some unexpected plot twist.

One such guest was the famous Professor Fun. You knew he was smart because he always wore a graduation cap on his head. One day on a family outing in Honolulu, we were thrilled to actually spot Professor Fun walking down the beach sans mortar board. Some nearby kid yelled at him. "Hey, where's your professor hat?" I don't remember what the man mumbled back, but I had the distinct impression Professor Fun had turned into Professor potty-mouth.

One year my mom took Kevin's third grade Bible class to be a part of the C&P live audience. We all saw our brother on television, live, in fuzzy black and white! When they panned the audience he, like every other kid, was flashing the most popular hand sign of the 1970s, shared by hippies and even President Nixon. Yes, I'm talking about the double peace sign! Unfortunately, Kevin was not picked to participate in one of the audience member games. These highly skilled contests featuring cracker-eating, then whistling, donut-hanging-from-a-string-eating, and butt-balloon-busting, all offered cool prizes for the winners.

Yet even losers didn't go home empty-handed. At the end of the show, every audience member received a goody bag of Li Hing Mui snack candy, sunflower seeds, Hostess Twinkies, a Checkers and Pogo activity magazine, and coupons for the restaurant sponsor, Tops in Waipahu. But the best goody bag treasure was the free Sky Slide ticket—eight seconds of pure ecstasy riding a burlap sack down a multi-humped giant outdoor slide.

It should be obvious why Checkers and Pogo were the Beatles of Hawaii. Everyone knew who they were. Like the Fab Four, whenever C&P went out in public they were mobbed by sobbing girls. The only difference was that their female fans were crying because they needed to be changed or they had missed their afternoon nap.

We knew some people who had actually gotten autographs from Checkers and Pogo at the opening of a local shopping center. The report was that jolly Mr. Checkers, like his pal Professor Fun, was actually a bit surly. Though shocked at the time, I can probably understand why now. Here was a middle-aged man, an actor who at one time had dreams of Broadway, or acceptance speeches on Oscar night. Instead of basking in the adulation of beautiful actresses and the American public, he was now basking in the suffocating heat, surrounded by a hundred screaming seven-year-olds at the Grand Opening of the Waialua Kroger's. Who wouldn't be surly?

Yet, on the local celebrity scale, Checkers and Pogo were right up there with Don Ho and Jack Lord from *Hawaii Five-o*. Interestingly, I recently purchased the DVD set of *Hawaii Five-O's* first season. In episode four, Steve McGarrett bursts into the Hawaii Attorney General's office. The very debonair man behind the desk, speaking with perfect diction, was none other than Pogo Poge! The change in voice, look, and demeanor was so startling that I almost didn't recognize him. The man could actually act!

A Chance at Marcia Brady?

As I mentioned before, *The Brady Bunch* paid a visit to our tiny island of Oahu in 1972. This was a big deal to me because I'd been a Brady Bunch fan since I was a mere third grader in Millington, Tennessee—and a particularly big fan, naturally, of Maureen McCormick (i.e., Marcia)! In early 1972, I heard that the cast was staying at the Royal Hawaiian Hotel for two weeks while filming a three-part episode that involved Greg's famous surfing accident and Vincent Price trying to relieve Peter of a cursed tiki god necklace.

During the Brady's visit, I briefly considered riding my bike to Honolulu and looking for Maureen McCormick at her hotel. Who knew, it could possibly lead to a romantic walk on Waikiki beach. I imagined my quivering hand gently holding hers as I placed those beautiful feminine fingers across the seams of a baseball, showing her how to throw the curve. That dream, like many others, was crushed by cold reality—my bike had a flat tire and I had too much homework that night.

Of course my brothers and I continued our pattern of taking in Saturday morning cartoons such as *Scooby Doo, The Bugs Bunny/Roadrunner Hour, H.R. Puffinstuff, Lidsville*—and naturally, the back-to-back pop rock cartoon classics, *The Osmonds* and *The Jackson 5*. But we boys (particularly Eric and I) were growing older and looking to branch beyond kiddie cartoons and kid sitcoms, to watching more grown-up fare. Dad and Mom allowed us just a taste—but what a memorable taste it was!

Never before had there been a sitcom like *All in the Family* (with Archie Bunker, his liberal daughter, Gloria, his leftist son-in-law, Michael "Meathead" Sivic and the sweet but often befuddled, Edith Bunker). All of America could sing the theme song which began with Archie and Edith dueting at the piano, "Boy da way Glen Miller played.... Songs that made the hit pa-rade....Guys like us we had it made... Those were the days...!" And with jokes and story lines that hit on subjects of race, religion, sex, gangs, counter-culture, the show became an early 70s phenomenon. The kind of show they would never DARE make in the 21st century!

Our family also enjoyed *The Odd Couple, Sanford and Son,* and *Mary Tyler Moore Show*. These comedies also touched on some adult themes and humor compared to sitcoms of just a few years earlier, but these shows didn't hit you with the sledgehammer bluntness and grittiness of *All in the Family* (though *Sanford and Son* came close at times).

For drama, action and gravitas, our go-to television show was a natural: What else could it be but...? **Hawaii Five-O**

How could our family not follow *Hawaii Five-O* on a regular basis? Actually we had started following the show back when we lived in Tennessee, but we took particular interest in it when we heard that Dad's next duty station would be Hawaii. Now that we lived in Hawaii, what a thrill it was to watch a show filmed almost entirely on the island of Oahu where we lived. Once a week, we could watch a nationally broadcast detective drama and spot locales that we often drove past or visited personally: Pearl Harbor, Waikiki Beach, Ala Moana Shopping Center, the Punchbowl (a military cemetery within a small extinct volcano overlooking Honolulu), the Honolulu Airport—even the old Hawaii Islander Stadium where we occasionally went to see ball games!

In short, every week we watched as the criminal underworld terrorized the tiny little island of Oahu we called home. The show was exciting to watch, but it was also sobering. Sure, I knew it was just a TV show—but it did enlighten me to the fact that there were indeed dangerous felons, murders, kidnappers—perhaps armed with those deadly silencer guns that so often made an appearance on the show—who inhabited our tiny dot in the Pacific. If there were shady characters like that around, they surely lurked within fairly easy reach of Manana. This truth would become all too real in the not-too-distant future.

I guess you could say those years in Manana could be defined as my real-life transition from a world that resembled that of *The Brady Bunch*, to one that increasingly resembled the more gritty world of *Hawaii Five-O*. But leading up to

1974, my most major traumas were on the ball field. Ironically, it was an episode of *The Brady Bunch* that should have been an ominous forewarning of things to come.

Chapter 17
Mound of Trouble

All you *Brady Bunch* enthusiasts out there, you remember the episode. No doubt you've watched it many times over the years in reruns. Yet while *The Brady Bunch* is generally known for stretching the bounds of credible reality in its often-sunny depiction of early 70s family life, the episode I speak of is different. In fact, no other *Brady* episode (at least to me) is infused with this much true-to-life authenticity.

The scenes I speak of begin when Greg, Peter, and Bobby walk into the family kitchen, having just returned from the big Little League baseball game. Their brother, Greg, was pitching. "How did it go?" asks Mrs. Brady in a chirpy voice. Greg, still in uniform, walks sullenly past his mother, not speaking a word. His eyes say it all. Peter, however, is more than happy to give a game report: "They...*clobbered* him!"

From there, Peter and Bobby describe the gruesome details of the shellacking Greg experienced at the hands of the opposing team. Soon, however, Mr. Brady enters the kitchen and tells the boys to cool it. Then, Mr. Brady tells Mrs. Brady that he better go have a talk with his humiliated son.

By this time, Greg has already raced up to his room, closed the door, and has climbed up onto the upper berth of the bunk bed. When Mr. Brady enters the room, Greg is trying to fight back the tears, but he's having no better luck doing this than he did trying to get batters out in the earlier game. Greg is sure about one thing. Through his tears, he blurts out, "I'm never going to play that stupid game again!" Greg's pain is even more acute considering how confident he had been going into the game. You see, Greg had been *certain* that this game was going to be his coming out party, a stepping stone to his eventual career as an All-Star Major League baseball player. The reality was, Greg Brady—long before Tom Hanks—discovered that there is indeed crying in baseball. In the spring of 1972, I was about to learn that sobering lesson for myself.

Yes, I too was a Little League baseball pitcher. During three summers in the early 1970s, I did my best to throw baseballs past the bats of small, steely-eyed boys wearing huge helmets and baggy uniform pants. Unlike most of my friends, I didn't view Little League as recreation, something fun in which to fill time until football season began. It was much more important to me. So when things went badly on the field, I was—like Greg on that *Brady Bunch* episode—utterly devastated. Why? Because (again, like Greg) I envisioned a future as a professional baseball player—a *star* professional baseball player. Consequently, I was determined to be the hardest working ten-year-old ball player in the United States, and in 1972, I may have been.

Little League was my apprenticeship, my proving ground, the place where I would begin to hone my maturing skills. I wasn't sure what "honing" was, but all the baseball books said it was important, so that was good enough for me. During those summers, every strike, every ball, and every hit became a personal referendum on whether my dream would succeed or fail. Driven by this self-induced pressure, my Little League experience produced soaring highs, gut-wrenching lows, and on occasion, even tears. It was wonderful. It was agony. It was the greatest time of my life.

Saturday morning, May 1972. The sun is shining—a beautiful Hawaiian day on the island of Oahu. Most kids in my neighborhood are still in their pajamas stretched out on living room floors watching TV, chomping on a breakfast of Captain Crunch cereal. Without a care in the world, they lazily gaze as Shaggy and Scooby Doo run frantically down yet another endless cartoon hallway. You know—the hallway that has the little table with the vase on it that the characters keep passing every two seconds. But I am not in my pajamas, and at this moment have several cares weighing upon my small shoulders.

I am standing on a pile of dirt, clothed in a Pearl City Navy/Marine Little League Cardinals uniform and things are not going well. The good part is that from my vantage point high atop the pitcher's mound, I can see everything that's going on. The bad part is that I can see everything that's going on. It's ugly. One by one, the opposition's bats are taking my pitches and spraying them to every corner of the ball field. In my defense, these thirty-two-inch clubs of destruction are not wielded by your average ten- to twelve-year-olds. No, these are the first place Pirates, a Little League version of the New York Yankees. They are big, they are skilled, and they are killing me. It is only the first inning and the score is already 7-0. My stomach hurts.

In those days, I seemed to get stomach aches on a fairly frequent basis. My mother couldn't figure out why and finally took me to the doctor. After examining me thoroughly and finding nothing physically wrong, the doctor offered his best guess: It was all in my head. He said that some people's anxieties are manifested through headaches, others through their belly. I was a "stomacher." Over the years, I fulfilled his observation and today was exhibit A. It felt like a Boy Scout troop was earning merit badges knot-tying my intestines.

The game had actually started rather well. Just twenty minutes earlier I had strode confidently to the pitcher's mound, armed with a 2-0 record and an array of what I believed were mystifying pitches. I began the game by serving up a little "now you see it, now you don't" in the form of my fastball. In no time, the first Pirate batter proved unable to see three of those pitches and returned to the dug-out as victim number one.

It was a point of immense pride to me that even as a ten-year-old rookie, I could really "smoke" it in there, bring the "heat," or throw some "gas" as we say in the business. Unfortunately, I apparently hadn't paid my heating bill, because after that first batter, the Pirates turned off my gas. The next few batters nailed fastballs into the deep regions of the outfield, sending our outfielders scurrying about like startled deer. Five minutes into the game and we were overwhelmed. Although this early display of Pirate power was a bit unsettling, my confidence was not totally gone.

Hammerin' Hank

With two runs already in, and two runners on base, I looked toward the Pirate dug-out and saw what could easily be mistaken for a coach striding to the plate. But I knew better. This was my idol and Pearl City Elementary living legend—Hank Buchanan. Hank was who I wanted to be some day. He was the league's most feared pitcher and greatest home run hitter. His gargantuan oak tree-clearing drives and bat-melting fastball were the stuff of school cafeteria legend.

Hank was not only larger than life, he was larger than anyone else in the league by a good four inches and twenty pounds. We were in awe. It was hard to believe that this baseball god actually lived just two streets down from me. I wondered what his life was like. Did he actually go to school, use the bathroom, or take out the trash like the rest of us mortal kids? I couldn't picture it. Like all fans, we were fascinated by our idol's life. Any Hank sightings in our neighborhood were immediately reported in minute detail and with breathless excitement. "I just saw him in the 7-Day store! He was reading a *Mad* magazine, wearing a blue shirt, and sucking on a fudge pop!" We couldn't have been more thrilled if we'd spied Bigfoot in the breakfast aisle comparing the fiber content of different cereals.

However, this Saturday morning there was no time for hero worship. Baseball was my business and I needed to get this guy out. As Hank stepped into the batter's box, he loomed even larger than I remembered. I also made a mental note that my last Hank sighting report had failed to mention chest hair, which I could now clearly see peeking out of his uniform shirt. This kind of physical evidence had the dual effect of unnerving young pitchers and making their fathers skeptical that Hank met Little League age requirements. In fact, this was such an issue that Hank's birth certificate had been examined closer than the Dead Sea scrolls. To all our distress, he was a legitimate twelve years old, born in 1959.

Unlike Hank, I was completely hairless south of my earlobes. Since I could not match Hank strength for strength, I decided to beat him with cunning. It was time to dig into my bag of mystifying pitches and pull out the ol' curveball, or, as we say in the business, "the snake." My theory was that Hank would be so anxious to jump on my fastball that he would be totally surprised by a slow curve and whiff harmlessly. Just in case he wasn't fooled, I turned towards my outfielders to let them know they might need to back up a bit. It was somewhat annoying to find that they were way ahead of me. All three were already leaning against the fence with arms crossed, like Florida tourists waiting for the *Apollo 11* launch at Cape Canaveral. Disgusted at their blatant lack of faith, I turned back towards home, determined to prove them wrong.

I wound up and twisted off the best spinning curve I could muster. *"Break! Break!"* I wordlessly pleaded as the snake slithered on its 44-foot journey towards the plate. My "surprise" theory was tested and found wanting. Hank Buchanan was not only unafraid of snakes; he was in fact a very proficient snake killer. Seeing mine slither his way, like any good farm boy, Hank swung his big club and beat that snake to death. Houston, we have a problem. The last I saw of the snake, it was slipping the surly bonds of earth, rocketing upward on its historic journey to become the first reptile in space. Hank lumbered like a giant around the bases to the cheers of his teammates as the kid scorekeeper posted Pirates 5, Cardinals 0.

Since there was no time to take a bus into town and retrieve Hank's ball, the umpire threw me a new one. The new ball somehow gave me a ray of hope. With this brand-new white ball I would throw a whole new array of baffling pitches: curves, drops, change-ups. But things only got worse. Of the next six batters, I walked four and gave up two more hits, both on pitches that were well out of the strike zone. Before Dionne Warwick could sing the first verse of "Walk On By," it was 7-0. Still only one out. My composure was now officially lost and gone. If my pitching was intended to be a test, someone had slipped the Pirates the answer key. The fight-or-flight instinct had kicked in and flight was looking pretty attractive.

Coaches and Catchers

During this whole fiasco, Coach Snyder calmly watched from the dug-out entrance. He seemed concerned, but not nearly as alarmed as his young pitcher. By now, after each batter I was giving him my most pitiful, *"please take me out of the game"* look. He acted as if he didn't notice and continued to clap his hands and shout encouragement: "You've got-em, buddy! Rock and fire, son. Rock and fire." Remember, back in those days, no one had yet invented the magical phrase, *You got this!* That surely would have turned things around. I had to settle for Coach Snyder's hand claps, each one essentially saying, "I believe in you, but I'm not bailing you out. Learn to work through your own problems." It wasn't the message I wanted to hear, but it was the one I needed. Today, members of the Self-Esteem Preservation Society would have probably stormed the field and spirited me away, saving another fragile child from the trauma of experiencing a potential "non-success." Mr. Snyder would be accused of child cruelty and packed off to sensitivity training. But in 1972, things were very different. I wasn't rescued. Thank goodness.

By now the game was getting quite loud. My teammates and our fans were yelling encouragement. The Pirate players, sensing blood in the water, added to the din by chanting and shaking the dug-out's chain link fence behind them: "We want a pitcher, not a belly itcher! We want a pitcher, not a belly itcher!" they yelled in unison. One of the great mysteries of the twentieth century is how such a lame taunt could become the most famous Little League chant of all time. I easily blocked out their witless harangue. Not as easy to block out, were the sobbing cries of my own brother, Eric, coming from right field: *"Come on, Alan! Can't you just throw **one** strike?!"*

At last the crisis was broken up by the welcome sight of my catcher calling time and walking out to the mound. For those unfamiliar with baseball, there are normally only two reasons a pitcher receives visitors. One is if the coach thinks a pitcher is in trouble and makes a kind of house call to the mound for a closer look at his patient. The second reason for a visit to the mound is when the catcher feels a need to talk strategy or to give the pitcher a pep talk. Oh, and by the way, it's never a good sign when your catcher comes out to the mound, crying.

"Alan, get it over the plate! You're killing us!" Josh cried as he proceeded to slam the ball into my glove. I waited for more, but that was it. That was my pep talk. With our sharing time concluded, Josh did an immediate about face and headed back to home plate, his shoulders shaking as he sobbed.

Barry Glad to See You

At long last, the coach of the Pirates seemed to take pity on me. Instead of sending yet another of his power hitters to the plate, he substituted in... little nine-year-old Barry Felton. This pleased my heart so much. Finally, someone in power was letting me off the hook. This ever so gracious coach was sending in his weakest batter to face me. An easy out! God had sent a sacrificial lamb.

Barry was my brother Eric's age, only nine years old. In a league primarily dominated by eleven- and twelve-year-olds, he and Eric were a rarity. They were certainly skilled for their age but not experienced enough as rookies to get much playing time with boys two to three years older. *Come on*, I thought, *If I can't get Barry out, I can't get my mom out*. Besides, I was already a little miffed at Barry. According to a reliable source working undercover in the third grade, Felton had been mouthing off at school about how he was a key cog in the Pirate baseball machine. The nerve of the little squirrel! Barry sauntered up to the plate with a smirk on his face. You would have thought he had personally driven in all the seven previous runs.

Barry stepped into the batter's box, all four feet two inches of him, and waved the bat back and forth like he was ready to do some damage. Then, just before I started my windup, he went into a deep crouch, pressing his belly almost completely against the top of his chubby upper legs. I threw a fastball that was right down the middle of the plate but it zoomed by Barry about neck high. "Ball one!" yelled the umpire.

It dawned on me what Mr. Felton—and his wily coaching staff—were trying to do. With a normal size little leaguer at the plate, a pitcher has a box about eighteen inches wide and two feet high as a target for a strike. Barry was already small, but by crouching, he was making his strike zone appear to be about the size of a saltine cracker. The weasel! He had no intention of swinging that bat. He was going to stand there in an upright fetal position and take four balls for a walk. It was all legal, but totally without honor in the world of Little League. Now I was really miffed.

I was determined NOT to give Barry Felton an easy walk to first base. Instead I... beaned him with my next pitch. It wasn't intentional, but then again, I was beyond flustered. Barry toppled over, crying out in pain. The crowd gasped, but I inexplicably felt a wave of satisfaction flow over me. I'd actually hit something I'd aimed at. After a cursory examination by his coach revealed no life-threatening injuries, Barry staggered to his feet and limped off to first base, giving me the evil eye each painful step. That bean ball had forced in another run. We were now down 8-0. It was still the first inning.

After I let in two more runs, Coach Snyder finally decided that there were better things to do on a Saturday morning in Hawaii. Mercifully, he came out to the mound, patted me on the shoulder, and relieved me of the ball. "Don't worry buddy. It's just not your day. We'll get'em next time," he said.

Embarrassed but very relieved, I hung my head and jogged towards the dug-out as the crowd gave me the standard pity applause. We all know the kind. It's the kind of ovation given to hide an embarrassed silence—the kind offered to a player who has let a fly ball hit him on the head but finally arises from the turf and limps off the field after lying on the ground for five minutes feigning injury. I felt like I had been hit in the head too, but this was just wounded pride.

After what seemed like the longest run in my life, I made it to the welcome shelter of the dug-out and slumped down on the bench. No longer in the unblinking spotlight, I finally felt the dam of emotion break; a flood of humiliation and despair overwhelmed me. I put my head in my hands and began crying. Josh Butler, my ever-sensitive catcher, happened to be passing by the bench at that moment and stopped, affected by the sight of his pitcher's distress. He thought for a moment, searching for just the right words. Finally he shook his head, pulled his mask back down, and said, "Man, what a baby!"

The Rest of the Story

Despite that nightmare game, I actually did pretty well my first year as a pitcher. Although not overpowering, I soon found my fastball was quick enough to strike out most batters. One kid told me that the last part of my wind-up was distracting. Apparently, totally without my realizing it, I had developed a quirk where I shook the ball back and forth in my wrist just before moving my arm forward to release the ball. I was told it was the same motion a person used to vigorously salt a plate of eggs. Luckily for me, batters found the shaking ball hard to pick up as it was released forward. Not only that, there is a famous saying in baseball is that lefthanders have "a natural curve." I'm not sure if that's true, but I had developed a decent "hook" and loved to throw it against left-handed batters.

Long story short, I did get better as the season progressed. By the end of that illustrious First Baseball Season of 1972, I was ready to press forward and reach for the stars—both as a hitter *and* as a pitcher.

Chapter 18

It's Awesome to be a
Kid in Manana!

Manana was a neighborhood tailor-made for forts and club-houses. Backyards with uneven grassy terrain, pockmarked by bushes and thick-trunked trees with low, overhanging branches were in abundance – all the better to add not only a vaguely eerie atmosphere, but also seclusion (from too much parental snooping). Most importantly, forts and clubs not only needed to be constructed by someone, but also populated by someone. Those someones, in Manana, were kids. Lots and LOTS of kids!

In 1973, kids were swarming neighborhood streets of the U.S.A. like ants, and in Manana, far more so. Unless there was a hurricane or the child's arm had accidently become detached, parents would not allow their children to be indoors during sunlight hours. And if an arm was detached and the bleeding profuse, even that wasn't usually enough to allow a kid through the front door. Instead, a couple band-aids would be pushed through the mail slot accompanied by a cheery "You'll be all right. That's why God gave you two arms."

Even the teenagers seemed to live outside, usually roaming around in mixed gender groups, sporting long hair, wearing green army jackets, and playing music very loudly on transistor radios. The only headphones available were the size of an air traffic controller's head-gear and only plugged into the family stereo. In 1973, instant messaging someone meant turning to your left and speaking directly into your buddy's ear.

What about adult supervision you say? Parents' monitoring their child's play was thought to be about as necessary as wearing a helmet while riding a bicycle. During the summer, fathers were at work and moms were enjoying their kid-free homes by either performing vigorous cleaning rituals or taking a break to watch one of the many TV soap operas such as "Dark Shadows," whose main character was a vampire (I kid you not). I'm sure some mothers worked outside the home, but I can't recall any that did in our military community. So, although locked inside, they were technically available to dispense sympathy if you ran home with some injury.

Parents in the 1970s had this wild idea that fresh air and sunlight were good for kids. Something about "how they had grown up back on the farm." Driving around Manana in 1973 (okay, I wasn't driving but my folks were) was like maneuvering through an obstacle course of orange cones except the cones had arms and legs, wore ice cream-stained tee shirts, and scurried about. Kids were everywhere. Kids in trees. Kids sitting on the curb. Kids playing twenty on twenty touch football games in the middle of the street. Kids riding bikes. Kids wrestling on the lawn. Kids spraying water on each other. Kids hammering pieces of plywood together in their backyards.

Ah, yes, but back to the plywood clubhouse or fort. Boys loved to build forts in the 1970s. You could also put clubhouses in this category, but even a clubhouse is, essentially, a fort. Before homeowner associations took over the world, it wasn't uncommon to walk through a neighborhood and see various structures of abandoned planks and wooden panels nailed together and erected in or around some stately tree or up against a house. Many times these homemade castles would be adorned with flags flying on metal poles, extracted from some nearby construction site. Underneath, cardboard signs would hang from the curtained entrance announcing that all girls, little brothers, and feuding rivals were banned from entering upon risk of death. Most of these structures would not meet local building codes and were only constructed to withstand sustained winds of, well, anything just above a light breeze. In Manana, there existed an entire sub-universe of forts/club-houses inhabiting the backyard tracts of the housing area.

When the Cook brothers constructed a backyard fort, we were even more expedient than the hammer and nail crowd. Tools took too much time. We wanted a fort you could build in the afternoon, sleep in that night with ten of your closest buddies, then tear down the next morning. To achieve that goal, only three building materials were needed—cheap wire fencing, chairs, and blankets. So off we would go to "shop" for supplies inside the house. An hour later, every bed was stripped and the dining room table was going to be standing room only for supper.

After carefully laying down a layer of old blankets to shield us against bugs, itchy grass, and dew the next morning, we would tirelessly erect our fort. Our early forts were simply propped up by multiple chairs, but eventually we got ourselves some wire fencing for extra support. Then, we piled on more blankets for a roof and "walls." An old, tattered parachute Dad had obtained from a Goodwill or Army Surplus Store added extra fort covering. After ten minutes of this strenuous manual labor, it was time to take a break for cookies and juice. By the late afternoon our masterpiece was complete. Now for the final phase, inviting a few key friends for a sleepover and moving in supplies.

A Night in The Fort

That night the lucky invitees were all gathered inside. Besides the three Cook boys (littlest brother, John, was too little to handle this night's spooky activities) there were Steve Erdeman, Sean Schrader, and Dan Keen. Dan was Eric's age while Steve and Sean were in my grade. Space was somewhat limited. The fort was only three feet high, encompassing a 5'x6' rectangle—ample room unless you are trying to sleep eight. So, like so many pick-up-sticks dumped out of the can, we lay there, arms and legs over each other, smelly feet in people's faces, and an elbow in every back. There would have been more room except for the vital supplies we could not do without: flashlights, comic books, baseball cards, Cheetos, Hostess Ding-Dongs and Twinkies, popcorn, soda, candy bars, and for desert—Oreo Cookies. The festivities started at 8:00: Snack Time coupled with Camp Erdman stories.

Steve, Sean, and I had all attended Camp Erdman just a couple of weeks before. All the sixth graders had. In fact, Camp Erdman was a rite of passage for every sixth-grade class that passed through Pearl City Elementary. And there were usually plenty of weird and spooky tales to come out of each year's camp outing. Ours was no different.

Steve was the first up with his Camp Erdman story. I knew his wouldn't be as good as mine, because he wasn't in my cabin. My cabin was at the center of the "incident." But that would come later. For now, Steve went into his story.

"We were all horsing around in our cabin—it was like after midnight. We were all laughing, cutting up. Then we hear a knock at the door. Jerry goes, 'Friend or Fart?' BOOM, the door busts open and Mr. Lee comes in all pissed off. 'Uh oh,' goes Jerry, 'It's Fart!'"

Naturally we all burst out laughing. Steven had a way with a story, though who knows if there was any truth in it at all.

Thus encouraged, Steve's story accelerated: "Mr. Lee grabs a mattress and pressed Alan's head against the wall, then he grabs Paul by his undershorts and I swear, he's giving Paul Neely a wedgie...!"

We burst out laughing again. If a wedgie by the science teacher would happen to anyone (besides Cory Beetle), it would happen to Paul Neely! Anyway, Steve completed his story, punctuating it with how Mr. Lee let out a string of four-letter words before he threatened them all with death if he heard one more word out of them.

A good story. A funny story. But we all knew why we were here. Spooky thrills and eerie chills. My story would provide that. And now it was my turn. "You all heard what happened by now," I began. At least Steve and Sean had heard. They were at the camp. But they were not where it *happened*. I was!

"I've heard like twenty different stories," said Sean. "I wanna hear what really happened!"

I nodded my head solemnly. "Well I know, because I know Kimberly and she told me herself!" At this, Steve and Sean's jaws both dropped. I had them in the palm of my hand. "Here's how it all went Friday night...," I continued.

As I eluded to earlier, Camp Erdman was the traditional send-off event for the sixth-graders and involved a weekend of cabin living by the ocean filled with fun recreational events. The camp was anchored by a large administration/cafeteria building that looked out on a field of crab-grass bordered by boys' cabins on one side and girls' cabins on the other. Farther on was the sandy beach and the roar of the Pacific Ocean. Towering over the road behind the camp were lush mountains thick with foliage. A kid's dream. For weeks we had been excitedly counting the days, furiously planning who needed to bring what vital supplies (snacks and games) and worrying that all our gang might not be able to bunk in the same cabin.

On the appointed day, the four sixth grade classes boarded two large, but rickety, buses for the trip around the island. For many of us, the three-day event would be our first overnight experience without parents. With newly-purchased sleeping bags, which would be used, and mom-packed sun-tan lotion, which would be ignored, we waved excitedly to our families as we pulled out of the school parking lot.

The trip was everything I had dreamed about and more. All my best friends made the Cabin Seven bunk list: Charlie, the funny Hispanic kid; David, my brace-faced Little-League buddy; Charles, the excitable boy; and, of course, Cory Beetle. We enjoyed three days of typical male bonding. Smelly socks were stuffed in the face of anyone napping, gas was deliberately passed in the direction of any classmate lounging on the grass for relaxation, treasured personal items were hidden from their owners, pillow fights were started, insults were flung, and other cabins were attacked viciously with water balloons. Just a group of boys showing affection.

To re-energize ourselves after all this activity, three square meals were served in the Camp Erdman cafeteria. Everyone sat at designated cabin tables and took turns serving as waiters for each meal. This of course was another opportunity to harass fellow classmates as all took great pleasure in ordering the poor waiter to bring more Kool-aid, another napkin, or seconds of mashed potatoes. After the noon meal, there were more formal activities such as hikes up into the nearby mountains or archery practice behind the cabins.

By nightfall, everyone was pretty much worn out. We retreated to our cabins and the teachers to theirs which were right next door in case of an emergency. Lights had to be out by 10:00 PM, but that just meant it was time for flashlights, ghost stories, or daring each other to sneak outside and peek into the girls' cabins. That dare was never taken because, wisely, the Camp had placed about one hundred yards of open field between the boys and girls living areas, well-lit by a couple of floodlights on tall wooden poles. Stalag Erdman!

I went on with my story. "Like I said, we were all in Cabin Seven." Now I paused a long time for dramatic effect. "Right next to Cabin...Six!"

"Ha-Na!" said Steve, exercising the Pidgin Hawaiian expression of awe. Hey, all haole kids used pidgin slang after we'd been on the islands for a while—some used it almost as adeptly as the locals! Now Eric interrupted.

"What's so big about Cabin Six?" asked Eric. Sean and Steve threw a look at Eric that seemed to say, '*Oh man, I feel sorry for* you!'

I proceeded to set my brother straight. "Cabin Six is where a man was murdered, like, fifty years ago." I could almost see the hairs on Eric's arm stand on end.

"I heard he hung himself," said Sean.

I wasn't sure myself. "Well, it was something like that. Anyway, they don't use Cabin Six anymore. Nobody goes in there by themselves and you better not go by there at night! A lot of people have seen his ghost."

"Woaaaa!" gasped Eric.

I went on. "I'm serious, we doubled locked our cabin door every night. We didn't go to the back washroom unless a buddy was with us."

Already Steve was chomping at the bit. "Get to what happened!"

I didn't want to lose my audience so I cut to the chase (after wolfing down a couple of Oreo Cookies though). "It was Friday. Second night at camp. Right about eleven o'clock we hear a scream. All the guys comes running out the front door of their cabin and we can see the girls across the field screaming, running out too."

"Yeah, we came out too," agreed Sean.

"We see some teachers with flashlights run over and try to calm things down. Everybody is goin' beserk. We're all going,

'What happened?! What happened?!' We're down by the girls cabins now."

"So what happened?" urged broken-record Steve.

"Kimberly Burnside saw something." Kimberly was a girl I actually knew from Sunday School at Camp Smith. Her family were faithful attendees of Camp Smith Protestant Chapel.

Steve's eyes were now bulging. "Kimberly told you?!"

I shook my head. "No, no. Well...she told me later. But that night Sheila told me what happened."

"So what did Sheila say?" demanded Sean.

I drew a deep breath. "Here's what happened—and Kimberly told me all this a few days later. Kimberly was in the bathroom in back of the cabins. She looks up, and she swears this is true, she sees a face looking at her in the window!"

Steve, Sean, Dan, and Eric all about fall over themselves reacting with a mixture of awe and delicious fear: "No way!"

"Ha-NAH!"

"For real?!"

Now I had to wrap it up. "The girls, they're still all screaming, running around. The teachers are yelling for everyone to go back to their cabin."

"Do you think Kimberly's telling the truth?" asked Sean, trying to bring logic and reason into the situation. "You sure she's not just prankin' everybody?"

This was easy to answer. I shook my head. "No way. I know her. She doesn't mess around like that. She's super serious." Sean looked like he wasn't sure if he was convinced. However, I hadn't even gotten to the best part of my story yet!

"But that's not the end of the story!" I announced. "It gets better!" Now everybody leaned in and quieted down, anxious for me to go on.

"Okay, me and my cabin buddies, we finally head back to our cabin. The teachers are making everybody go back, right?"

"Yeah, I remember," agreed Steve.

"Now everybody in my cabin, we're all thinking, *the Cabin Six ghost*! That has to be what Kimberly saw." I looked over. Young Dan was now hunkering down in his sleeping bag, as if not willing to hear more. I went on.

"So when we get back to our cabin, first thing, we push the dresser in front of the door. Then we pull all our beds close together in the center of the room. Kind of, added protection and all that."

"Yeah," nodded Steve, as if in agreement that this was a good move.

"After a while it gets quiet again, but I can tell nobody in our cabin can sleep. I can see their eyes open. Now we're hearing funny stuff—like muffled voices. Somebody moving outside in the grass..." My listeners were now transfixed. It was time for the climax.

"Me and Charlie are kinda talking... but all of a sudden Charles yells out, 'Cut on the light! Cut on the light!' Someone jumps up, switches on the light, and I look down to where he's pointing."

I paused again, but this time not so much for dramatic effect, as for the fact that now I too was becoming a little freaked out at bringing up this frightening recent memory: "Our pillows, they were facing each other, so he's only like about a foot away from me while we were talking in the dark. I look where his finger is pointing and he's pointing at my pillow—there's like three or four drops of blood on it."

There was an immediate outburst of exclamations from Eric and our invited guests. It seemed like they were all about to explode up through the blanket roof covering of our dimly lit fort. I had to talk over their now highly-agitated jabberings: "I jump back, check my head for cuts and for blood. I don't feel anything. This is blowing all of our minds and Charlie is losing his mind, half scared to death."

Sean tries to reason it out again. "Charlie did it. He had to!"

That dog wouldn't hunt. "No way. I was right next to Charlie. I would have seen him try something. Swear!"

I had opened up Pandora's Box of bedlam, and I had to virtually shout out the conclusion to my story: "We all tore off the pillow case and threw them in the corner. Nobody went near it. Finally we turned the lights off and tried to sleep. But I don't think I slept hardly at all that whole night!"

Now Dan was crying. Sean gathered up his brother to take him home. Dan insisted it wasn't the story, but rather, he had a bad stomach ache. When Sean returned, several minutes later, we changed the subject. Each (remaining) camper was interrogated about which girl they liked. All vehemently denied any amorous feelings for anyone, practically disavowing knowledge of the other gender. After that, large quantities of junk food and soda were consumed. Someone had brought a tape recorder. Everyone then took turns making belching noises into the microphone, then doing an imitation of well-known school teachers. Much laughing ensued

Suddenly a hairy hand appeared! It thrust itself through the blanket cover, right underneath Steve's elbow. Steve unleashed a torrent of English and pidgin cuss words at the sight of the monstrous hands. The rest of us nearly jumped out of our PJ's. The "hand" suddenly whisked away, as suddenly as it appeared. We all agreed it was probably time to go to sleep. We turned out the lantern light. As we drifted towards silence and sleep in the darkness, we all deduced that the "monster hand" was probably the paw or nose of the ever-curious Dachshund that lived next door.

Still, around midnight, we had awakened enough to do a sneak-out—a quick run around the darkened neighborhood streets until the headlights of an approaching Military Police truck came into view down the street. We all raced back to the fort, diving into the tent-ish fortress just as the headlights swept by.

Somehow we all woke up next morning on the living room floor in the house. It got too cold and wet for everybody in the fort, so around 3 AM we all made our way inside with our sleeping bags. After a breakfast of sugar cereal the next morning, all our fort guests went home.

Several decades later, I can't still explain what happened that night in Cabin Seven.

Chapter 19
Over the Fence

In Manana, kids were routinely seen playing away from home with no adult in sight. Playgrounds were full of small kids swinging and climbing by themselves. There were rarely any parents watching from nearby benches or hovering over them like some overgrown spotter. Older children were trusted even more, sometimes allowed to roam freely outside the security of our fenced-in housing area.

Manana was laid out on the side of a long, gradually sloping hill, each street on a tier directly above the other. At the top of this hill the land flattened out and the houses and fields backed up to a large chain link fence. Across that fence was dense underbrush that sloped down the back side of the hill and opened up into a low valley of dense scrubrush wilderness. Far below, the only man-made object visible was a single dwelling: an old wooden cabin with several beat-up cars parked out front. I could never figure out how the vehicles got down there because there was no road in sight and the house seemed to be marooned in a sea of thick vegetation. The only signs of life were the wisps of gray smoke constantly wafting from the crumbling chimney and the sounds of chickens squawking in a couple wire mesh cages outside. We had no idea who lived there and weren't anxious to find out. It was rumored that Japanese and Japanese-Americans were interred here in this valley during World War II, confined in makeshift camps.

Just a few hundred yards away from the old house was a stagnant pool of water called Pond #6. To reach the pond, one had to navigate down the back slope of a hill across the neighborhood's security fence. That area was strewn with trash deposited by the locals who arrived via a secluded dirt road which wound around the middle of the hill. The hillside was full of broken glass, old refrigerators, bottles containing unknown chemicals, and countless other abandoned objects that people didn't want to take the time to dispose of legally. To add to the ambiance, it was rumored that drug addicts would sometimes camp out in the dense underbrush to get high, hidden from the watchful eyes of the citizenry and local police. All in all, this was not the kind of area parents would want their kids to explore.

But kids did explore, all the time. In recent years, my friend Shelly shared that back in those days she and a girlfriend used to hike all the way down to Pond #6 by themselves to catch crawdads—a scenario one cannot even fathom a parent allowing today. My brothers and I rarely braved the other side of the fence. We always had this overwhelming sense of anxiety that someone or something was watching us from the bushes and scraggly trees. When we did go over the fence, we usually didn't wander too far down the hill, just in case we had to beat a hasty retreat.

Most of the time these excursions were driven by the need to retrieve wayward baseballs. One of our closest practice fields backed up to that fence and we were always fouling balls backwards or accidentally throwing them too far over the heads of our intended receivers. When one of us did have to crawl over to the "dark side," the other two would keep an eye out for sinister drug addicts while the searcher beat the grass trying to find the lost ball. This anxiety was not unfounded, and the primary reason can be summed up in one word: Redbone. That will be explained more later. But another good reason to not play around with "the other side of the fence" reared its ugly head one afternoon in '73.

Gunman in Manana

"Car!"

This was the standard call-out whenever someone spotted an approaching automobile while two or more of you were engaged in a sports activity... in the middle of the street. That was everyone's cue to immediately vacate the street so the car could pass. If this social contract was violated, should even one motorist complain to authorities, your street ball privileges could be immediately revoked. On this particular day, Eric, my buddy Charlie, and I were playing catch in the middle of the street. We played catch in the street many times. So we were well acquainted with the "*Car!*" drill.

Once the gold-colored with faux-wood side paneling station wagon rolled past, we resumed our spots in the center of the roadway. Once again we began tossing the ball back and forth. Moments later another rumbling was heard—but it wasn't coming from the road. It was coming from the sky. A low-flying helicopter appeared overhead. It looked like a policeman or MP was inside, slightly leaning out and speaking into a megaphone or bullhorn or some such thing.

It was hard to hear every word clearly—the speaker had a distracting reverb. Still, we caught the key words, something to the effect of, "Everyone get inside your homes" as well as something about "fugitive on the loose." There were more words but we were too freaked out to understand them. Charlie did though (or he insisted that he did) and he filled us in on the details we missed: "They said there's a guy with a gun in the neighborhood!" At this, we all tore off for our respective houses.

Fortunately for Eric and I, we were playing catch right in front of our house so we didn't have far to go. Charlie, on the other hand, had to tear down a couple of hills to the lower streets to reach his! I hoped he would make it alive.

"Lock the doors!" I ordered Eric once we were safely inside the house. And that's just what we did— Eric locked the front door while I locked the back door. Then we went around and locked every window, while also pulling down every blind. Along the way, I grabbed a baseball bat. Eric, seeing that this was a good strategy, grabbed a bat too. Thus armed, we sat with our backs against the wall so no one could sneak up on us.

It suddenly dawned on me that the house was eerily quiet. "Where's Mom?" I asked Eric.

"She's at the commissary," answered Eric. This had me worried. What if Mom happened upon this miscreant fugitive on her way home from the commissary (for the uninitiated, a commissary is the military base grocery store)? Even as I was mulling over the terrible scenarios, we heard the chugging of the family Dodge Van as it pulled into the driveway. The engine shut off. Eric and I leapt up. "We locked Mom out of the house!" I yelled.

We quickly unlocked the door before Mom could find the entrance locked. She entered holding a couple of sacks of groceries, little John following her and jabbering happily.

The expected order came quickly. "Alan. Eric. Help bring in groceries." Clearly Mom was completely in the dark about what was going on in our normally safe and secure Manana Housing neighborhood. I started to inform her as to what was going on, but she was distracted tending to John's messy face (melted ice cream was all over it). So Eric and I whipped out of the house and emptied the van of groceries in record time, adrenaline bursting out through every pore, our heads turning wildly to see if any untoward figures were lurking about in our driveway.

Once the van was unloaded of groceries, I finally got Mom's attention. "Mom, we have to lock all the doors! There's a man with a gun loose in Manana!" Mom stared at me incredulously. This was clearly information she was not expecting to receive on this normal-looking sunny Hawaii afternoon. "Who said so?" she said finally. Eric and I stepped over each other telling everything we knew.

"Let me call Darla Medlock," Mom said finally. Which she did. And our story was confirmed. But Mom also heard some more details—at least details that Mrs. Medlock had heard from *her* neighbors: Apparently a man had assaulted a young woman in the hilly brush area behind the chain link fences that backed the Manana Housing area. Now this hoodlum was (perhaps) running amuck within the housing area! In short, no one was safe! To add to the unsettling feeling of it all, few fathers were home at this particular hour of the day, ours included! Dad was up at Camp Smith, plowing through his usual workday. He wouldn't be home until evening. Still, Eric and I had noticed something else that alarmed us. Kevin wasn't with Mom and John when they returned home.

"Mom," I said in a shaky voice. "Where's Kevin?"

"He's down at the field having practice," answered Mom. This was a relief to hear. That Kevin was having practice (probably) at Franklin Field with his Minor League team, the Indians, put him a good ways out of danger. But I had to confirm.

"At Franklin Field?"

"No. Manana Field." Eric and I nearly blew a fuse. A gunman was on the loose and our brother was right out there in the open at the edge of the housing area! One coach and a bunch of 70-pound youngsters weren't much of a match for an armed and dangerous real-life nightmare straight out of a *Hawaii Five-O* episode!

Eric and I piled into the car with Mom to make the perilous drive down to the field to pick up Kevin. To our relief, we didn't pass any gunman on the way down, but the streets were ominously empty. We were even more relieved to arrive at the ball field to find the team practicing happily and safely. Mom informed the coach what was taking place—he was more than a little surprised as no one had told him anything! Nevertheless, he dismissed the players and offered to drive anyone home who didn't have a ride already. Kevin came home with us.

We were still at our post an hour later when the housing area was given the "all clear." The next day we gathered more information from friends and neighbors. From what we were told, it seemed that the fugitive had abducted a woman from the nearby Pearl Ridge Shopping Center, driven her to that service road over the security fence, and then proceeded to physically assault her. Somehow, she managed to struggle free from the intended rapist and scrambled up the hill where a Manana resident spotted her and helped her over the fence.

When the police canvassed the area, they found the car on the service road, but not the fugitive. Even for the most lenient parents, this was a little too close for comfort. Many immediately laid down the law to their kids. "From now on, young lady, under no circumstances will you ever, and I mean ever, go play over that fence—unless you wear this warning whistle! Have fun, see you at supper!"

The next school day, Charlie had some information of his own to share. A true eyewitness account. And I completely believed Charlie as he looked at me, bug-eyed, reiterating the horrifying events of that afternoon: "My neighbors looked out their back window yesterday and they saw the gunman run right across their backyard! I swear!"

Chapter 20
Hawaii: The Place to Rub Elbows with Greatness

In preparation for this great baseball summit meeting, I actually rehearsed what I would say. "That was really great how you pitched that shut-out against the Phoenix Giants. Sorry about the playoff loss against Tacoma…" Hey, I figured he would be impressed with my knowledge of Hawaii Islanders baseball, how I had faithfully followed not only the great victories, but the defeats as well. My greatest hope, however, was that the great Dennis Ribant, star pitcher for the Hawaii Islanders, might actually…throw the ball around with us!

Even for those who followed Major League baseball in the 1960s and 1970s, Dennis Ribant is probably not a household name. But to us Cook boys, he was larger than life. Ribant, the fire-baller star pitcher for the Hawaii Islanders Triple A baseball team, had once pitched for the Detroit Tigers. These days he was trying to work his way back up for one last shot at the Big Leagues. We had seen him pitch more than once at the old Honolulu Stadium. Listen, the Hawaii Islanders were nothing to sneeze at in those days. Two recent episodes of *Hawaii Five-O* had centered on the Islanders—one on an

Islander player (complete with game action) and the other, with Islander stadium serving as the primary murder locale.

So imagine our head-exploding reaction when our neighbor, Mr. Calcagno, told us that he had been a college buddy of Dennis Ribant—and that Mr. Ribant was going to pop over for a visit in the upcoming week! Would we boys like to meet him?

Would we like to meet him?!

On the fateful evening, a flashy red sports car pulled up in front of the Calcagno house. There could be no mistake as to who it was. Mr. Calcagno and we three older Cook brothers were all awaiting his arrival, standing expectantly on the sidewalk. We were all wearing ball gloves, and naturally, we had a ball handy.

We looked on in slack-jawed awe as Dennis Ribant himself climbed out of the sports car. He had a thick crown of longish, blow-dried brunette hair (think c. 1980 John Ritter of the classic sitcom, *Three's Company*) and, if I recall correctly, he was wearing sun glasses. He strode up to Mr. Calcagno and they greeted each other warmly. They chatted for a few moments as we boys, intimidated into stony silence, stood back and stared. Finally, Mr. Calcagno motioned over to us boys and said, "I believe we have some young fellas here who would love to meet you."

The local star pitcher couldn't have been more gracious. The first thing he did was shake each of our hands and then he signed the pieces of paper we held up towards him. Of course we made sure to proffer a profuse "Thank you!" when he signed. I can't remember if I spoke my rehearsed lines or not, but I have a feeling I forgot to say them, or more likely, chickened out.

The next thing I knew, my brothers and I were spread out in the street, standing in a semi-circle. We took turns lofting a baseball to Dennis Ribant, who caught the ball bare-handed as he stood on the sidewalk and continued chatting with

Mr. Calcagno. How can I even convey the thrill, to catch a ball thrown to me by *the* star pitcher of the Hawaii Islanders—albeit thrown at least 60 miles per hour slower than he normally threw? If there was a baseball heaven, I was in it!

This was my first brush with greatness, at least that I can remember. True, our family did actually have one of the Doolittle Raiders over at our house one Sunday for dinner. He was a missionary at the time and thus had spoken at Dad's church. But I was too young to remember that or to appreciate this man's greatness even if I did remember. But by the time we Cooks landed in Hawaii I had become familiar with celebrity. Okay, I'll admit it—by age eight I was a big fan of Barry Williams (aka Greg Brady of *The Brady Bunch*) and by age nine, I had a crush on his TV sister, Maureen McCormick (aka Marcia Brady)!

You know, I hate to keep bringing up *The Brady Bunch*, but come to think of it, wasn't our dreamlike game-of-catch with the great Dennis Ribant foreshadowed by that episode where Greg Brady thrills to a game of catch with L.A. Dodgers ace Don Drysdale (who, like in our scenario, actually showed up at his house)? Of course my own nightmare pitching game (see Mound of Trouble chapter) was foreshadowed in that very same *Brady Bunch* episode! It's almost eerie.

Actually, living in Hawaii afforded us the opportunity to brush elbows with greatness on more than one occasion. Celebrity figures tended to float in and out of the islands on a pretty regular basis. That even included the entire Brady Bunch whose 1972 visit resulted in a three-part Hawaii-filled episode later that year. A bit higher up the celebrity scale, our island was also paid a visit by The King of Rock n Roll: Elvis (Himselvis) Presley. He performed that famous live-around-the-world satellite concert at the Honolulu International Center Arena in 1973. That same year, fresh off his stunning destruction of Smokin' Joe Frazier to win the World Heavyweight Boxing Championship, George Foreman popped over to Honolulu where the local paper captured him paddling along the shores of Waikiki Beach in an outrigger canoe.

Okay, we didn't lay eyes on the Brady Bunch or Elvis or George Foreman, but we did have our share of "celebrity encounters." One such case occurred without we Cook boys even knowing it at the time. Only years later did we appreciate it. Our first year in Hawaii, Dad had a Marine Colonel and his gracious-mannered southern-raised wife over for dinner. They seemed friendly enough, but we boys didn't take much notice of the visit. It was not unusual to have company over to our house for dinner. That is how Dad and Mom often became acquainted with chapel parishioners.

Dad had gotten to know this Marine Colonel through his frequent visits to Dad's office. It seemed this elder soldier enjoyed discussing theology with Dad. Only years later did we discover that this (seemingly) friendly and mild-mannered Marine Colonel was none other than the nationally-known (thanks to a famous book and movie starring Robert Duvall) spitfire known as "The Great Santini."

Baseball celebrities, however, we were not bound to overlook. And if we thought we had reached the pinnacle of rubbing elbows with baseball greatness after the Dennis Ribant visit, well, we were wrong. About five months later, Heaven upped the ante.

One day, I happened to be glancing through the *Honolulu Star-Bulletin* newspaper (searching for the Sports section, no doubt) when I saw the nearly full-page advertisement. There was a large black and white photo of San Francisco Giants star slugger, Willie McCovery, holding a bat. The headline above it read, "COME MEET THE STARS OF THE SAN FRANCISCO GIANTS." Eagerly I scanned down to see just who those stars would be. My eyes nearly bulged out of their sockets.

"Dad!" I called out.

In the next moment, Dad was besieged by Kevin, Eric, and I, holding the newspaper up for our weary-looking dad to see. It was all there in black and white: Four San Francisco Giants would be in the nearby town of Waipahu—at a local Toyota dealership, no less—signing autographs! Yes, super star Willie McCovey would be one of the four Giants in attendance. The other three would be Barry Bonds, Hal Lanier, and... Willie Mays! *Willie Mays*!! Yes, *that* Willie Mays! The Say Hey Kid— one of (at least) the Top Five greatest players to ever live!

Yes folks, 1972 was such an innocent time in the world of pro sports wherein an outfit like Toyota of Waipahu could actually convince four Major League Baseball players—two of them future Hall of Famers—to sit in its showroom and sign autographs for local fans. Such a scenario could never happen today. Now days this would strictly be the stuff of big city convention centers. Mind you, Waipahu was no metropolis, not even a tourist destination, the kind of a big city that Major League ballplayers would naturally gravitate to. It was just a decent sized town, maybe a population of 30,000 to 40,000 at most. Oh, and by the way, one of the players signing autographs for the event, Bobby Bonds, was already father to a son who would grow up to become baseball's all-time home run king (with a little help from steroids, some say).

When we arrived in the early evening, a table had been set up on the showroom floor and the four ball players sat on folding chairs behind it. All the kids and their parents were asked to form a line that would pass by these four larger-than-life San Francisco Giants ballplayers. Eric, Kevin, and I all had pens and scraps of paper in our sweaty little hands and were nervously rehearsing what we would say to each player. "Sir, Mr. McCovey, sir, could I please have your autograph? Yes sir, that's Eric with a 'C.' And may I say sir, my deepest sympathies on you making the last out in the 1962 National League

Championship." John, at three years old, was not nervous at all. He slept through the whole thing.

When we finally got up to the long table, I felt like I was in a dream. It was hard to comprehend that I was standing across the table from men I had only seen on television or baseball cards—and indeed, read about in books! Willie Mays was especially riveting, the liveliest of the bunch, telling jokes, and every once in a while letting loose with that high crackling laugh I had read about in his biography. Instead of scraps of paper put before him, he was signing black and white photos of himself and passing them out to each person that came by.

Then it happened. In the middle of this baseball nirvana, Kevin blew it. "Mr. Mays, you accidentally gave me two." Inwardly, I winced. Willie Mays, one of the top five baseball greats of ALL TIME was not paying attention and had unknowingly slipped Kevin an extra autograph! Unfortunately, my brother has always had a very high sense of fairness and honesty. Here he was faced with a real ethical dilemma. Should he keep the extra autographed picture? But, what if Willie ran out of photos and some poor kid at the end of the line didn't get one because he, Kevin, had taken two? My sense of fairness was not as evolved, but before I could advise him, I watched in horror as Kevin handed the photo back to Willie Mays. My brother, Abraham Lincoln. Willie grabbed the autographed photo back with a feigned hurt look on his face and said, "Okay then!"

I won't judge my brother's actions too harshly, after all, he only had a second-grade education. The kid probably thought we would be frisked on the way out by the police or something. "Sgt Takumi, come over here please. I found this little boy trying to walk out of here with *two* autographed pictures of Willie Mays! Okay, son, please lean forward on the Corolla and put your hands behind your back. You have the right to remain silent, anything you say will..."

Chapter 21
The POWs
Come Home

It was some time in the dark, early morning AM, maybe three in the morning. In any event, it was dark, as only it could be in the pre-sunrise early morning hours. I don't think any of our family was fully awake just yet, hence, the drive over to Hickam Air Force Base was pretty quiet, chat-wise. Instead, we listened to a local late night talk show. The radio host was chatting with a young woman.

"What is it about the Japanese and Chinese that you don't like?" asked the radio host incredulously.

"I never said I didn't like them," replied the young woman defensively.

"Well it sure sounds that way."

"All I'm saying is... there's things about them I don't like."

"Such as?"

Now the young woman let her defenses slip. "For one, they're not friendly at all."

The radio host seemed aghast. "I don't know how you can say that. The Asian people I've met here have been, almost without exception, truly wonderful people."

The young woman was not about to back down. "You really think they're friendly?"

"Yes! I really do."

"I've never seen a smile on their faces."

The radio host pressed further. "So that's what you don't like about them? They don't smile enough?"

"No. It's... well, they just seem to be so aggressive. Like they want to take over your land."

The radio host laughed in disbelief. "Take over the land...? You're prejudiced, aren't you?"

Now it was the young woman's turn to be offended. "I am not prejudiced!"

"Yes. Yes you are. And I feel sorry for you."

The young woman would not give up. "I'm not prejudiced. I just don't like that they seem to do everything in secret and they seem to want to take over your land."

I suppose it's ironic that we were hearing this particular verbal exchange on this particular morning. After all, we were about to witness an event that signaled the end of an American-Asian conflict that had lasted 14 long years—32 years actually, if you count the Pacific War with Japan followed by the Korean War of the 1950s. And yet the war with Asia was apparently still being fought—only on this dark AM morning in 1973, it was being fought over the Honolulu airwaves. Our family rode on in silence as the radio host switched off the caller and bemoaned the young woman's unyielding attitude towards her fellow human beings.

The Hickam Air Force base passenger terminal was not much to look at. The terminal was a small cinderblock building right next to the flight line, usually giving shelter to airmen or soldiers taking military flights to the Orient or arriving there from. When we arrived there was already a throng of hearty souls waiting by the chain link fence, many with cameras or carrying big homemade signs. In those days, whenever a crowd with homemade signs was on TV, they were usually thrusting their fists in the air and screaming about getting out of Vietnam or impeaching President Nixon for war crimes. This was not that crowd. They were mostly military families and were in an excited, anticipatory mood.

After what seemed like a long wait, some Air Force C-130s landed on the far runway and taxied over by the fence. When the door opened, slowly one by one, gaunt men in uniform began gingerly descending the plane's stairs. As they walked towards the terminal, people began shouting and cheering. It sounded like the reception a rock group would get, but it was for something much more significant. These were prisoners of war from Vietnam, setting foot on American soil for the first time in over seven years for some of them. They had been initially processed in the Philippines before boarding Air Force transport planes headed for the States. As with Air Force One a year earlier, when Nixon paid a visit, Hawaii was a refueling stop.

Before my father had re-entered the Navy as a chaplain, he spent several years as an enlisted troop, serving some of that time as the navigator on an A3D bomber. At the time, one of the POWs had been a junior officer bombardier on his airplane. Dad had always looked up to this officer, who he called the "spark" of the crew. After 14 years, he was hoping to see him again and welcome him home. The POWs sat in the terminal while the plane was being serviced with security posted at the door to keep them from being overwhelmed by the crowd.

Because the soldiers were so frail, only a few people were let inside to speak to them. Visitors had to first send in a note saying who they were and who they wanted to see. If the POW recognized them and felt up to it, they were allowed in. My father's old crew mate agreed to see him.

On the ride back home that early AM, we asked Dad how the meeting went. "It went okay, but we didn't talk long," he answered hesitantly. "He seemed kind of weak and a little out of it. I don't think he was taking in a lot of what I was saying. He just didn't seem like the energetic, fun-loving guy I remembered."

It made us all appreciate even more the devastating ordeal these men had gone through. It was an exciting experience as a boy but only as an adult, with a much better knowledge of history, have I truly appreciated the honor it was to be there.

On a more personal level, the 1973 Little League baseball season was everything I'd hoped it would be, and more. With a group of new powerhouse players (like the Artis brothers) who moved to the islands, the Cardinals were first place! We weren't as dominant as the Pirates had been the year before, but first place is first place.

Individually I had a dream year. At the plate my batting average was just above .400, a watershed statistic that confirms star status in Little League—*mega*-super star Hall of Fame status if you are a Major League pro. What's more I hit not just one, but *two* over-the-fence home runs! As a pitcher, I also excelled. The number of strikeouts I threw that year skyrocketed from the year before. There were no nightmare mound outings like that one against the Pirates the year before.

Only the All Star tournament was a disappointment. The good news was that I was voted onto the Manana Navy-Marine Little League All Star Team! The bad news was that we lost to Waipahu, 7 to 1. I can't say our defeat was a shocker— our League had historically come up short against the local powerhouse Oahu teams. To put it in perspective, Wahiwa All Stars had made it all the way to the Little League World Series tournament in 1971. In 1972, our Manana League All Stars (I was not on that team) was crushed 16 to 1 by the Pearl City All Stars. Forget that stereotype of the short and slight Asian—the Pearl City All Stars were mostly Asian and they were giants! What's more, that same Pearl City All Star squad also went to the Little League World Series in Williamsport, Pennsylvania, and finished number three in the entire *world*!

Nevertheless, I was set up for a dominating 1974 Little League season. With all my success of 1973, I still had another year of Little League to go. In the short term, I was determined to lead Manana Navy-Marine Little League all the way to Williamsport, PA, and the Little League World Series. In the long term, my ride to the manicured and stadium-surrounded fields of Major Leage Baseball, was right on schedule.

Chapter 22
Girls, Girls, Girls!

I stood in front of Kevin wearing my ball mitt and pounding the baseball into my mitt. "Let's go play catch," I said.

Kevin was deeply immersed in a recent Batman comic. "Let me finish my comic first."

"Come on. We need to do it now. So we can throw some before supper."

Kevin simply did not want to abandon his Batman. "What about Eric?"

"He's over at Joe Kossler's."

My brother breathed a resigned sigh. He knew it was useless when I was determined to play catch. He slammed down his comic and got up. Being the thoughtful older brother I was, I had Kevin's glove ready, so he didn't have to go to his room and hunt it down. I handed him the glove.

Once outside, I started walking down the street—in the direction of the Medlock's house. "Where are we going?" Kevin asked.

"Just down the street," I said, trying to sound as casual as I could.

"Why?!" demanded Kevin. "Let's just throw in front of the house!"

I shook my head and kept walking, in fact, quickening my steps. "I don't like throwing out there. Down the street it's wider and we can see cars coming better."

Kevin whined. "We can see cars coming okay on our street!" I wasn't listening and I wasn't about to turn back. This had nothing to do with wider streets or being able to see approaching cars better. I was a man on a mission—but I didn't want Kevin to be the wiser. And what I didn't want him to be the wiser about, was that my love life was at stake.

You see, the week before, me and a group of pals were throwing the football around in the street near the Medlock house. Pretty soon, Brent came out and joined us. But it's what happened next that blew my mind. Cindy—*Cindy*—Medlock came out of the house and sat down on the curb, watching us. She didn't say anything, she just observed. And she seemed to have eyes only for me! Okay, sure, I was with three of my other buddies, but they were complete goofballs. Cindy would never be interested in the likes of Jeremy, Franklin, and Cory Beetle (Cory in particular was so devoid of social graces that you always felt compelled to refer to him by first *and* last name). Out of our motley little group of hombres, I was the only one with all-star baseball credentials.

I came to a halt. "Okay. Here." I took my place in the center of the street and Kevin backed up about 45 feet away. Cleverly, I didn't plant us directly in front of the Medlock house— that would have been too obvious, even for a kid as young and clueless as Kevin. Instead, we were positioned in front of the house one up from the Medlock place. Even so, I made sure we were within easy view from the Medlock house side windows and carport (in case Cindy should happen to pop out of the house to empty the trash).

Kevin and I tossed the ball casually back and forth. Granted, I made sure to look cool and professional as I expertly threw sharp pitches. But I wanted to save my best stuff in case we had an audience. And pretty soon...

"Hey, guys!" called out a familiar voice. It was Brent, and he was striding towards us wearing a ball glove of his own. Boy, was I glad to see him! Sure, I liked Brent as a great older brother type guy, and not just because he was Cindy's brother. But I also knew that if Brent came out to hang out with us, then Cindy might just see fit to tag along! It was all working according to plan.

"Mind if I throw with you guys?" asked Brent.

I smiled and waved him in. "Yeah! Come on in!" We immediately formed a triangle and began throwing three-way.

"Seven hundred-twelve!" Brent yelled out. I knew right away what he meant by that.

"I know!" I exclaimed. "I heard it on the news yesterday!"

"Yeah," grinned Brent. "The sportscaster guy on the radio today goes, 'He's gonna do it this year, folks! He's gonna do it!'"

It was an exciting summer of 1973 in the world of baseball. In fact, it was making national news, and not just the sports pages. Thirty-nine-year-old Hank Aaron of the Atlanta Braves was only three home runs away from breaking Babe Ruth's all-time home run record! But the 1973 season was drawing to a close and he had only a few games left to tie, then break, Ruth's record. And the night before, he had just hit number 712!

Now Kevin wanted to share *his* Hank Aaron news. "Hey, Brent! I was card trading with my friend, Lee, and I got a Hank Aaron 'In Action' card!"

Brent nodded his head appreciatively. "All right! Outta sight!"

I then started to say something about Hank Aaron being 39 years old and that he might hit 40 or more home runs before the season was over. I don't think I completed my thought. Or if I did, I was highly distracted while doing so. That's because my heart leapt into my chest when I saw *Cindy* walking up the street towards us. She was wearing a tank top and cutoff shorts. Her hair was pulled back in a ponytail and she was packing a baseball glove!

"Can I play?" asked Cindy as she strode up. "I need some exercise."

"Sure!" I spoke up, without hesitation. I couldn't think of a good follow up to that. So instead, I spread out so that our triangle turned into a four-square throwing pattern. I happened to glance over at Kevin who looked more than a little disgruntled. I knew what he was thinking: bringing in Cindy now completely ruined our serious baseball throwing practice. Me, I couldn't have been more ecstatic, though I did my best to act cool about it. Why would Cindy come out to throw with us unless she really wanted to? And why would she really want to...unless she enjoyed my company?

I was very deliberate with my ball-throwing strategy as it pertained to Cindy being in our foursome. When I threw to Cindy, I threw it gently, and with care. I remember smiling at her as I tossed her the ball, just so she knew I was glad she was there. She smiled back! But when I threw to Kevin or Brent, I very suavely went into a professional ball player semi-wind up and snapped an impressive line throw their direction.

"You're getting' some good zip on your fast ball," Brent said after I threw him a particularly good hummer. I hoped Cindy heard that, and as for me, I just softly chuckled as if to say, *'Aw, it's nothin.'*"

We tossed the ball around for a few minutes more before the sound of Eric's hollering wafted down the street towards us: "Alan! Kevin!" I knew that was our cue to head home. Mom had sent Eric to call us home for supper. We waved goodbye to Brent and Cindy and started home. I paid particular attention to what Cindy said in parting.

"'Bye Alan. Bye Kevin.' Thanks for letting me throw with you." I was thrilled. She had clearly enjoyed our (my?) company! I didn't so much walk home that evening as *float* home, on Cloud Nine.

"See?" groused Kevin. "We should have just played catch in our yard. When she came out it ruined everything. We always had to throw soft to her!"

"Aw, grow up, Kevin," I said in my most worldly, cosmopolitan manner. Kevin was just going to have to get used to a world where girls didn't necessarily all have cooties.

Sadly, I wasn't as cool and cosmopolitan as I thought when it came to the opposite sex. Not that I didn't try to follow up on my successful Cindy Medlock throwing-the-baseball-around encounter. I made my follow-up move just three days later (I had to allow a little time to pass, so it wouldn't look obvious). Since Kevin had been such a downer about my otherwise glorious experience with Cindy, this time I cajoled Eric into being my partner in crime. Like before, I gave Eric the song and dance about wanting to play catch down the street so I had more room to try out new, crazy pitches (knuckle balls, sliders, extreme curve balls) while also being able to see approaching cars better. He bought it. So we headed down the street in the direction of the Medlock house. So as to not make it look—at least to the Medlock family—like I was going for an encore of the previous throw-around, I positioned our catch game a little further up the street from the Medlock house than we'd been previously. Still, we were within easy viewing of the Medlock family, should Brent happen to look out the window. And if Brent came out, perhaps Cindy would follow?

Eric and I threw for a few minutes, but there was no sign of life. After a while, I began talking and laughing a little louder, so that my voice would waft down towards the Medlock house. Then, my heart quickened as someone emerged from the Medlock house. This time, however, it wasn't Brent—it was Cindy! My heart began beating wildly. What would I say to her? How would I greet her? Was she wanting to throw with us, like last time? I did notice, however, that she wasn't carrying a baseball mitt.

"Hi guys," said Cindy as she sat down on the curb near us.

"Hi!" I said, probably a little too enthusiastically. Then, my mind went blank. What would I say next? I panicked. So I just turned to Eric and continued throwing. Cindy just smiled as she sat there watching, her arms thrown around her knees.

Cindy's unexpected company had the dual effect of making my heart pound like it was hitched to a pogo stick and also propelling my sweat glands into overdrive. I hadn't been this nervous since the pitching outing against the Pirates with no outs and the bases loaded. Self-conscious doesn't begin to describe it. Not knowing what to do, I threw even harder, eliciting a yelp of pain from poor Eric as my fastball smacked into his thin glove.

Like a passenger who has to take the controls of an airplane when the pilot has a heart attack, somewhere in my brain the calm voice of an air traffic controller spoke: *"Okay son, just calm down and let me talk you through this. First read me your gauges."* I reported back my high sweat levels, increased heart rate, and light-headedness. Before I could listen to his reply another voice, this one panicky, suddenly blurted out, *"You have to leave now! Run inside! Pull the curtains! Hide under the bed!"*

The calm voice took control again. *"Don't listen to him! You've been waiting two years for this—don't blow it now."* I felt the time had come for me to now nonchalantly tell Eric my arm was getting sore, give him the ball, then go over and talk to Cindy. It never occurred to me to ask her to join us. She didn't have a mitt! I had to say something to her. But what was I supposed to talk to her about? The Baltimore Orioles' chances in the upcoming playoffs? Ask her what brand of tube socks she wore?

Finally, Cindy got up and waved goodbye. "See you guys at church."

"Bye Cindy," I said, trying to infuse my voice with a deepness that wasn't there, yet also somehow trying to convey that despite my failure to communicate, I was still happy to have had her company. Maybe my smiling at her as she walked off would let her know what my words failed to convey. Inwardly, though, I was kicking myself. Eric and I tossed the ball around for five more minutes or so, before I called out, "Okay. I'm done."

And I pretty much was. I tried a couple more times to re-ignite the magic of that first throw-around by bringing Eric down the street to throw the ball in the street within eyeshot of the Medlock house. One time, Brent came out to throw with us and a few minutes later, Cindy made an appearance. This time, though, she just sat on the curb again. She only watched for a few minutes, though; before long, she seemed to get bored. She got up and left. Again I kicked myself inwardly because once more I couldn't think of anything clever—or really, anything at all—to say to Cindy while she watched us. How could I, with Brent and Eric right there!

I tried the play-catch-in-front-of-the-Medlock-house strategy a couple more times in the ensuing weeks, but Cindy made no more appearances. I was crushed. What's more, I knew I had blown it. My window of opportunity had slammed shut—on my fingers. But it hurt elsewhere.

Not that I didn't have crushes on other girls (not to mention my TV crush, Marcia Brady) but Cindy was simply a cut above. Now I had to resign myself to the reality that, at least at this stage in my life, she would never consider me as any kind of romantic suitor. How could I compete with the teen studs—the kind who had chest hair and sideburns and could drive cars—who vied for her attention? How was I, an elementary school kid, going to turn her head away from Eddie Tangen? But I was still hopeful that someday...

By late 1973 I had become—and I am ashamed to admit this—reduced to "spying" on Cindy. No, not the way you're thinking; I would never have stooped *that* low. A group of my neighborhood buddies and I were hanging out at one of their houses, and we were bored. We were looking for some kind of excitement. So one of our group, Randy, suggested we spy on a group of teens who always seemed to be hanging out at the Medlock house. We all agreed that could be kind of fun, so off we went.

Nearing the grass hill just below the Medlock backyard, we ceased our jabbering and got into military stealth mode. We plopped down face first on the grassy slope and slowly, methodically, began crawling on our stomachs up the hill. Nearing the crest, we peered across the backyard lawn. Sure enough, about half a dozen teens—a few girls, Cindy being one of them, and a few boys—were hanging out in the garage, talking and horsing around. "Bang a Gong" by T Rex was blaring out from a transistor radio. A couple of the girls seemed to be turning our direction so we quickly ducked back down, trying to stifle our laughter. The music suddenly stopped. Uh oh. Had we been spotted? Then, a girl's voice wafted down to us. "Hope you punks are enjoying spying on us!"

That was all it took. My buddies and I virtually leaped head first down the hill, crash-landing near the bottom of the slope. In the next instant we were on our feet, tearing across the playground at the bottom of the grass hill. I didn't look back. Had Cindy seen me? I hoped not.

If Cindy had spotted me that afternoon, she never let on. In fact, just a few weeks later, I experienced a truly amazing and quite unexpected encounter with Cindy, one that was actually (at least for me) romantically charged! I happened to be walking home from one of my regular errands to the 7-Day Store one evening. Usually every week Mom would send me down there to pick up a few odds and ends, usually stuff like milk, eggs, sugar.

After completing my purchases, I headed home, skirting the Little League ballfield adjacent to the 7-Day Store and then trudging up the first big hill that led into Manana Housing. Reaching the summit, I crossed the first empty grass lot, heading across the street ahead after which I would jog up a series of three other hills to my street. As I was marching across that first grass lot, I heard a voice behind me: "Alan! Wait up!"

Stopping to turn around, I was stunned. I could not believe my eyes. Jogging across the grass lot to catch up with me... was Cindy! She held a small bag herself so apparently she too had been doing some shopping at the 7-Day Store (how did I not see her?). She quickly caught up with me. "Mind if I walk with you?"

Did I *mind*?!

Amazingly, I don't remember a whole lot of what we talked about as we walked to upper Manana together. What I *do* distinctly remember is feeling like I was walking on clouds of peppermint green, basking in the presence of my dream woman, having her smile, laugh, and joke with me as we walked—just she and I. Needless to say, by the time we reached Birch Circle and parted ways, my feet never touched the ground— for the next few days!

In retrospect, something she said to me came back to haunt me years later. "Do you walk down to the 7-Day Store every day?" she asked me.

"No," I said. "Usually it's just Tuesdays before we have supper."

Chapter 23
Diamonds, Druggies, and Redbone

Growing up, our athletic interests gave my brothers and I a well-lit avenue to discover companionship, belonging, achievement, and discipline under our various coaches. For other young people in the early 1970s, their interests led them down darker roads to much more self-destructive places. Places far from the potential saving influence of the Mr. Dixons and Coach Snyders of the world. By 1973, the Vietnam War was almost over, but another war, a domestic one, was still raging between American teenagers and their parents. Experimental drug use had just a few years earlier seemed confined to inner city ghettos, the hippie culture, and college campuses. Now, to the alarm of parents and teachers everywhere, it had spread to middle America and its high schools.

The families in our military housing area were certainly not immune to this drug epidemic. Navy enlisted families seemed to be hit the hardest. Their lifestyle, which combined low economic status, frequent moves, and fathers constantly deployed to sea made their children especially vulnerable. These sons and daughters, already feeling isolated from the new communities they were thrust into every two to three years, also had to deal with a Vietnam-weary culture that many times had nothing but disdain for their father's military profession.

Without the daily guidance of a father, and with a mother frequently overwhelmed by her single-parent duties, these teenagers looked to their friends for a sense of belonging. Seeking acceptance by distancing themselves from their military background, many adopted the anti-establishment philosophy, dress, hairstyles, and recreational drug use of their peers. To military parents, their teenager's lifestyle was both an insult to their own traditional values and a deep emotional wound. Hurting people on both sides of this "generation gap" did not know how to talk to each other about the root causes of the rift, so they just fought. It was kids my age, and the age of my brothers, who were often witnesses to this ever-present generational and cultural war. It was a war in which, sadly, there was often collateral damage.

Some of the generation gap warriors we feared the most were the "druggies." These were teenagers, sometimes from our own neighborhood, who, whether legitimately or not, had earned a reputation for unpredictable behavior when under the influence of narcotics. In the 1970s, a worried alliance of parents, teachers, and politicians, sensitive to what we younger kids were seeing, created comprehensive drug education programs to spare us the fate of our older counterparts. We became the first generation of students indoctrinated with anti-drug messages throughout our entire public-school education. Unfortunately, looking back at my generation's extensive use of cocaine and marijuana during the 1980s, it's hard to view those programs as a resounding success.

At Pearl City Elementary, we were warned incessantly about dangerous hallucinogenic drugs like LSD. Our teachers told us about college students who, after taking these drugs, jumped off buildings thinking they were birds, or tried to kill their parents, imagining that they were the devil. Smoking marijuana, although not as scary, was portrayed as a stepping stone to other, harder drugs. We read stories about young junkies shooting heroin with dirty needles in ghetto back alleys and middle-class kids hiding out in the garage sniffing glue or other chemicals, risking permanent brain damage.

Once, a former drug addict who looked like she could have been Janis Joplin's twin, came to our classroom, accompanied by a police officer, to deliver an anti-drug lecture. I'm sure this was a community service requirement for her as part of some prior drug violation. She was a little coarse and may have only been on the straight and narrow since she was arrested the previous week. After the officer showed us a kit of actual drugs they had confiscated in Pearl City, the girl related her life-story which included running away from home, getting strung out on drugs, and sometimes seeing people's faces turn into cat heads during some especially "bad trips." We were mesmerized, but I wasn't sure if her lifestyle came across as repugnant or kind of adventurous. And so it went. The constant anti-drug message was one that by the time we were high school seniors, had become so familiar it had lost most of its effect.

Whether or not it scared us away in later years, these stories did have one immediate impact on us in elementary school. They made us very afraid of any older kids we thought might be drug users. The media of the early 1970s fed that fear. There were constant articles and television news segments, trumpeting episodes illustrating the unpredictable violence that could be leveled against citizens from—and this came to be a popular culture phrase—"drug-crazed hippies." The month we moved to Hawaii, the Manson family trial was just wrapping up in Los Angeles. If ever there was an individual that embodied every paranoid fear this country had about drugs and the youth culture, Charlie Manson was it. Being attacked or stabbed to death by some maniacal hippie was a thought that, at times, hovered in the back of my mind whenever my brothers and I left the security of our housing area.

Redbone

We didn't have a Charlie Manson in Manana, but we did have Redbone. That was just a nickname. I don't remember knowing his actual first and last name. But like other boogey-men from popular culture such as "Freddie" or "Jason," that single name struck fear in our hearts. After all, first and last names were reserved for regular people with parents, pets, histories, talents, hobbies, and other things that made them normal.

To the kids in Manana, Redbone was someone without any of those humanizing attributes. He was a walking, breathing, urban myth. A ghost. Someone that boys told unbelievable tales about to scare each other in backyard tents or forts during sleepovers. An apparition, that when spotted, sent us scurrying to our bikes to escape. But why? Where was the evidence of his evil deeds? None of us had ever seen Redbone perform any sort of violent act, but we knew that he looked a little funny, was a known drug addict, and that was proof enough.

I remember the first time I became aware of Redbone. My brothers and I, along with some neighborhood friends, were playing pickup sandlot baseball in the open field behind our house. At the far edge of the grassy field was a chain-link fence behind which was a brush and tree-covered hillside. As we threw the ball around, a teenaged boy, he looked to be around 17 or 18, came striding across the open field. His eyes were sleepy, his manner spacy. He took no notice of us at all. The teen had thick sideburns, almost David Cassidy-like facial features, and sported a thick head of blonde, Art Garfunkel-like hair. He wore an over-size Army jacket and bell-bottom jeans.

The teen made his way towards the chain-link fence, and without once looking in our direction, scampered up and over the fence, dropping down into the brush area below. Then, he disappeared.

"Who's that?" I asked in a low voice.

"That's Redbone," said my buddy. "He's a drug addict. He goes behind that fence to sniff glue."

I was floored. "Whoa, really?! He's doing drugs…?!"

"Glue, heroin, LSD… you name it. Stay away from him."

Over the coming days and weeks, my curious queries about Redbone turned up more information—or at least, more stories. I can't recall which pal told me this one, but it went something like this: "And one night Redbone comes home and he's super high on drugs. He's covered himself all in yellow paint, he was so high! It took five MPs to cuff him!"

For a monster, Redbone presented a fairly tame figure. He was thin, pale, and was more "pretty" than rugged looking. He lived on the street below us, the teenage son of a Navy family. Even on hot summer days, he always seemed to be wearing a pea-green, long-sleeved army jacket, a piece of counter-culture apparel that was highly popular with young rebels back then. My friends said that was just to hide needle marks on his arms, perhaps also to hide cannisters of spray paint cans when he headed out on sniffing outings. We had never seen him sniffing with our own eyes but had frequently spotted him carrying containers.

Despite his reputation, I never saw Redbone display any kind of aggressive behavior. He was usually shuffling along, almost in a trance, seemingly oblivious to everyone around him. But as a kid you believe what you want to believe. It was more fun to imagine him as a dangerous person lurking in the neighborhood than to see him as most adults did: a sad, lonely kid with a drug problem.

Because drugs were illegal, Redbone apparently spent a lot of time behind the fence of our housing area where he could get high in seclusion. Once, when we were back in that same underbrush exploring, we stumbled onto a clearing with an old camping stool and spray cans strewn about on the ground. We knew this was one of Redbone's hideouts and a collective shiver raced up our spines. Was he watching us from the bushes even at this moment, enraged that we had invaded his lair? Would he jump out and attack us at any second? Scrambling over each other, we beat a hasty retreat, our hearts pumping and our heads on a swivel. Upon reaching the housing fence, we propelled ourselves over it like boot camp recruits with a Marine drill sergeant screaming in our ears.

One time, Kevin and Eric were playing catch in the field behind our house. I wasn't with them. But when they came home, Eric confessed to sending Kevin over the fence to fetch an errant ball. I was incensed and I read them the riot act: "You stupids! Don't you ever go over that fence when I'm not there! How do you know Redbone wasn't there watching you?!"

Sometimes we would encounter Redbone when we were playing at the Manana baseball field. One time he slipped into one of the dugouts and sat motionless, clutching what looked like a jug of water. One kid told me that Redbone was crazy and thought water was precious like gold. Looking back, I think the "water" was actually mineral spirits, another chemical good for a sniffing high. At those times when he sat watching us from the darkened dugout, the only thing that kept us from gathering up our equipment and leaving was the fear that he would get angry and chase us.

One Sunday afternoon, Dad accompanied my brothers and I down to the Manana ballfield for some fielding practice. Being quite familiar with the drill by now, we all spread out in the outfield as Dad stood at home plate with a bat and a few scuffed-up baseballs scattered around his feet. He began throwing them up in the air one by one and hitting them out to us. As we fielded them, we would throw the balls back into home plate where Dad would stop them from bouncing past with his foot or the bat.

After a few minutes, I almost froze as Redbone, from seemingly out of nowhere, sauntered into one of the dugouts and sat down. I was concerned about what he might do, or even worse, that my dad might try to engage him in conversation. This called for quick action. I began to jog towards the infield where Dad was. My plan: nonchalantly as I could, warn Dad that we should all get the heck out of there. But before I could deliver this message, my worst fears were realized: Dad casually began to make his way over to the dugout. My mind virtually screamed, '*Dad! Don't say anything to him*!' Again, too late.

"Hi. Would you like to join us?" No! Dad had done the unthinkable! He had asked Redbone to come out and join us on the baseball field! All mayhem was about to break loose! I held my breath as Redbone seemed to just sit there for a moment. But then, to my shock and amazement, Redbone slowly rose to his feet and took a couple of hesitant steps towards the dugout doorway. Dad strode over and extended his hand. Now I *knew* nothing good was going to come of this!

Once more, to my greater shock and amazement, Redbone shook Dad's hand. His demeanor was almost bashful! Dad spoke: "I'm Chaplain Darren Cook. Your name?"

"Greg." Actually I don't remember what the actual name was, but it wasn't Redbone. It was some name that sounded oddly normal.

Dad smiled. "Well Greg, I'm going to hit some fly balls out to the boys and I could use a catcher. How about it?"

Redbone nodded his head. He removed his army jacket, laid it on the grass. As Dad grabbed a bat, I tossed Redbone an extra glove. And since I happened to be standing close, I knew Dad expected me to be neighborly. So I walked over, held my breath, and extended my hand. Redbone shook it. He was polite. Almost soft spoken. It had to be a trick! I turned and ran back out to the field.

Redbone flipped Dad a ball and for the next several minutes, a surreal game of fielding practice took place there on that Manana ball field. Dad hit fly balls out to us boys; we caught them or chased them, threw the balls back to Redbone. Redbone caught or chased down our throws and dutifully flipped the balls back to Dad. After a while, Dad actually let Redbone hit a few fly balls out to us!

I recall that Redbone did not have exceptional baseball skills. He was just average, perhaps just a little better than average. How come I remember that? Because back then I judged *everybody* on their baseball skills! But the most remarkable aspect of that afternoon was the fact that the notorious Redbone actually seemed to enjoy this highly normal and American activity of playing ball on a Sunday afternoon—with a chaplain and his bratty kids!

I know I've already described this all as surreal, but I feel this point has to be emphasized again. This was like playing ball with the Joker or the Penguin. But Redbone kept up the competent fielding, even jumping to snag a few high throws. I wondered, could Redbone have actually played Little League baseball in his earlier days? The possibility had never entered my mind that he might have led a fairly normal life before now.

Dad finally waved us in. As we came running in from the outfield, Dad again shook hands with Redbone, who emitted a soft smile. There was some brief small talk, then Redbone turned and headed on his way.

On the car ride home, Dad filled us in on what we'd missed. "He was a really nice young man," said Dad. "He says he's going to be joining the Marines."

Still, I felt it my duty to inform Dad as to just who we had just been sharing the ball field with. "Man, I was nervous when you asked him to play!" I told Dad.

"Why?"

"Everyone says he takes drugs and sniffs glue! Kids have seen him go behind the fence—probably to sniff glue!"

Dad set us straight. "All the more reason we need to pray for him, right?" This admonishment quickly brought us down to earth and we grew quiet. We knew Dad was right. Still, Dad had another thought. "I need to get him and his family to chapel."

Chapter 24
Entering the World of Youth!

Sure, it was my house, but it had somehow been strangely transformed into a whole 'nother world. For one thing, I was sitting, cross-legged and cramped, shoulder to shoulder on our golden shag rug living room carpet with about 30 other "youth" aged 12 to 18 or so. Like most everybody else, I was dutifully singing along to perhaps the most iconic song of the 1970s Church Youth Group songbook:

I wish for you my friend
This happiness that I've found
You can depend on Him
It matters not where you're bound
I'll shout it from the mountaintops
[Praise God!]
I want the world to know
The Lord of Love
Has come to me
I want to
Pass it on

Setting the pace and leading the way, was none other than Eddie Tangen on acoustic guitar. By virtue of his advanced age over the other kids (he was 19 or so) and likewise advanced skill with a guitar, Eddie had beaten out several other would-be youth meeting guitar players—all of them boys. What's more, the reason there was so much competition to be the guy with the guitar, was visible right before my disapproving eyes. Seated on the floor around Eddies' feet, and gazing up at him with adoring eyes, were half a dozen or so attractive teen and pre-teen girls. Even so, it was Cindy Medlock who had the seat of honor, her right arm propped up on Eddie's knee. Naturally, Eddie Tangen wasn't singing along with this cherished Christian contemporary chorus, but then as lead musician, I guess he got a bye. Cindy, being the talented singer she was, made up for her surly boyfriend by lending her soaring vocals to the group harmony.

I wasn't big into the long sing-sessions. Then again, chorus singing was a big improvement over the activity we'd done preceding: namely, the little-too-wild-and-wacky-for-me contest of passing an apple around the large circle with our chins. Of course my recipient couldn't have been a cute girl—I had to get up close and personal with burly, often sweaty, Tommy Marshall, as he had insisted on sitting next to me. Not that the previous get-to-know-each-other game was any better: passing a small wad of peanut butter around the large circle with our noses. My peanut butter recipient of that game? Tommy Marshall. Again.

From previous years, I knew that Cindy and Brent Medlcok regularly attended Sunday evening Youth Group (usually held at our house). By the time I began attending as a "youth" myself (just barely, at age twelve) Brent was still a regular attendee, but to my dismay, Cindy Medlock only attended sporadically. When she did, it was only in the company of Eddie Tangen. Even worse, for pretty much the entire evening, those two huddled together in a corner spot, hardly socializing with anyone except each other.

I was still fuming over the sorry spectacle of Eddie and Cindy rubbing their love affair right in my—and everyone else's—faces as the singing time drew to a close and the meeting moved into the "Rap Session" phase of the evening. If you're thinking something along the lines of Snoop Dog, Jay-Z, or Drake, you're in the wrong decade. We did a lot of "rapping" in the early 70s, but it had nothing to do with boasting or threatening. Early 70s rapping was all about relating, sharing—brother to brother, sister to sister, and various combinations thereof.

Chaplain Dale Fimbers, only a 26-year-old Lieutenant himself, was the facilitator. Chaplain Fimbers had a thick brown moustache and thin sideburns and wore round, wire-rimmed glasses. He enjoyed a good laugh during a group game, but he also knew when to "keep it real" during the group rap session. First, he played us a record wherein the narrator gave a simple talk pertaining to youth, and tonight's topic was, "Hey, Buddy." After the narrator gave his homily rap, there was the strumming of an acoustic guitar and a singer sang a quick ditty asking the narrator to "break it down."

> *Break it down*
> *Break it down*
> *Break it down!*
> *What's that got to DO with me?*
> *Break it down my friend*
> *So I can see*

The record came to an end and the room got uncomfortably silent. Chaplain Fimbers was taking a deep breath and slowly turning his intense gaze around the room. I lowered my head so our eyes wouldn't meet. Then, I heard Chaplain Fimbers speak: "I don't know about you all, but that blows my mind."

There were murmurs of agreement coming from around the room, mostly from the older teens who were on that wavelength. I wasn't. Chaplain Fimbers went on, "Here's what I want you all to do. Scoot up closer to the brother or sister sitting nearest you. Place your hand on their head, look them right in the eye, and tell them three things that are wonderful about them." Chaplain Fimbers clapped his hands. "Let's do it. Rap with each other."

Immediately there was commotion and movement throughout the crowded room as attractive guys and girls leaped to partner up with someone of like attractiveness, or at least someone they deemed to be cool. Me, I tried to turn in the opposite direction, but, fast as lightning, Tommy Marshall had reached out and clamped me on the shoulder. "Looks like it's you and me again, Alan buddy!" Arrrrrrrrrrrgh!

Tommy didn't exactly gaze deep into my eyes and for that I am grateful. I was even more grateful that, at LEAST, Tommy was not going to get "heavy" on me. "Okay," began Tommy, huffing a deep sigh, "I think you're cool. You're super good at sports. And you're a good friend." Done.

Now that's a "rap" I could be in tune with. So I reciprocated. "All right. Let's see. You always have a good thing to say about your friends. You're one of the best throwers in Sham-Battle, and .. you tell some funny jokes." Tommy seemed pleased to hear all this, and just like that, our "group" was done with the activity. We looked around the room. All the other teens and sub-teens didn't look to be anywhere near done—especially the pairings of attractive guys and girls. So for the next ten minutes, Tommy and I debated who the worst teacher was at school.

Finally, the Rap Session portion of the evening came to an end, and now it was time to go even deeper. This was Sharing time. "Who would like to share?" intoned Chaplain Fimbers in a soft voice. The room went silent. Finally, seventeen-year-old Christine May raised her hand to volunteer. Actually, come to think of it, the first volunteer to share was virtually *always* a girl. Only a few seconds into Christine's testimony, I was already squirming with discomfort. This was heavy, grown-up stuff she was talking about, and what's more, she was speaking through her tears!

As Chaplain Fimbers softly prodded her to "let it all out," Christine talked of constant conflict with her parents, smoking pot, and sometimes going too far with her boyfriend (who also being in the group, sat there and looked to be in shock, not expecting to be part of the sharing).

When Christine finished, her friends swarmed about her to hug her, place tissues in her hand. Aside from the sniffling and sympathetic whispers of love and support, the room again grew ominously quiet. Eventually, you could hear the proverbial pin drop—only it wasn't a pin, it was my stomach making hugely embarrassing wheezy noises from the Coke I drank. Naturally, Tommy had to turn towards me and spit out a laugh. Then, it grew quiet again.

Then, to my horror, it happened! I couldn't have drawn it up any better in my worst twelve-year-old nightmares. Chaplain Fimbers turned to his left and fixed his intense gaze directly on... me! "Alan. After hearing that, what would you like to say to Christine?"

Say to Christine? I thought. I panicked like I had never panicked before. My eyes glanced across the room. Cindy Medlock was looking at me with expectant eyes—waiting for me to be the cool, suave baseball hero she knew. Talk about pressure! I drew a complete blank. What could I say that would even be remotely heavy enough to rise to the occasion of the hour?!

I had to say something—something that showed concern but wasn't judgmental. Something that was encouraging but didn't come across as forced. Sweat began to form on my forehead. I looked over at the still teary-eyed Christine, and now she was waiting for the pearls of wisdom that would fall from my lips. Finally, I cleared my throat and offered, "Hearing you talk about all that, I thought to myself, 'Wow!' It made me think of what we talked about. Being open and everything." Someone suppressed a snicker but Chaplain Fimbers nodded, as if I'd just uttered words of wisdom worthy of King Solomon himself! He looked deeply into my eyes and said in a half whisper, "Thanks for the good word, man. Thanks for the good word."

The meeting finally broke up into the welcome "Social Time" phase of the evening. That's when I got to hang out with the kids in the group who were more my age. We talked and joked together as we drank more soft drinks, wolfed down more frosted cookies. The older teenagers broke into various guitar groups, each hovering around their favorite guitar hero. You never heard so many versions of Creedence Clearwater tunes being played at one time.

It's now the 2020s and I don't think things have changed much in the world of Church Youth Group. Just a few years ago, as I walked my daughter into *her* youth group meeting, I stopped and took in the scene for a few minutes. All the same personality types I remembered were there. The shy ones sitting in the corner. The girl talking very loud, supposedly to a friend, but in reality for the attention and benefit of others in the room. The same boy/girl games (tease and slap). The same awkwardness. The same need to be noticed, to be cool. Even the 1970s clothes and hair styles have somewhat returned. Take away all the smart phones and it could be 1972 again. I did note one sign of progress though—not an acoustic guitar in sight!

Chapter 25
The Great Streaking Debate

Though moving up into the "Youth Group" subculture of church involvement may have come as somewhat of a culture shock for me, there were already harbingers of things to come in what was formerly a comforting and familiar institution: namely, Sunday School.

In the elementary school phase of Sunday School, you pretty much knew what you were getting. Wholesome game playing (usually with small prizes given out), some arts and crafts, practicing group prayer, memorizing bible verses, and finally, your hour anchored by a bible story lesson.

I had several Sunday School teachers during our stay in Hawaii. My first and favorite was Mr. Dixon. The term "an officer and a gentleman" was created for men like him. He was a southern boy from South Carolina who, before joining the Marines, had achieved regional fame as an All-Conference tailback for the state university. He was tough, exuberant, funny, a dedicated Christian, and family man. He was also quite a storyteller.

During my fifth-grade year, we kids were transfixed as his booming voice filled our Sunday mornings with vivid descriptions of Daniel in the lion's den, Jonah in the whale's belly, and countless other Bible stories. I was best friends with his son, King Dixon III, a boy who shared my love of baseball. But whether you were his son or the new kid in class, Mr. Dixon treated every student the same—like a little adult. He addressed all of us as "Mr." or "Miss." This practice had the dual effect of making us feel more sophisticated than we were while also subtly encouraging mature behavior.

It's not easy teaching Sunday School. Your discipline options are limited—no principal's office to send kids to, no homework to assign, no taking away of recess. Even verbal reprimands are tough to administer. How stern can you be with a kid misbehaving when the lesson is about Jesus turning the other cheek? However, Mr. Dixon had a presence about him that made all thoughts of acting up disappear. God was in control of the world, but Major Dixon was definitely in control of classroom 5B in the Camp Smith Sunday School building.

But by my third year in Hawaii, I had graduated to the Pre-Teen echelon of Sunday School. Herein, I had another memorable teacher: Mrs. James. She was in her late twenties, the wife of a Marine Sergeant. Although she lacked Major Dixon's charisma, Mrs. James took a backseat to no one in her dedication to helping kids. Still, this would not be Sunday School as before. Sure, we would still have a bible lesson, but now these were augmented by discussions of modern-day "issues," especially as they pertained to youth. Now, topics such as boy/girl relationships and drug abuse were acceptable items to delve into. Mrs. James was determined to tackle any subject which could be an obstacle to our faith. And I mean *any* subject.

Take the controversial 1974 fad known as "streaking." At college campuses all across the nation, male and female students were taking off their clothes and running through the streets, through large public gatherings, seemingly just for the thrill of it. Every day there were reports of a naked person gleefully sprinting across the field in the middle of a big football game somewhere, in full view of thousands of spectators, and with a squad of security guards giving chase. A streaker even ran across the stage during the Academy Awards on live national television! On the more amusing side of this phenomenon, there was the hit song by Ray Stevens, "The Streak," which achieved massive popularity due to it being embraced by both pro-streakers *and* anti-streakers:

> *Oh, yes, they call him the Streak*
> *(Boogity, boogity)*
> *He likes to turn the other cheek*
> *(Boogity, boogity)*
> *He's always makin' the news*
> *Wearin' just his tennis shoes*
> *Guess you could call him unique*

Not wanting to be left out of the hottest trend in the country, some teenagers had recently been caught streaking in our housing area. This alarmed our very conservative military community. They supported jogging, of course, but not without the modest covering of a regulation Marine Corps tee-shirt and shorts. Even more distressing was the nonchalant attitude of the local teens who viewed the fad as just harmless fun.

This did not set well with Mrs. James who knew some of the kids involved. She was determined to set them straight regarding the biblical position on casual nudity. So one Sunday morning she announced that next week we were going to have a debate on streaking! I was pretty sure that this broke new ground for junior high Sunday School lessons. It would certainly be more exciting than making crosses out of Popsicle sticks.

Her plan was to invite some streaking supporters to our Sunday School class for the debate. After all, no one in our class wanted to defend streaking. We students were supposed to do most of the debating (on the anti-streaking side of course) with assistance from our teacher as needed. However, in case we eleven- and twelve-year-olds didn't do our Bible homework, Mrs. James dove into her own research like she was preparing for a Presidential debate. She would come loaded for bear (or is that bare?). Knowing this, I was surprised that the streaking defenders agreed to even show up. I could only conclude that these rebels had no idea what they were getting into.

The next week, four long-haired teen boys with smirks seemingly tattooed on their faces, arrived at our classroom door. Mrs. James entered soon after, her arms full of Christian reference books, stacks of notes, and a Bible with little paper placeholders sticking out of the edges. Her opponents had brought nothing with them except that one essential teenage accessory: attitude.

Our determined teacher set up two rows of chairs facing each other on opposite sides of the room. Not wanting to force anyone into one position or the other, she then told everyone who *supported* streaking to sit on the left side (how ironic) and everyone who was opposed, to sit on the other side. After a few seconds of seat shuffling, we were aligned for battle. But wait—there'd been a defection! Now sheepishly sitting on the streaking side with the four smirkers was my friend from school (and yes, I had somewhat of a crush on her as well), Shelly Light!

I couldn't have been more shocked than if Ted Kennedy had joined the Right-Wing Conspiracy! Mrs. James was not pleased but masked it well. My displeasure was not as disguised. I was still somewhat enamored with Miss Light and couldn't believe that she was a closet streaker-supporter. My gut feeling was that her position was due more to peer pressure than deep conviction. Obviously, these obnoxious guys were her friends. Not supporting them would severely damage her current "cool" rating. I couldn't understand why these rebels, whose hobby in life seemed to be thumbing their nose at the world, were so attractive to girls. But that subjective assessment may have been slightly tainted by my smoldering resentment at Shelly's defection.

Before I could further ponder the mysteries of boy-girl attractions, the debate was on—such as it was. It was immediately clear that the streaking crowd was very inexperienced in the art of logical argument. Although they may have been burning something the night before, it definitely wasn't the midnight oil in preparing a vigorous defense. The argument for the civil right to run naked through the streets like toddlers escaping a mother's clutches after a Saturday night bath, was not in good hands.

One of the teen boys on the Pro-Streaking side tried to get things off on a sardonic note by giving our class the once over before flipping his forelocks back and heaving a heavy sigh as he sat down. "Wow, man, did I walk into the right class?" His friends thought this was hilarious and they broke out into guffaws. We Sunday School regulars didn't get it.

The streakers' debating strategy was to rely heavily on improvised wit and an air of indifference. The first item, they apparently forgot to bring with them. The second unfortunately had not served them well in their public-school education and would, likewise, be of little help today. There was no need to pat them down at the doorway, they were intellectually outgunned. Still, they might have had a chance if their opponents were just us Sunday School kids. They knew how to handle us. We could be intimidated, our arguments made to seem dumb by a few well-placed sarcastic comebacks.

But they hadn't counted on our Goliath: Mrs. James, not willing to leave such important matters to her students. She stepped confidently into the debating ring carrying the two-by-four of Truth firmly in her hands. She swung early and often. Mercifully, it was over quickly. The streaking crowd threw a few half-hearted punches, were clubbed severely for their trouble, then decided to quietly lie down on the canvas and take a nap until the bell rang.

The following is an excerpt from that historic, not-so epic battle. Mrs. James lobbed the first volley. "First of all, let me ask the streaking side—why do you think streaking isn't wrong?"

The kid with hair flopping down over his eyes smirked (or, should I say, smirked even more acutely than he'd been doing up to that point) and then heaved his shoulders. "I dunno." That said, the kid looked around at this buddies, and they, in support, started to giggle. Thus encouraged, the kid with the hair over his eyes went on. "Because it's fun I guess."

Mrs. James didn't ease up one bit. "It's interesting you say, 'fun.' Is that how we should judge right or wrong? By the 'fun' it gives us? I'm sure sleeping with another man's wife can be considered fun—but it wrecks marriages and families. I'm sure smoking pot can seem 'fun' but it can put you in jail and cloud your judgement. Stealing money may allow you to have fun, but it's still taking someone else's property. What do you say to that?"

The Kid with the Hair over his Eyes figured he would put up a fight (and naturally, try to look cool and unaffected in the process). "Man, it's not like we're stealing anyone's money when we we're streaking. Everyone is just truckin' down the street, you know?"

Mrs. James came back. "No, you're avoiding the point. I was making an analogy."

"A what?"

"Don't you think it's wrong to be naked in front of other people?"

The Kid with the Hair in His Eyes smiled. He had anticipated such a line of questioning and he was ready. "Naw man, it's natural. We were born naked. Why should we be ashamed of our bodies? Hey, God made us naked, right? Adam and Eve, man."

Oh no! Had this punk checkmated our beloved Mrs. James? We looked on nervously. As it turned out, we had nothing to fear. Mrs. James leaned forward. "It's not a matter of being ashamed. Going to the bathroom is natural too, but if I pulled a toilet stool in here, I don't think you'd perform that natural act in front of the whole class."

A couple of the Pro-Streaking teens tried to giggle off this toilet analogy but that tapered off quickly as Mrs. James glared at them, awaiting a response. The classroom went silent for a few tense moments. When there was no verbal rebuttal form the Pro-Streakers, Mrs. James continued, "But as you get older there is a sexual component to seeing people of the opposite sex..."

After hearing the word sex used twice in the same sentence, the whole Pro-Streaking team giggled or tried to stifle a laugh, but Mrs. James was not distracted from her mounted offense. "Besides, if it's all right to be naked, how come you guys wore clothes here today?" Me and the other kids on the Anti-Streaking side all exchanged looks as if to say, *That's a brilliant point!*

It was at this juncture that another teen, with an even thicker shlock of blonde hair that fell even further over his eyes, tried to counter with a joke, "Lady, it was too cold this morning!" Everyone on the Pro-Streaking side giggled, but not Mrs. James.

From there our astute teacher broke out her Bible and proceeded to quote every verse in scripture where God showed displeasure with nakedness. We started in Genesis with God commanding Adam and Eve to put something on, moved to God telling Noah's sons to cover the shamefulness of their father's nakedness, plowed through the Mosaic Law which mentions clothing one's self several times, and ended in the New Testament with the teachings of Jesus and Paul.

Instead of having the intended effect of swaying our streakers' opinions, the avalanche of references put them into a dazed, almost catatonic state—the same state I'm sure they experienced when their Math teacher covered algebraic equations. At the end, we all stood up, shook hands, and left the room with basically the same beliefs we had when we entered. However, I do not fault Mrs. James. Whether or not she handled the issue correctly, the lady saw something that concerned her and took action. She genuinely cared for those boys and thought they needed help.

As for me, I wondered if I had become one of those proverbial biblical "hypocrites" when it came to my stance on streaking. Not that I was a participant, but I still turned the radio up louder when the familiar emergency news bulletin came over the airwaves:

Once again, your action news reporter
In the booth at the gym
Covering the disturbance at the basketball playoffs
Pardon me, sir, did you see what happened?

[Inevitably, the interviewee turned out to be one of those all-American good ol' boys who spoke with a deep southern twang]

Yeah, I did
Half time, I's just goin' down thar to get Ethel a snow cone
And here he come, right out of the cheap seats, dribbling
Right down the middle of the court
Didn't have on nothing but his PF's
Made a hook shot and got out through the concessions stands
I hollered up at Ethel
I said, "Don't look, Ethel!"
But it was too late
She'd already got a free shot
Grandstandin', right there in front of the home team

I admit, I burst out laughing nearly every time. But I did try (sometimes) to make confession of sorts with a self-debriefing: 'Ok, *this isn't really funny. Not in real life.*' Not sure that it worked.

Chapter 26
Fear and Loathing in Junior High

I pedaled faster but the bus continued to gain on me. Despite rising off my seat, leaning forward, and pumping my legs like two pistons gone wild, it was not enough. Within a few seconds the gray government school bus pulled even with me, its immense size dwarfing my yellow ten-speed bicycle. I could sense its critical occupants, noses pressed against the windows, peering curiously down at me. Embarrassed, I stared straight ahead and waited for the exhaust-belching machine to pass on by. As it did, I imagined the driver speaking into a microphone, acting as a tour guide to my Highlands Intermediate School classmates:

"Ladies and Gentlemen, on your right we are passing the Manana mudflats, a popular weekend destination for the local dirt bike racers. If you look out on the left side, almost hidden by our exhaust, you can see Alan Cook, a local seventh grader, riding his bicycle to school. Some of you may wonder why he isn't on the bus like the rest of us. No, he isn't training for the Olympics, but good guess. Allergic to close social con-

tact? The truth is, his parents thought the 50-cent bus fare we charge is too exorbitant. That's called saving $2.50 a week the hard way. God bless him.

Despite my vivid imagination, I'm sure if anyone on the bus did notice me, they didn't give much thought to my choice of transportation. Like every seventh-grader, I assumed everyone else was as pre-occupied with myself as I was. Although over the years I have tried to wring out buckets of guilt from my parents for making me ride my bike to school every day, it really wasn't the cruel Oliver Twist experience I made it out to be. Yes, there were some days when I had to pick up the pace to lose a kid who was trying to hijack me for my lunch money. And yes, the three-mile trip to King Dixon's house was mostly uphill. And true, once I arrived at King's house, I still had another mile to walk to school. But, by the end of seventh grade, I was in tremendous physical shape, although somewhat disproportioned. I used to scare small children at the beach with my skinny little torso sitting on top of tree trunk legs. However, I credit my ability to dunk a basketball just a few years later as a direct result of the tremendous leg strength I developed pedaling up those hills for nine months.

My biking experience, in fact, came to symbolize my entire seventh grade life. The whole year it seemed as if everyone else was on the same bus and I was somewhere outside pedaling to keep up. My peers were losing interest in our previously shared interests such as sports, toys, and building forts. These pastimes were quickly being replaced by more teenage hobbies such as girls, parties, hanging out (not playing anything—just sitting on the curb), talking about how dumb or boring everything was, and, did I already mention, girls? Not that I didn't share some of these interests, but such a drastic shift in social activity intimidated and perplexed me.

It was the same at school. Although Highlands Intermediate was only four miles from my home, it seemed a thousand miles from the world of Pearl City Elementary. Highlands was a much larger school, encompassing seventh- and eighth-graders from four other feeder elementary schools in town. The buildings were two-story concrete structures that projected an institutional coldness more closely associated with a prison than a school for young people. Litter was abundant. The bathroom walls had graffiti scrawled across them, but the classrooms had minimal decoration. It was as if someone had taken a large vacuum cleaner and sucked out every bit of color and warmth. Depressing.

The teachers, although cordial, displayed a harder and more aloof exterior than the elementary school instructors I was used to. I'm sure that shell was formed from years of confronting disruptive behavior and apathy in their young charges. There would be no surrogate-mother figures here.

Happily, I moved from one class to the other with the same core group of students, a good bunch of kids that made my classroom hours fairly enjoyable. However, in between classes and during lunch or activity periods, we were once again thrown in with the general school population, most of them older and not nearly as friendly as my classmates at Pearl City Elementary.

Hippie Teachers

As in my previous Hawaii schools, all my teachers at Highlands were Polynesian or Asian. In 1973, many of them were young and greatly influenced by their college experiences in the turbulent late 1960s. Two of my seventh-grade teachers, both in their early twenties, exemplified this new generation of tradition-challenging instructors.

My favorite of the two was Miss Tieko, my Social Studies teacher. She was very into positive reinforcement, wearing short skirts, and sharing her personal life, philosophy on love, and thoughts on other subjects her older peers would have considered inappropriate for the classroom. A glimpse into her unique teaching Modus Operandi came early in the year, when I was working on my Tiki god project. During workshop time (the last 20 minutes of each Wednesday and Friday class session) she came over to see what I was working on.

"Very interesting, Alan. What do you call that?"

I wasn't sure what she meant. "I'm making a Tiki god."

"Far out. Why did you choose that subject to work on?"

I wasn't sure. "Uh, I just think they look cool."

Ms. Tieko nodded enthusiastically. "They really are cool. And what's really groovy is that these carved gods are infused with such power and significance in the Hawaiian culture."

"Yeah." I said. What else *could* I say to that?

"How does working on something like that make you feel?"

What was it about reaching junior high age in the early 70s that was prompting every other adult to ask you how you were feeling about something?! I tried to come up with something that would satisfy her. "It makes me feel good. Like…I'm going back into time and seeing Hawaii in the old times."

Ms. Tieko closed her eyes, took it all in. "Groovy. That is so groovy. Keep it up." Ms. Tieko moved on to the next student. She seemed no less enthused about Frank's ugly lump of whatever it was he was working on.

As for my Tiki god, in reality, my amateur attempts at whittling a face looked more like a pair of rabid beavers had attacked a random stick for a few minutes, then spit it out. I knew it wasn't any good. That's one of the problems when teachers go overboard with positive reinforcement—they lose credibility. Kids are pretty savvy about when they've done well and when they haven't. Yet, credible or not, I appreciated her attempt to promote my interest in art.

It was in Miss Tieko's class where I was assigned the task of keeping a daily journal for two weeks. I still have that notebook, and although my rambling scribbles are somewhat embarrassing, I am impressed by the time Miss Tieko took to write detailed comments on each entry. Words like "groovy," "cool," "out of sight" frequently punctuated with multiple exclamation marks were generously offered on even my most mundane musings. At one point she even commented on my smile in class and said, "I really dug it!!!" You have to admire such optimistic, out-to-change-the-world enthusiasm. I wonder how many years that lasted?

Then there was Mr. K. He was my Physical Science teacher. Like Miss Tieko, he was also very young and exhibited all the signs of a man influenced by university life during the era of hippies and college anti-war protests. At the start of class, he would remove his shoes, roll up the pant legs of his jeans, and sit cross-legged on the lab table in front of the students—perfect "rapping" position. The first time he did this, I wasn't sure if we were going to learn about the three forms of matter or the three steps to higher consciousness.

Unlike Miss Tieko, Mr. K. seemed to come from the school of partying rather than the school of changing the world. He was definitely more interested in earning his cool teacher credentials than imparting knowledge. He was all for positive reinforcement as long as it was directed at him. I could imagine his senior superlative from teacher's college being "Most Likely to be Caught Smoking Weed with a Female Student at the Windjammer Motel." If he never lived up to that superlative, I'm sure it wasn't for lack of effort. The cute girls in class seemed to enjoy more than their share of personal instruction and affectionate nicknames. In the meantime, my affectionate nickname was "Hey, you with the blue shirt, I'll be with you in a moment."

One morning, Mr. K had an important class announcement to make: "Our first science project this term is going to be a little different than what many of you are used to. We're going to be making wine."

Several of us laughed. Yeah, that Mr. K had a weird sense of humor. But he wasn't laughing. "I'm not joking. We're going to make wine. It's an ancient and honorable art. But I would like you all to promise not to talk to your parents about this. Many of them will not understand and, what the hell, I don't want to get fired or some shit like that, you know?"

Mr. K. liked to pepper his speech with curse words. I imagine he thought that kind of rebellious persona would win our admiration. It didn't. We didn't really want our teachers to act like us. We didn't want to be their buddy. We wanted them to act like adults and teach. To my relief, Mr. K. soon forgot about making wine and proceeded to spend almost the whole year passing out worksheets full of questions we were supposed to answer through personal observation. A typical 1970s "learning through independent study" class. Books and class lectures were for squares (old-fashioned, conservative geek types).

Sadly, the deep inner longing for acquiring knowledge was in short supply amongst my peer group. But then who were we to complain? On many days we would be released like doves to flit around campus, supposedly observing rock formations, basking in the wonder of soil compositions, and drawing interesting plants we encountered. As you might guess, we instead threw rocks at each other, basked in the wonder of cute girls sitting in classrooms we passed, and quickly scribbled in the blanks of our worksheets right before the bell rang so we would get credit. Ah, education!

Since I was not female, I managed to escape Mr. K's attention for most of the year. That is, until the day he started pontificating on the great theory of evolution. After proving beyond any doubt that this was the most airtight theory of all time, he decided to poll the class: "Everyone in this class who still doesn't believe in evolution, raise your hands." Only I and a couple others were brave enough to do so. Shocked that his logical arguments had not erased all doubts, Mr. K angrily zeroed in on me.

"Mr. Cook, why do you not believe in evolution?" There was a disconcerting sharpness in his voice and demeanor.

I swallowed hard and went for broke. "It's because, you know, I believe God created humans like it says in the Bible."

This did not go over well. Turning red as a baboon's behind (evolved over millions of years via natural selection in order to attract a mate), Mr. K. sputtered with indignation. "Okay then, you say evolution is wrong. Show me your proof. Tell me your proof."

I hesitantly offered a few facts from a Chick Publications poster in my room at home which listed the various "missing links" that had turned out to be hoaxes or derived from animal bones over the years. This made him even more angry. "Do you have any idea what you're talking about? Clearly you don't. A poster in your room? Put out by some church group? That's your proof?" Now he was jutting his finger at my chest. "The next time you come to class, I want to see some physical proof of your arguments. Otherwise, I don't want to hear any more of your [now he imitated me] 'Well the Bible says it's not true!'"

That evening, when Mom asked me about homework, I noted that I had to do twelve geometry problems, an essay on George Washington, and, oh, I had to gather enough physical evidence to disprove the theory of evolution. By the way, could she drive me to Africa so I could pick up some dubious carbon-dated fossils?

The next day I was ready to answer Mr. K's challenge. And he started right in on me, first thing. "So, Mr. Cook, have you come up with the evidence that Evolution is a completely false theory?"

I nodded my head. "Yes."

"Well, present your proof."

"I know that evolution never happened because when I get to Heaven, I'm going to ask Adam and Eve if they evolved from monkeys."

Mr. K threw back his head and roared with laughter. "Okay. So then what if you get up to Heaven and you find out Adam and Eve aren't there?"

I leaned forward and let him have it. "Then *you* ask them!"

The class roared with laughter, so much so that the windows rattled. Mr. K's face turned beet red (again) and he looked like he was about to blow a fuse. Instead, he wheeled around, punched the chalk board hard with the palm of his hand and stormed out of the classroom. In his absence, my classmates swarmed me, hoisted me atop their shoulders, and paraded me around the room in a victory parade.

At least that's how it should have happened. It's like that old scenario where you only figure out the perfect verbal comeback a day later—or in my case, several years later (when I heard that joke in church). But the reality was, I tried to present my anti-Evolution proof to Mr. K the next day. But like Mrs. James in my Sunday School class, she of the famous Streaking Debate, Mr. K came prepared to shoot me down. He threw quotes from Dawin's *On the Origin of Species* at me; he threw Dr. Leaky anthropology findings at me; he threw a 1972 article from *National Geographic* at me; he even demanded that I refute recent studies in animal proteins as they pertained to shedding light on molecular evolution! My defense was to shake my head repeatedly as if to say, 'Yeah, yeah, right.' In essence, I was trying to pull the old Jerry Seinfeld trick of refusing to be drawn into this debate ("I choose not to run!").

Needless to say, there was no allowance for a difference in opinion on this hallowed subject in Mr. K's class. No encouragement of independent thought. Just anger and accusation at those that thought differently. So much for fostering a free exchange of ideas in the classroom.

Chapter 27

Art of the Autograph and Can I Get a Do-Over?

I finally had my pal, King Dixon, right where I wanted him. I was in the driver's seat now! After two years of getting bested by King in baseball card trades—and constantly turning green with envy whenever I looked over his mind-boggling card collection—King finally had to grovel before me for something he wanted.

"C'mon, Alan," whined King, "I've traded you some good cards in the last year!"

I scoffed openly. "Oh yeah, right. 1972 Milwaukee Brewer Rookies for my Frank Robinson."

"Rookie cards are a risk. I told you that before we traded! But if they become stars, you've got a cool card everybody wants!"

"I want your '65 Mickey Mantle, your '63 Willie Mays, your Rookie Johnny Bench, and at least ten extra Hall of Fame guys."

King broke in with mounting frustration. "Oh come on, Alan, be reasonable. I traded cards with you whenever you wanted!"

"You wanted to trade too."

"Not as much as you did, and you know it. So come on. Here…"

I shook my head, a resolute refusal. "Boog Powell and twenty 3-D's ain't gonna cut it."

"Twenty 3-D cards I'm offering you!"

"Yeah, but there's no big stars in there—you're offering me Ray Fosse, Don Michner, Sonny Siebert, Cookie Rojas..."

"I'll throw in Tom Seaver. Okay, there!"

I still wasn't impressed. What I had was too good. "You're gonna have to do way, way better. Where else are you gonna get this autograph?"

King whined some more, but this time I knew I had him. Even if he flew to the mainland and attended the Major League All-Star Baseball Game, he had no hope of getting the autograph I had in my possession. He didn't get it from me that day either. He didn't even come close.

Beyond mere card collecting, another—and more personal—way of connecting with my favorite Major League baseball players, was to accumulate player autographs. If I couldn't hang around ballplayers every day, at least I could carry around pieces of paper that were actually scribbled on by my idols.

I've already told you about the time Willie Mays, Willie McCovery, Bobby Bonds, and Hal Lanier of the San Francisco Giants all showed up at the car dealership in the town next to us to dole out autographs (and we three brothers all got one of each!) but that kind of event was an aberration—a lightning-striking-once kind of blessing. You can't sit around your Oahu lanai waiting for *that* kind of opportunity to roll around again! Hey, even as far back as the early 70s, the days of the Hawaiian Islands being a baseball barnstorming destination for the superstars such as Babe Ruth and Joe DiMaggio were long over.

In short, because Hawaii was so isolated from major league cities, I wasn't sure how I was going to get more Major League Baseball player signatures. Then, one day I was flipping through a baseball magazine and came upon an interesting article. It was written by a kid about my age who had amassed a vast autograph collection. For the first time in print, he was offering to share his time-tested methods for landing these treasures. Eagerly, I read on.

The young author said the key was a standard fan letter that he sent (short, flattering, to the point) to every ballplayer accompanied by a self-addressed stamped postcard for the autograph. That way the player, who was inundated with fan mail, just had to scribble his signature on the postcard and drop it in the outgoing mail pile. It sounded like a brilliant plan to me. It certainly was easier than traveling to big league cities, paying for tickets, and joining the pushing, shoving, and screaming mob by the dugout wall trying to get the attention of players who wandered by pretending they didn't see you. So, I gathered some old postcards, begged a few stamps off my mom, sharpened my no. 2 pencil and sat down at the kitchen table to write. My standard fill-in-the-blank autograph request letter usually went as follows:

Dear (is "God's gift to baseball" a little over the top?),

My name is Alan and I am ten years old. I have been closely following your career for many, many years and think you are great. I was especially impressed with your performance in the (fill in specific game to personalize letter) *when you* (fill in outstanding feat). *My goal in life is to become a major league baseball player just like you. In the meantime,* (time to get to the point) *I would be honored* (flattery with class) *if you would send me your autograph. I have enclosed a stamped self-addressed postcard* (I wonder if he will mind that it's a picture of the Free Methodist Church Headquarters Building at Winona Lake, Indiana?) *for your convenience. Thank you and good luck in the 1973 season.*

Your biggest fan,
Alan Cook

P.S.
By the way, please don't let some personal assistant forge your signature or stamp my card with an autograph maker. I would be greatly hurt and so would my lawyer who will sue you for everything you've got from World Series rings down to your jock strap.

I sent a version of that letter to Nolan Ryan, Johnny Bench, Vida Blue, and Roberto Clemente. Three of them did not send me my postcard back. Maybe church postcards were a hot collector's item in the big leagues that year. Instead, they sent their own postcards with pictures of themselves and an autograph. Although the pictures were cool, despite my warnings about possible litigation, the three signatures looked suspiciously "stamped." As soon as I could save up enough allowance, I was determined to litigate. At the time, however, my brothers and I split one dollar a week so it was going to be a while before F. Lee Bailey would be working my case.

But then my faith in ballplayers was renewed when a few weeks before Christmas I received one of the postcards back in the mail. It was stamped Dec 14, 1972, and on the back was a message written in flowing blue ink. The words were difficult to read, but finally I deciphered them to say, "To Alan, Best Wishes, Roberto Clemente."

Clemente, of all people! He was the Dominican outfielder for the Pittsburgh Pirates who had almost single-handedly beaten my beloved Orioles in the 1971 World Series! Although an outstanding all-round player, he had spent much of his career in the shadow of more glamorous homerun hitters such as Hank Aaron and Willie Mays.

Back then Latin American players seemed to not be as appreciated for their skills as players born in the states. That may have been due partly to the language barrier. Many of them did not speak good English or even live in the states in the off-season. This meant that many baseball writers didn't know how to relate to them as much as they did their American counterparts. The result was that their feats were under-publicized and many times, just taken for granted. Clemente had just begun to get his due recognition with his 1971 World Series performance and then in 1972, by reaching the cherished milestone of 3,000 career hits.

On the night of January 2, 1973, a little over two weeks after I received Clemente's autograph, we were watching the evening news. It was announced that a small plane had crashed on its way to Nicaragua from Puerto Rico. All the people on board were killed, and that included baseball superstar, Roberto Clemente. He was on his way to Nicaragua to bring supplies to refugees left homeless after a recent earthquake. He was only 37 years old and left a wife and three children.

Eventually we all learn there is no such thing as Santa Claus. And ten-year-old boys eventually learn that professional athletes, even ones signing autographs in car dealerships, are human like everyone else. For every Brooks Robinson, there are many others who are not necessarily thankful for the wonderful opportunity they have been given to make a living in sports. I had already read about some of these less than stellar attitudes, but one quote from my hero Vida Blue really hit me like a punch to the stomach. It was the fall of 1973. I remember it as vividly as I do the events of last week.

The *Honolulu Star-Bulletin* had just been thrown in our front yard. I slipped off the rubber band, pulled out the sports section, and spread it out on the sidewalk to read. My eye caught a picture of Vida Blue over an article about the Oakland A's upcoming World Series against the New York Mets.

Excited, I started to read. Suddenly I came upon a quote by my pitching mentor that sounded like he was speaking directly to me there in Hawaii. I recall little of what was said during my own wedding ceremony, but I still have that Vida Blue quote burned in my memory.

> *"I refuse to lie to all the Little Leaguers out there. I don't love baseball, I like it. All that matters to me is the money we're going to get, win or lose."*

What? Don't *love* it? It's just the money, not the winning? This wasn't Mickey Mantle practicing for years in the choking dust and stifling heat of Oklahoma, just for the honor of putting on a big-league uniform. This wasn't a dying Lou Gehrig crying at a Yankee Stadium tribute and saying he was "the luckiest man on the face of the earth!" I knew Blue had become very cynical since the salary dispute the previous year, but this...? I was stunned and hurt. Today, a remark like that would elicit nothing more than a resigned yawn from young fans. But in a world before free-agency, multi-million-dollar salaries, huge endorsement contracts, and the "it's all about me" athlete, that quote was like John Wayne saying he was afraid of horses. It was inconceivable. Although I continued to love playing the game, that article was the beginning of my disillusionment as a fan of professional athletes.

In the Spring of '74, despite the cynicism of my former hero, Vida Blue, I still considered a career in professional baseball as not only my ultimate dream, but also as all but inevitable. Saying I wasn't going to be a major league baseball player was as ridiculous as saying that in 2007, the 1974 Mr. Olympia (and former Mr. Universe) was going to be to be Governor of California. Or, as crazy as saying that by the time I was forty there were NOT going to be flying cars or cities on the Moon. Hah—right!

Of course I knew the statistics. According to the experts and my parents, who would weigh in on this subject from time to time, the odds were astronomical against my reaching that goal. Probably in the same ballpark as my mom saying one Sunday morning, "I think we all need a break from church. Let's sleep in today." Or my dad saying, "I don't care how much those shoes cost—money is no object!"

1974: My (Not So) Dominating Final Year of Little League

I looked forward in great anticipation to my final year when all the hours of practice would finally pay off. Granted, Coach Snyder would not be our coach this year—he had moved away. But his baseball lessons had paid off so much in my case that I didn't really need a top-notch coach. In my dreams, I would assume the crown of the league's most dominant player, solemnly promising previous kings Hank Buchanan and Ray Smith that I would wear the title with humility and class. I would triple my home run count to six and lead the league. I would win almost all my games on the mound, cooled by the breezes of swinging bats hitting nothing but air as my blazing fastball streaked past them.

After the regular season ended, I envisioned our all-star team finally breaking through at the district tournament, winning State, trouncing competition in the West Regional, and becoming one of the final eight teams in the world to compete at the Little League World Series in Williamsport, Pennsylvania. Before the game, I would be interviewed before millions of viewers by major league pitcher Tom Seaver and broadcasting legend Jim McKay. Despite the heady attention, I would speak humbly of God and country, thanking my parents for their support, and giving a special hello to "Cindy" back in Pearl City. Autographs would be signed and then I would trot to the mound to shut out Taiwan, bringing the championship back to the United States where it belonged. My teammates would mob me and ABC would show it in slow motion with the Love Unlimited Orchestra playing "Love's Theme" in the background.

Cue the banana peel.

Only one thing was standing in the way of '74 Season domination, and that "thing" could be summed up in one word. No, not Pirates (as in '72) but... Giants. More specifically, Giants coached by the masterful Mr. Redelman and manned by a team of crack players, the most dominating being none other than my good friend, Duane Macgregor.

Duane and I were good pals and friendly rivals. He was over at the house quite a bit and we frequently picked him up for Sunday School since his parents didn't attend chapel services. He was my same age but a year behind me in school. We both loved sports and practical jokes. Duane had an easy disposition and a funny high-pitched giggle which made me laugh just hearing him. As an opponent, though, Duane was very serious and very intimidating. He wasn't a graceful ball player, just an energetic ball of raw ability and power; the best kid athlete I've ever seen. Duane wasn't tall but he had the physique of a little weightlifter (I have yet to see another eleven-year-old with muscles and a cut torso like that). He had a herky-jerky batting swing, but still hit the ball a mile. His pitching motion was mechanical and simplistic, but the ball came out of his hand like it was shot out of a cannon. And oh, could he run. Like the road runner.

The Giants beat us 5 to 3 on Opening Day. While that may not sound so bad, for me it was devastating. Not only did I manage just one measly hit at the plate, but my pitching had also not flustered the Giants hardly at all. They simply crowded the plate and rendered my fastball ineffective. To add insult to injury, Duane knocked the ball several leagues over the fence off me! Afterwards I told myself that this game had to be a fluke. We—and ME—would get our revenge next time we played them. Hardly. The Giants spanked us 22 to 1 the next time. That game ended with a hard-hit ball going through my brother Kevin's legs in the outfield. At that, Coach Artis waved our team in. He might as well have held up a white flag or thrown a towel onto the infield.

The unthinkable had happened. In what was to be my final superstar season, I went into a pitching and batting slump! Hitting home runs? Not even close—I could hardly hit a good line drive! Dominating pitching? I was struggling to get the ball over the plate and was giving up way too many unearned runs. Forget being the league's top guy—Duane MacGregor already had that sewn up. Would I even be good enough for the All-Star team?

Then, Mr. Gary Redelman stepped in. He was the coach of the Giants, father to their second-best star player. After one of my particularly bad outings, Coach Redelman walked up to me, put his arm around my shoulder, and said he knew I was a better hitter than I was showing. If I wanted to, he would be willing to come over to my house the next Saturday and work with me on my hitting stroke. I could hardly believe the offer but accepted right away. The next Saturday he showed up with his bat and worked with me for about 45 minutes.

Employing the tips he showed me, I broke out of my slump the very next game, getting three hits. From that time out, my batting average soared and even my pitching was falling into line. I was striking out players again. My fastball was again popping into the catcher's mitt. To this day I am grateful, and in awe, of this opposing team coach who went beyond the call of duty in coming to the aid of a faltering, and highly discouraged, young ballplayer.

Unfortunately, I will also remember that 1974 baseball season for another reason. It was in the midst of that all-important baseball season when the Cobra came calling.

Chapter 28
Enter the Cobra

As the weeks passed and the Patricia Hearst story kept unfolding, I, like many other Americans, just assumed the F.B.I or the Marines would storm the hideout of the so-called Symbionese Liberation Army kidnappers and rescue this millionaire heiress who had recently been dragged out of her Berkley, California, condo. Yet every night on the evening news, this band of crazed radical kidnappers seemed to always be one or two steps ahead of the Law. Instead of being brought to heel, the SLA instead delivered a steady stream of tapes to the Bay Area news outlets, tapes bearing the spoken messages of the captive, Patty Hearst. Then, one night as I happened to be watching the news with my folks, the story took a bizarre turn. On the latest tape delivered to the media by the SLA, the emotionless, robotic-like spoken words of Patty Hearst stunned the world:

"Mom, Dad, I have been given the choice of being released in a safe area or joining the forces of the Symbionese Liberation Army and fighting for my freedom and for the freedom of all oppressed people. I have

chosen to stay and fight."

Mom let out an audible gasp. Dad shook his head and wondered aloud, "Have they brainwashed her?" Me, I was angry—angry at this female traitor who had sided with a bunch of yippie criminals. But the surrealness of this story didn't end there. A few days later the newspapers were treated to a photo of Patricia Hearst (who had now changed her name to "Tania," to reflect her new freedom-fighter status) holding a semi-automatic gun and wearing a beret. And just when you thought the story couldn't get more outrageous, the following evening's newscast showed the SLA gang in action, bouncing around the lobby of a San Francisco bank and aiming their semi-automatic weapons at the customers. And there was Patty Hearst, right along with them, robbing the bank! It seemed to me the entire world had gone insane—or at least they had over there in California.

Back home in Hawaii, however, my brothers and I were plowing through the '74 Little League season. As noted earlier, my plan on this being my breakout superstar year was riddled with minor highs, major lows, then back to major highs again. By the time it happened, Eric and I both were on track to co-pilot the Manana Navy-Marine All-Stars all the way to Williamsport, Pennsylvania. Every day I daydreamed of just how it would all be accomplished. Then, one late spring afternoon, Mom's voice interrupted my late day baseball musings, "Alan, I need you to run down to the 7-Day store and pick me up a half gallon of milk and a carton of eggs."

I groaned. In addition to interrupting another Little League All-Star fantasy, one of my favorite episodes of *Gilligan's Island* was on. "Mom, whenever something good comes on you always..."

"Not another word!"

"Can I wait until this is over? It's almost over!"

"No, you can do what I say right now."

I grumbled and mumbled as Mom handed me the money, then I pushed open the door and stepped out into the street. I wanted to get this errand done and get back home as soon as I could. Then I could resume my TV watching.

As I headed down the sidewalk, I noticed an old beat-up van chug past me. As it passed me, it sped up. That seemed a little unusual, but then old beat-up vans weren't too uncommon in 1974 Manana. It seemed almost every rebel, counter-culture leaning teenage male dependent drove one. I continued on my way.

My hike down to the 7-Day store was like many others I'd done. Once inside the brightly-lit store, its shelves and refrigerators crammed with basic food and snack items, daily toiletries and a few basic auto supplies, I quickly found Mom's items, then took them to the counter. I dutifully showed the cashier my dependent military ID card and paid for the items. Upon exiting the store, I spotted Eddie Tangen's van parked at the edge of the parking lot—the same van that had passed me on my street. I figured it had to be Eddie's van since he was now loitering beside it wearing a tank top and Jo-Jo hat. At the moment he was laughing it up with a young man with a large afro who looked to be about 18 or 19. I had never seen him before. I can still recall the music track that was blasting from the van speakers: the bopping, bouncy, vaguely Native-American soul hit, "Come and Get Your Love." Eddie and the man were glancing over at me, then quickly looking away. I didn't like this. So I started quickly on my way home.

I trudged up the tall grassy hill next to the ballfield and entered the environs of the Manana Housing area, just as dusk was falling. I felt I was in safe confines now. Yes, the 7-Day Store was actually within military boundaries, but the truth is, it was located in a kind of open border area where military and civilians pretty regularly mixed together. I felt better being up the hill in Manana.

A couple of minutes later, I had cut up another hill and was merrily trudging across an empty lot dotted with plumeria trees. This grassy lot was not far from my house. I must have been daydreaming about upcoming pitching duels against Duane MacGregor when I suddenly looked up and saw two frightening figures blocking my path. It was Eddie Tangen and the guy with the large afro I'd seen earlier at the 7-Day Store.

Eddie smiled. It was an evil smile. "How ya doin' little brada'?"

Before I could answer—not that I was capable, frozen in fear as I was—Eddie's companion whipped out a switchblade, "We're the SLA! You know who the SLA is?"

I could only nod, terrified and in disbelief that this was actually happening. The young man with the afro, who I was soon to learn was named Keith, barked out, "Damned right you do! And you comin' with us, bra'!"

I was hurriedly prodded towards Eddie's parked van at the edge of the lot. Eddie hopped up ahead, motioning for Keith and myself to halt. He checked to make sure all was clear. Satisfied, he waved Keith on. Keith proceeded to shove me into the van and I flopped down on the cold, dirty metallic floor. Eddie and Keith both leaped in quickly behind me. At once I tried to yell but I was quickly gagged by a filthy bandana. Keith took this opportunity to harangue me about protocol, "Now dig what I say to you, honky. You are a prisoner of war and we will kill you if you try any shit. Dig?"

But that warning wasn't enough. He yanked my head back by my hair and stuck his face close to mine. "I said, do you dig?!"

Fear and humiliation began to overtake me, and I began to feel tears well up in my eyes. I could only offer a weak, "Yes."

"Keep your damned head down," demanded Keith. With that he crawled up to the front passenger seat and climbed in. Eddie had already started the unmuffled engine and soon, the van started to roll. My head was down on the van floor, but as we motored slowly along the road I could hear Eddie urge Keith, "Hey man, blindfold him!"

With that, Keith climbed back out of his seat and slunk back to where I was. In a matter of seconds, yet another filthy bandana was wrapped around my eyes. What was I thinking at this moment? My mind was a cauldron—I kept vacillating between terror at my predicament to assuring myself that, surely, this was some kind of sick joke. At any moment I would be unblindfolded and escorted into some kind of surprise party—maybe one initiated by the Medlock family. But to do it this way? With knives and four-letter word expletives? No, I was truly in trouble. Terror again filled my mind. I began to pray. Hard.

We rolled quietly for a while. I could sense when we were on municipal streets, but eventually, all sounds of traffic, noise of people, faded off. I could sense we were now on some rural roadway for now I heard nothing but the engine and the sound of dirt and rock beneath the wheels of the van. After what seemed like several minutes, the rough-running engine suddenly cut off and I felt the van jolt to a halt. I heard the front doors open and slam shut, followed by the back van doors being thrown open. Humid air rushed into the van as did a sense of dim light through the blindfold. It was either Eddie or Keith barking to me, I couldn't tell, "Let's go little dude."

I was pulled out of the vehicle then stood upright outside the vehicle. Still blindfolded, I was led up a pathway and soon, I felt myself entering an old wood plank building that smelled as stale and musty as could be. The footfalls and voices echoed in the room I was led into, leading me to presume I was entering an empty building. "All right, man, it's cool," I heard Eddie say. In a rough manner, my blindfold and gag were removed.

I blinked and squinted, trying to clear my eyes, my senses. Gazing at my surroundings it was clear I was inside an empty old, abandoned cottage—probably a field worker cottage built many years ago. There seemed to be a lot of brush and overhanging trees outside. The only furnishings were a floor lamp and some blankets spread out on the floor. A back room was visible. Hanging on the wall of the back room was a white sheet with "SLA" crudely painted on it in big red letters. A bean bag was on the floor of that room. Eddie and Keith marched me back to that small back room. "In there, punk honky," ordered Keith.

A thought suddenly struck me. I wasn't going to submit to this. Not this easily. I suddenly turned and bolted for the front door, yelling at the top of my lungs, "Help me! Someone help…!"

I didn't get far. Eddie was on me in a second, leaping on my back, grabbing my face, clasping my mouth. He slammed me face first onto the floor. I heard Keith bellow that he was going to, "kill that little…!" The term he used was a stronger variation of the F word I heard fairly frequently at school—this one had a big 'M' at the front and the 'F' part in the middle. In fact, Keith and Eddie would pepper their speech a lot with this particular vulgarity. At this moment, however, I didn't have time to show disdain for Keith's language, for now he too was on top of me. He had again whipped out his knife and was menacing me with it. "Do it, man," urged Eddie, laughing. "Cut him!"

Now Keith had the knife at my throat, but then raised it to just under my chin. At that moment the dam broke, and I truly began to sob aloud. Even as I did so I was ashamed—ashamed that they had browbeaten me into this display of weakness.

Keith snarled. "You do that one more time you'll be dead. You can believe that!" At this I was dragged to the back room and tied to a chair. Again I was blindfolded. I tried to turn my mind, my all-encompassing fear off. I simply prayed for God to send in the Marines. Quickly. Surely it would happen. I had only just turned twelve. It couldn't all end like this.

I'm not sure how much time had passed. I was only conscious that it had grown dark. It had to be nighttime by now.

Then, I heard the sound of the front door opening. I could hear a girl's voice. There was much conversing back and forth between the girl, Eddie, and Keith. After a while, the frantic back and forth of muffled voices ceased. The door to my back room opened. I could sense what I perceived to be lantern light filling the room. I could hear a female voice gasping. The door to the back room quickly closed shut again.

Now there was the sound of loud arguing. The girl was yelling, cursing at Eddie and Keith. They cursed back. Though the vulgarity in the language was hardly familiar, the female voice became more so. It was Cindy. I knew it had to be! My hopes now skyrocketed. She would see to it I was freed!

Finally, I heard the back-room door open and again I sensed lantern light flood the room. Soft steps padded up to me and gentle hands began untying my blindfold. Again, I blinked as my eyes tried to adjust again. What a beautiful sight I beheld. It was Cindy, kneeling in front of me, her lighted kerosene lantern set on the hard wood floors and illuminating our small, shared space with angelic-like light. She began to stroke my hair. She gazed at me with sad eyes. She seemed about ready to cry.

"I am so sorry about this," Cindy said softly. At hearing this, my heart soared. This was all about to end. Cindy was about to see to it I would be let go! She took out a white handkerchief and began to dab the encrusted blood on my chin. "They were not supposed to hurt you like this. I am not going to let them keep doing that."

Keep doing that? Alarms started to go off in my head. I pleaded with her in urgent whispers. "Cindy, help me! Can't you get them to let me go?"

To my dismay, Cindy slowly and sadly shook her head. "Alan, I know... but trust me. This is not going to last long. We have to do this."

My head was exploding. I couldn't believe what I was hearing coming out of Cindy's mouth. "You have to do... *what*?!"

"We're doing this to help poor people, Alan. Your parents would want to help poor people too, but they just wouldn't understand our way of doing it."

Cindy had gone mad! If it's possible to scream in a whisper, that's what I was doing. "Get me out of here! Please! I won't tell!"

Cindy stroked my shoulder, but now her comforting touches sickened me. She cooed in a soft voice, "We *will* let you go, sweetie. I promise. But first we need to raise money to help poor, hungry people. We think your folks can get us the money we need to do that."

Now I was furious. I raised my voice above a whisper now. "They said they were going to kill me!"

Cindy vigorously shook her head. "Oh, no, no! We aren't going to..."

The door to the room burst open and in barged Eddie and Keith. "That's enough," ordered Eddie as he yanked Cindy to her feet. "You got your time alone with the prisoner. Our turn now." Cindy yanked her arm back and grumbled something to Eddie, but now it was clear: Cindy was not in charge. She stepped aside, lowering her head as if in shame. But I didn't have time to regard Cindy very carefully for now Keith was pacing in front of me, glaring at me all the while.

Now, in a boisterous drill-sergeant-like voice, Keith began to read me the riot act, "You are a prisoner of the Hawaii Chapter of the Symbionese Liberation Army. Your white, bourgeois family has gotten rich off of money taken from the people...!"

What was he talking about? Keith went on:

"Your family is guilty of the crime of oppression and enslavement of black and brown-skinned people from the beginning of this country's history."

Gazing at me with far kinder, far more sympathetic eyes, Cindy chimed in. "I'm sorry, Alan, but it's true."

I glared angrily at Cindy and Eddie, but now I was actually more angry with Cindy. She had turned on me! "What about you two?!" I shouted at them. "You're both white! Your dad is a Marine…!"

At this, Eddie rushed me and got right in my face, screaming, "Punk, we've joined the fight to help! Your old man could be joined in the fight but instead all he's doin' is holdin' church for a bunch of baby-killer jar heads!"

I lowered my head, not wanting to enrage Eddie further. Still, I couldn't let his remarks pass. "You're a liar," I muttered. Of course, he heard me.

"What did you say?" said Eddie in a voice way too calm to be trusted. I waited for the expected smack across the face, but Keith jumped in before that could happen. Now Keith was in my face.

"I don't think you understand, you little white pig," he yelled. "We in a war! Your family is under a sentence of death for crimes committed against the people! The revolution is here, bra'! If your pig family ain't educated, we gonna educate them."

Finally, Eddie said it. "Your family has bread, man."

I looked over at Cindy in disbelief. Her sorrowful eyes said it all. "I had to tell them, sweetie. It's important we get that money. We can help so many people." Now it suddenly dawned on me: Cindy had told them! She had gone to Eddie and Keith with the family history I had shared with her that night we played the board game at our house! She had clearly told them that because my ancestors had owned land in Los Angeles, we were rich! That we were loaded with money! Cindy—you traitor!

Keith interjected. "And if we don't get that money, we kill you and your entire pig family! Believe that!"

Cindy protested, but it was way too weak: "Keith…!"

Again tears welled up in my eyes but I still tried to put on a brave front. "My parents aren't rich…"

"They own half of L.A.!" interjected Eddie, though he used several strung-together adjectives to describe Los Angeles that were among the foulest expletives I'd ever heard.

Cindy wheeled on Eddie. "Stop trying to scare him!"

"He better be scared!"

Now Keith grabbed the front of my shirt and twisted it in his fist. "Your pig parents gonna come up with a half million dollars. *Then*, we let you go."

Chapter 29

In the Hands
of the Cobra

It was late that same night. I was awakened from a fitful sleep by Keith and Eddie. This time a small floor battery lamp provided light. Eddie plopped a black Panasonic portable cassette tape recorder on the floor in front of me, then handed me a few sheets of paper filled with crudely written script. I was to read the lines and say them into the tape recorder. When I was ready, Eddie pushed PLAY. I began to read in a shaky voice.

"Hi Mom and Dad. It's me, Alan. I am a prisoner. Um..."

Keith suddenly shut off the tape and snapped at me. "Of the Hawaii SLA, man! And you say, 'I'm okay and ain't nobody hurt me.' Dig?" I nodded, yes. Keith pressed PLAY again, and again I began to speak, my body and soul filled with numbness:

"A prisoner of Hawaii SLA. I'm okay. Nobody's hurt me..." I went on to tell my parents—and anyone else listening to the tape—that the Hawaii SLA wanted half a million dollars in cash. It was to be dropped off on the green bench in front of the Kam Shopping Center in Waipahu. At this point, Keith pushed me back and he broke in:

"Don't think we fuckin' with you. We fightin' for the revolution and we fight with our SLA comrades in California. We fight for the other oppressed peoples of the world. We will kill if necessary. All power to the people and death to the white insect fascist…that preys upon the life of the people!"

As Keith shut the off the tape, he fixed upon me a menacing glare. "Don't think it's just us three cats, that we the whole SLA on the island, man. We got a whole army out there. They gonna make sure we take over this pig island." And with that, he got up and left me in darkness.

I had nightmares as I slept that night. I dreamt that Eddie, Keith, and several other unrecognizable, masked SLA radicals blasted into our house on Birch Circle and sprayed the house with M-16 gunfire. Though I couldn't see any of my family through the smoke of the gunfire, I knew they had to be in the room, relaxing on the sofas and easy chairs, reading or watching TV. I jerked awake, panting in fear. After a few moments, I realized it was a dream, but my reality was hardly better.

Normally when you wake up from a nightmare, there is that rush of welcome relief when you realize it was all just a bad dream. This time I woke up from one bad dream to my reality in another. I gazed into the other room. I could make out the forms of Keith, Eddie, and Cindy sprawled out on the bare floor of the main room. The thought occurred to me that now was the perfect time to make a break for it. But two things prevented me from doing so: one, I was tied up; second, I just knew one of them would wake up and then I would be killed.

Early the next morning, at my urgent request, Eddie led me outside to go to the bathroom. I had to relieve myself in the woods behind the house, with Eddie watching me the entire time. The humiliation I felt was total, and with it, the feeling of abject helplessness. I squatted down but couldn't do a thing. I had no choice but to plead.

"Can I go behind those bushes? I can't do it if you're standing there."

Eddie waved his pistol with angry impatience. "Go! But I'm still watchin' from here. You try somethin' I'm comin' after your ass!"

I quickly pushed my way into a patch of briar bushes. Turning back, I could see Eddie staring in my direction but he was obscured by brush and branches. A moment later, Eddie seemed to get distracted and he turned to stare in the other direction. A sudden epiphany hit me—I could make a run for it! Not hesitating a moment more, I hiked up my pants and started barreling through the bushes in a mad dash. I came to a sudden halt.

There, standing in the open field and staring right back at me...was Redbone! He gazed at me, without moving and without expression. Just beyond him, I could see Pond 6. So *that's* where I was—in the ravine just behind Manana Housing! Still, I froze. The horror of it all suddenly hit me: *Redbone was one of them*! He was in on it, standing sentinel for the SLA! I quickly turned and high-tailed it back into the brush. I could now see Eddie pushing through the prickly branches and bushes towards me. "What are you doing, man?" he called out in a menacing tone.

I quickly squatted down again. "I'm almost done!" I called back.

I didn't try to escape after that. Keith was right. I was surrounded by a seen and unseen SLA army. I couldn't tell how many days had passed—it could have been three, maybe four. Maybe just one. I just know I spent the daylight hours tied up in that tiny back room. Every now and then, TV dinners or sandwiches were brought to me. And every so often Eddie would lead me out back to go to the bathroom, often browbeating me to hurry it up. I despised him.

Naturally I wasn't given a TV or radio, but Eddie, Keith, and Cindy had a little battery-operated TV in the main room. Through the open door I could sometimes see, or at least hear, what they were watching. They seemed particularly interested in the national and local news. One evening they were all huddled in front of the tiny TV as a newscast was on. Suddenly all three of them became very excited, virtually bouncing in their crouch-seated positions. My eyes, too, suddenly lit up. There, on the screen, a local news anchorwoman stood in front of my house—the Birch Circle COOK house! Eddie turned the volume up.

From my back room I could clearly hear the anchorwoman saying something about, "...was kidnapped by a group claiming to be the Hawaii Chapter of the Symbionese Liberation Army...When he did not return home..."

I could not hear the entire spiel because Eddie, Keith, and Cindy were besides themselves with excitement—cheering, congratulating themselves. Eddie and Keith continually slapped palms and performed the "Right On" clasp of hands.

"They know us now!" crowed Keith.

A moment later, I heard the anchorwoman reveal more pertinent information: "The cassette tape was left on the front porch of the Cook home behind me." Eddie and Keith then broke out in loud laughter as excerpts from my speech on the tape were played, followed by Keiths demands for ransom. Cindy hardly said anything as she watched, transfixed. Then, the anchorwoman revealed something that even I had no knowledge of: "The group has even left mocking clues as to their whereabouts."

At that point another excerpt of the tape was played—and this time it was the voice of Cindy that wafted over the airwaves. She spoke in an odd, mocking, bravado-filled tone, one that I had never heard from her before: "And for all you pigs out there, here's a clue for you. There's two snakes in Hawaii: one at the zoo, and a cobra in Waikiki."

Eddie and Keith burst out laughing, again slapping palms. Cindy was smiling.

"Now the pigs gonna be all *over* Waikiki, man!" exclaimed Keith. "All we gotta do is keep truckin' right here!"

Eddie turned and began mocking the TV anchor people, jabbing his finger at the TV screen, "Wake up, pigs! The Cobra is in your own backyard!"

I lost track of time. It seemed like I was a prisoner in that house for months. For a few minutes the next day they untied me, allowed me to move around a little—under close watch of course. Later in the afternoon, I actually indulged in something pleasant: Cindy had returned from the 7-Day Store with a box of peanut butter caramel "Space Food Sticks." I was allowed a couple and began to eagerly devour one, when suddenly, a rumbling was heard overhead. All heads looked skyward out through the windows.

"Everybody down!" bellowed Eddie, and we all hit the floor so as not to be seen. Actually, I had to be pulled to the floor as I most definitely *wanted* to be seen.

"The pigs are lookin' down here, man," said Keith.

"How did they find us?" whimpered Cindy.

"We can't stay here, man," continued Keith. "They's gonna be pigs all over this place, boots on the ground. We gotta split."

I was brusquely pulled into the back room and shut inside. Still, I could hear my three captors frantically trying to come up with an exit strategy. A few minutes later, our group made its move. Eddie handed Keith his van keys. "Be careful, man. It's an old machine. Don't hammer the clutch too much."

Keith just nodded as he took hold of the keys. "Right on. I meet you guys up there later tonight." With that, Keith turned and left. That's the last I ever laid eyes on him.

As soon as Keith drove off with the van, Eddie, Cindy, and I began winding our way along the back trails. "We'll come up behind the fence on Shafter Road," I heard Eddie tell Cindy.

"It's too close!" Cindy protested.

"It's the best the place to hide, man," insisted Eddie. "Right under their nose."

"Eddie...!"

"Shut up, man!" Eddie bellowed at Cindy. "We have to go there. That's where I told Keith to pick us up!"

Helicopters continued to swarm overhead and now we could see police cars and official-looking *Hawaii-Five-O*-like sedans swarming into the ravine, blocking the main roads out. We huddled in a thicket while it got darker.

Once the ravine was sufficiently enshrouded by the night and mist, we crept our way towards Manana, working our way up the hill as silently as we could. At last reaching the fence, Eddie surveyed the other side, making sure there was no police or Marine presence to be seen. When he was sure the coast was clear, he had Cindy scale the fence first, followed by me and Eddie right on my heels. All of us reached the other side, plopping down on a dark, grassy field. The nearest house was about fifty yards away.

"Okay, let's move," said Eddie. "Casual. Any funny moves, little man, you're dead."

As we walked through the darkened Manana streets, Cindy kept trying to reassure me in soft whispers, "This would all be over soon. Everything would turn out all right. One day my parents would understand."

Chapter 30
The Cobra Makes Their Move

After several minutes of silent walking and keeping to the shadowy side streets, we reached our Manana "safe house." Even in the darkness I recognized it immediately. I had ridden my bike past these housing units at the far end of the Manana Housing area many times. These units fronted the back fence behind which was the dirt road leading down to the old cottages—including our own SLA hideout—in the ravine below. This particular empty house had always stood out to me as somewhat creepy. For some reason it always seemed to be empty, not to mention those tall black tiki torches that rose in crisscross fashion in the empty grass lot next to the house. The house, as well as the tiki torches, all sat under the low hanging branches of a large banyan tree. The scene always struck me as my idea of an ancient Hawaiian graveyard.

The house was dark, yet Eddie had no trouble getting in through an open back window. Apparently they had prepped this unit beforehand as a possible fallback SLA safe house. Once inside, I was tied up again. Cindy set up her small floor lamp in the living room. Through the open window, the roar of a motor could be heard. Eddie dashed over to the window and crouched down, being careful to stay out of sight. He peered out. "Car comin', man," he said in a low voice.

Cindy quickly switched off the small floor lamp, rendering the house completely dark, completely quiet. The headlights and engine sound of a slow-moving vehicle rolling past reverberated through the empty house. I was hopeful—*every* time I heard a car engine I was hopeful. But the headlights and sound of the engine receded into the darkness.

Once the vehicle was safely past, Eddie offered an update. "MP's." They waited a few more moments until all was completely quiet. Eddie gave the final update. "Pigs are gone. The coast is clear." Cindy flicked the floor lamp back on.

That night I was forced to make another tape recording. I dutifully read what was written on paper for me: "This is Alan again. I'm still okay. Today Elvis Presley was in the news. He bought a car for a lady he didn't even know. Mom and Dad, you said you would leave the money at the shopping center but we checked and it wasn't there. The SLA isn't kidding. They are really serious..."

My captors passed the time mostly by listening to their tiny, portable transistor radio. To this day I have distinct visions of my ordeal when I hear the quirky circus-blues strains of Three Dog Night's "I Must Let the Show Go On," the Latino-flavored remake of "Hooked on a Feeling" by Blue Suede (complete with its wild, caveman-like intro chant of 'Ooga-Chaka! Ooga-Chaka!'), the driving power-pop of Paul McCartney & Wings, "Jet," but most eerie of all, the ominous and foreboding keyboard and brass soul of Chicago's "I've Been Searching So Long."

As the minutes slowly passed, my captors always kept one eye towards the front window until the next of our voices heard was Cindy blurting out, "Car!" At this, Eddie would shut off the radio. The lamp light would be shut off. Then, the house would grow deathly quiet as the vehicle in question drove past. Once the coast was clear, Cindy or Eddie would say, "Gone." The festivities would then resume.

Every so often Cindy leaned down to address me. "It's almost over, sweetheart. We're going to pick up the money tonight. Tomorrow at latest. If it's all there we can let you go."

I detested it when she called me, "Sweetheart." Even at my age, I recognized the term as phony and patronizing. I wasn't a four-year-old who needed to be placated with sugary platitudes, especially by a girl who was only six years older than me. Not that I cared for Eddie's blunt verbal brutality.

"Don't get him thinkin' like he's about to go home, man," Eddie snarled at Cindy. "I don't think his pig parents are going to come up with the bread."

Cindy wheeled on Eddie and spat out in a shrill voice. "Eddie, shut up!"

It was a long, quiet, tension-filled evening. Eddie and Cindy continued listening to the radio, hardly speaking to each other at all. Cindy peered anxiously out the window. "Keith should have been back by now."

"He can't rush this, man," said Eddie.

Cindy turned to Eddie. "Eddie, he can't get through the *gate* after dark!"

"My van has a base sticker."

"You should have gone. Not him!"

"If there's too many pigs at the front gate, he'll just park the van at the 7-Day store and walk up. Don't get all freaked out!"

Clearly frustrated and flustered, Eddie pushed himself to his feet and headed down the dark hallway of the empty house. A few moments later he returned, holding a guitar. Clearly, my captors had hidden out in this unit before and had stored a few "provisions."

Eddie plopped back down on the floor, sitting cross-legged and tuning the strings of his instrument. Finally, he started strumming the chords to *Love* by John Lennon. Softly, he began to sing:

Love is real
Real is love
Love is feeling
Feeling love

Now Cindy joined in. As I took in this bizarre duet, it struck me as both sinister and oddly beautiful—or at least the execution was beautiful, I do have to admit. It wasn't a parody. There was no ironic distance as they harmonized. They weren't making a mockery of Lennon's "love" lyrics. Quite the contrary, there was a sincere, heartfelt quality to what they were doing. Such scenes, unfathomable to 21ˢᵗ century sensibilities, seemed utterly natural in the universe of the early 1970s. I assure you, those same moments could not have found air to breathe in a post-1974 atmosphere. They continued to sing:

Love is wanting
To be loved
Love is touch
Touch is love
Love is reaching
Reaching love
Love is asking
To be loved
Love is you
You and me
Love is knowing
We can be

Only later, when I thought back to that night, did the scene strike me as more than a little surreal. Here were these two young radicals, at least one of them having no qualms about committing mayhem and violence to achieve his ends, softly rendering a musical paen to love. And they seemed to mean every word they sang. Having lived several decades since then, I can now make some sense of it. To Eddie and Cindy—and probably to Keith, as well—what they were doing *was* love, in the truest sense. By doing what they were doing, by risking everything, including their lives, they were expressing a higher form of "love" for the people. But just like the Jacobeans of late 18th century France, not everyone was worthy of their love for the "people." Those who got in their way... would have to be eliminated.

It was getting late now. Eddie and Cindy were again crouched silently on the floor near the soft light of the floor lamp. Eddie moaned, "Keith, come *on,* man!"

"Turn on the radio," suggested Cindy. "Maybe there's a news bulletin or something." Eddie flicked on the radio, switching through the channels. There was only music, talk shows, but no talk of the SLA.

Eddie shook his head. "See? Nothing, man. That's good." Grand Funk's "Locomotion" was now playing. Eddie got up and danced wildly. Cindy laughed at this. A few moments later, she joined him.

An hour or so later, Cindy and Eddie were cuddled together on a big pillow next to the floor lamp. Cindy had started to weep softly, "Something must have happened." Eddie whispered some (presumably) words of comfort and assurance to her but I couldn't hear what he was saying. Suddenly, Eddie's body rose with a start and he clamped his hand over Cindy's mouth. He reached over and switched off the lamp. "Quiet!" he said in an urgent whisper.

Now Eddie bolted over to where I sat, bound in my chair. He whipped out a scarf and gagged my mouth with it. "Make one sound, you're dead!" he warned. In the next instant flashlight beams bounced against the front windows of the house.

Cindy crouched on the floor. She appeared terrified. I could actually hear her whimpering. A face peered in through the front window. It appeared to be a young Marine! He called out in a commanding voice, "Is there anyone in there?"

Eddie was still hovering over me when the Marine called out. Whispering frantic obscenities, Eddie pulled out a handgun from his over-sized Army jacket. He crawled towards the back kitchen. By now, the flashlight beams had disappeared from the front of the house, but now they lit up the lights of the back bedroom windows. Now we could hear the voice of the young Marine again, this time from the back of the house:

"Police! Someone in there?" In the next instant there were two loud pops—gunshots. My heart leaped in my chest. This was followed by a pained grunt, then the heavy thud of a body slamming against the outer wall of the house. From the next room, Cindy screamed.

My sudden flicker of hope was dashed when Eddie bolted into the house from the back door. I could still smell the smoke from his fired pistol. Now Cindy was hysterical. Eddie bolted past me and yanked Cindy to her feet. He yelled at her. "I had to, man! You want the pigs on us?!"

As if suddenly remembering they were trying to lay low, Eddie switched off the floor lamp. Cindy was inconsolable. "We can't just leave him out there!"

Eddie took a quick look out the front window. All appeared dark. "We have to split, man. We have to split now! We can cut through..."

Before Eddie could finish his sentence, a low-flying helicopter swooped over the house. Floodlights from above engulfed the safe house. There was the sound of a man on a bullhorn, "Attention! Stay in your homes! Do not leave your homes! Police action! Do not leave your homes!"

Eddie cursed. The voice from the bullhorn kept up his commands. At that time it faded out, but then returned stronger when the chopper swooped again over the house. Eddie peered out the window. It was starting to get light. "Pigs everywhere," seethed Eddie through his teeth.

Now Eddie crawled over to a nearby closet. To my horror he began pulling out a startling collection of guns and ammunition. I had no idea they were armed to this extent. Eddie slid a gun over to Cindy. "This is it, man! We make a stand here. For the people!"

Cindy seemed to be breaking down, but as if by reflex, she loaded her gun. Looking back, it was clear she had been trained for this moment, weeks or months in advance. Nevertheless, reality was hitting her. Hard. "I don't want to die!" she wept.

"We all gotta die, baby," moaned Eddie. "But we'll take some pigs with us."

I was terrified. There was going to be a shootout. People were going to be killed. And I could well be one of them. I said my prayers of confession. I was almost certainly going to be standing in front of my maker soon. Yet this could not be. I was only twelve. Surely my parents and my brothers weren't going to be subjected to my funeral! Please, God, stop this from happening.

Now Eddie came rushing to where I sat in the back room. I was sure he was going to shoot me but instead, he untied me. "Let's go, man," he said, jerking me to my feet. "Try something and I blow your brains out!"

Then came a voice, bellowing through a bullhorn, "Come out of the house with your hands up! You are surrounded! Come out slowly with your hands up!"

Suddenly Cindy panicked. Eddie yelled at her to stop, reached out to grab her arm but he was too late—she was already dashing out the side door of the house, pistol in hand. As Eddie held me fast, screaming at Cindy to stop, I caught a glimpse of Cindy raising her weapon.

I cannot describe the horror and heartsickness of that next moment. As I looked on, Cindy crumpled to the ground in a hail of gunfire. She had let out one last piercing scream before suddenly growing silent.

Screaming in anguish and rage, Eddie hurled me to the floor, forgetting I was his one and only bargaining chip. He then proceeded to smash the front window glass with the butt of his gun. He started firing wildly. Bullets ripped back into the house in answer. I lay flat, face down on the floor, my hands covering the back of my head. There was the sickening sound of bullets ripping into flesh and bone, a loud cry of agony, then the heavy sound of Eddie's body dropping to the floor. I allowed myself a peek over at what had taken place. There lay Eddie. All I could see was the bottom of his tattered Keds sneakers. But I could also see the blood spreading out on the floor. I closed my eyes and laid where I was, not daring to move. Not daring to breathe.

A terrible quiet fell over the back neighborhood semi-circle where our safe house was located. But then I heard the thud of boots on the floor of the living room. They came over to where I lay. A deep, calm voice spoke to me, "Get up, son. It's all right."

Chapter 31
Aftermath

I had only been captive for three days. It had felt like five months.

I was led out onto the front lawn by a law officer in a suit and tie. To me, he was like the real-life *Hawaii Five-O*. Outside, awaiting me, were a gaggle of armed policemen and MPs. And my parents. They smothered me in hugs and kisses. Mom's face was covered with tears of happiness and relief. In the street, newsmen with cameras were starting to gather. Just a few feet away along the front curb, covered bodies were being loaded into medic trucks. With all the activity swirling around me, I stammered reflexive assurances of 'I'm okay' to my folks. At the same time, I was awash in a hazy stupor of wildly mixed emotions—lingering fears that SLA radicals were still lurking, happiness, grief, embarrassment. Policemen were already rolling yellow crime scene tape around the perimeter of the "safe house." This unit had no doubt been chosen by my SLA captors as it was one of three back cul-de-sac units that always seemed to be empty.

As I was to later find out, something had indeed gone wrong with Keith's mission the night before. Upon being stopped at the guard entrance to Manana, Keith had panicked. Just as

Cindy had done. Keith tried to shoot his way through. It didn't last long. In the moments that followed, with a large crowd of Manana residents and nearby civilian locals gathered around the bullet-riddled van and Keith's bloodied body lying in the road, it was not hard to figure that the "Hawaii Chapter of the SLA" was somewhere in the vicinity.

Of course it was a poorly thought out and executed plan. I also later learned that the full SLA "gang" unit consisted only of Eddie, Cindy, Keith, and some other guy I'd never met. None of them had any connection whatsoever with the California Symbionese Liberation Army. Despite this, the apparent plan was to link up with Patty Hearst and her SLA comrades in California. Somehow. To this day, I'm not even sure how any of the "Hawaii SLA" planned to even get off the island.

What Cindy, Eddie, and Keith did not realize, however, was that they were trying to squeeze money from the wrong family. Mom later enlightened me to the fact that while great grand-dad did indeed own a lot of prime property in what would become the business district of Los Angeles, he had actually lost it all during the Great Depression.

That first night home, I lay in bed with the lights out, staring up at the ceiling. While it was great to sleep in my own bed again, all I could think about was Cindy. I thought about the first time I had seen her, singing "Love Can Make You Happy" with her family. She was such a vision of loveliness, and I never lost my infatuation with her. I couldn't believe she was gone. I couldn't hold back the tears, though I did my best to weep silently (so my brothers wouldn't hear).

Naturally Dad officiated at Cindy's memorial service and funeral. While the graveside funeral would be a private family affair, our family attended the memorial service and reception afterwards. That reception was held at Leeward Hall on the grounds of lower Camp Smith, overlooking the city of Honolulu.

The Hall was filled with friends and relatives, all offering condolences to the bereaved Medlock family. Mr. and Mrs. Medlock, along with Brent, stood in a receiving area near the panoramic windows. Just off to the side was a display table bearing a large, framed picture of Cindy, adorned with Hawaiian flowers. Mr. Medlock, a Marine Major, stood stoic, never once removing his dark aviator glasses. Mrs. Medlock, by contract, wept openly. Yet even through her tears she made it a point, as did Mr. Medlock, to profusely apologize for what Cindy and her companions had put me through. I said it was all right, mainly so they wouldn't have to feel any worse.

As for Brent, he stood with his parents, shook hands, and exchanged hugs with those who came forward to express their condolences. On this day, however, the normally smiling Brent seemed to be fighting back tears. There was finally a moment when Brent was standing off by himself. I chose that moment to go over to him. Eric came with me. Brent saw us coming and smiled warmly. I was amazed that he could manage to smile at all.

"Hi Brent," I said.

"Hi Alan!" chirped Brent. Brent then turned to Eric and called Eric by his little league nickname (a nickname he'd earned during an impressive showing in batting practice): "Hey, little Dynamite!" Eric smiled, but didn't seem to know what to say.

As for me, I was the older brother. I had to say something. "I'm real, real sorry, Brent."

Brent turned more serious. "Thanks. Hey, I'm sorry too. She shouldn't have done to you what she did."

"She was still nice to me. Way more than those two other guys. She was the only one that didn't want me to get hurt."

Brent forced a smile. "Yeah, that's Cindy."

"I never wanted anything to happen to her."

Brent smiled again, but this time tears welled up in his eyes. He lightly punched me on the arm. "You're all right. Outta sight!"

I laughed. I wanted to cheer him up. Eric laughed too. But then, Brent lost his composure. The tears took over and he turned away. A relative came over to embrace him. I felt so bad for him but there was nothing more I could do. I led Eric away.

A few moments later, I saw a middle-aged man in uniform—he looked to be Italian or Greek—approach Mrs. Medlock. He took her by the hand and squeezed. He leaned in to whisper some words to her. He too seemed to be highly emotional. They embraced.

At that moment, Mr. Medlock stormed across the room. Cursing, Mr. Medlock grabbed Mr. Tangen by the shirt lapels. There was a brief choking and shoving scuffle before a couple of younger Marines pulled the men apart. Dad also jumped in to help put the bear hug on Mr. Medlock. But the father of the deceased would not be placated. "What the hell kind of son did you raise?!" bellowed Mr. Medlock. "God damn you!"

Mr. Tangen yelled back, "You're not the only one who lost a child!"

Mr. Medlock wasn't through. "Your son deserved what he got! My daughter didn't have to die like that! She did *not* deserve to die like that!"

Several men were now pulling Mr. Medlock away from the reception area. Mr. Tangen turned and walked out. Things calmed down. It was a shocking outburst, but I understood it. After what I had gone through, I understood it.

A few minutes later, I wandered over to the far side of the reception hall. I happened upon one of the side rooms. The door was ajar. My eyes caught the sight of Dad praying with the huddled and grieving Medlock family. Brent briefly looked up. Our eyes met, but then I averted my eyes. I felt like I was intruding (which I actually was). It was the last time I would ever see the Medlock family.

Chapter 32
Another Manana Goodbye

Though I didn't realize it at the time, the day I saw Redbone down near the SLA hideout, he was actually supposed to have been in the Marines. The fact is, however, he had washed out of the Marines some two months earlier and had simply returned home to Manana. Once again, Redbone had taken to wandering around with the same vacant, defeated expression. Worst of all, Redbone had gotten back on drugs.

I always wondered how Redbone's parents felt, though I had never even seen them. Were they ashamed of him? Embarrassed? If his dad did hit him, was it because he didn't know how else to deal with this? Did his mom sit in the dark at home all day like some of my other friends' moms, depressed about her son? I was starting to realize that although both our houses were just one street apart, Redbone and his parents lived in a different world that even the Hawaiian sun couldn't penetrate.

One evening, shortly after I'd returned home from my SLA kidnapping ordeal, I was dangling—somewhat precariously—on a high branch of a favorite climbing tree in the front yard of our house. You could say I was showing off my monkey-like skills when Dad and Mom came walking up into the yard. I said something somewhat facetious in greeting. In answer, Dad looked up at me with a somber face and warned me to get down off that branch. "We've already lost one boy this evening. We don't need to lose another."

When I heard what happened, me and some friends jumped on our bikes and pedaled down the hill to the street below ours. A large crowd of neighbors was gathered in front of Redbone's house. Many were talking in hushed tones while others just stood silently with stricken faces and hands over their mouths. There were a couple of security trucks parked out front and an ambulance with emergency lights silently rotating.

Someone said Redbone had shot himself. Another person said, "No, he overdosed." I never found out which was true. But I remember the front door opening and two EMTs wheeling out a stretcher with a figure strapped to it, completely covered by a sheet. The "boogey man" was dead.

As I pedaled home, my mind kept replaying that Sunday afternoon at the ballfield. He had seemed so happy, just standing there playing baseball with a dad and three boys he didn't even know. Maybe it reminded him of when he was younger, before he wandered into that bewildering maze of drugs from which he never found his way out. Some of us, like my brothers and me, saw the allure of that maze, but our faith and families had a tight hold of our hands and quickly pulled us away.

Yet others are able to slip their parents' grip and wander inside the maze. At first parents tell themselves that it will be all right. They can see their son over the hedgerows, making his way around the outskirts of the confusing path. He is still close, close enough to grab. He will see the maze doesn't go anywhere and come back out soon.

But then the boy begins to make his way farther and farther into the labyrinth. If the boy is lucky, he will turn a corner and find a Coach Snyder or Mr. Dixon waiting. They are always on the look-out for boys like him. With a baseball glove or a scouting trip to aid them, these men will put an arm around a boys' shoulder and gently guide him back to safety. For others like Redbone, no such lifeguards appear and they keep wandering deeper into perplexing rows of ever-higher walls. Soon, the walls are so high they block out the sun and any chance of gaining their bearings. Now they are truly lost.

For parents it is too late to go in. All they can do is hurry around to the exit and wait. And wait. Wait for their son to emerge. In some cases, they do. They come stumbling out into the sunlight, legs wobbly, skin cut and bruised from years of abuse. But somehow they have escaped and are moving on with their lives. A few years later they will be telling jokes about how "wasted" they were back in the 60s and 70s. Many will laugh at these stories as if a trip through the maze is some endearing rite of passage.

But for other parents, the wait ends not with their son walking out of the maze, but being wheeled out. A nineteen-year-old boy, covered by a sheet, being wheeled down the hall of their home. Past the kitchen with handmade Mother's Day cards from third grade still tacked up on the fridge. Past a living room with the seventh-grade school picture of a smiling boy who likes Batman comic books and skateboards. Then out the front door into the glaring sun amidst the shocked stares and muffled whispers of the entire neighborhood. No rewinding the tape to do things different. No waking up. This is it. This is the moment they will have to come to terms with each day for the next fifty years. No endearing rite of passage here—just pain.

That night I did not fully appreciate how easily I might have been in Redbone's place if not for the family and faith I was blessed with. While Redbone's family faced an agonizing night one street down, I was tucked peacefully in the three-tiered bunk bed with my two younger brothers, John already asleep in the next room. We three told each other funny stories for a while, suppressing giggles so Dad wouldn't come in and tell us to be quiet. Soon, the sounds of heavy breathing from below my bunk told me my audience was done for the night.

As with the loss of Cindy Medlock, I took Redbone's death hard, though I internalized it more than I deigned to show outwardly. The fact is, Redbone probably saved my life. That time I had seen him down by the Pond 6 cabin? He wasn't a lookout for the "Hawaii Chapter of the SLA" at all. Redbone had simply wandered down there that day I saw him, as he had so many times before. As it turns out, after we happened upon each other, he returned to Manana and told some authorities that he "may have seen that chaplain's kid who was missing." At this, the local police sprang into action.

I lay awake in the dark with my thoughts. The only light was a sliver of gold coming from underneath the door, letting me know Mom and Dad were still up. There was no crying, no yelling, no slurred accusations—just the usual sounds: coffee cups clinking, the rustling of the *Honolulu Star-Bulletin*. There was the happy sound of Mom laughing at Tim Conway accidently giving himself a shot of Novocain in a skit on some *Carol Burnett Show*. Shortly after, there were muffled discussions between my parents about the events of the day and schedule for tomorrow. The sounds of security and a happy home.

I pulled out my transistor radio, a Christmas present from two years earlier, and tuned in to KKUA. Pressing the small speaker to my ear, I slowly drifted off to sleep as the static-y voice of Elton John lamented a lost brother:

> *Daniel is travelin' tonight on a plane*
> *I can see the red tail lights*
> *Headin' for Spain*
> *Oh and*
> *I can see Daniel wavin' goodbye*

God he looks like Daniel
Must be the clouds in my eyes
Oh God, he looks like Daniel
Must be the clouds in my eyes

God he looks like Daniel
Must be the clouds in my eyes
Oh God, he looks like Daniel
Must be the clouds in my eyes

Chapter 33
Going, Going, Gone

I became a celebrity of sorts after I returned home and once more resumed "normal life." I went back to school and was heartily welcomed back by, it seems, everybody! Even by the kids who menaced me when I walked down the hallway before. Granted, though, it was hard to concentrate on my final week of studies with cameramen and newscasters lurking outside the windows of my classrooms. For a while I kinda enjoyed the fame—everywhere I went, kids were clamoring for my attention. My recounting of how I heard all those bullets hitting the house as I lay on the floor of the safe house seemed to satisfy most of them. That story alone was enough to leave them staring wide-eyed, their mouths agape, gasping, "Hun-*nah*!"

As it turned out, I only missed two of my last three Little League games. On that final game day, those same cameramen and newscasters were massed behind the fence along the first base line. Sure, they were distracting, but I was used to them by now. I still managed to have a good last game, going two for four and hitting a double. More and more each day I was able to push my captivity and the SLA behind me. I was determined to return to my life of pursuing my baseball dream.

As my last Little League season wound to an end, I was seeing stars. Not the real ones that come out at night, but those cartoon ones circling my head, the result of multiple blows to my ego, sustained over a long season. Yet, beyond these punch-drunk stars there emerged much brighter ones signifying the start of All-Star season: my final chance to redeem myself and to write a happy ending to the last four months. But somebody forgot to tell the Pentagon.

Right before the coaches voted on the 1974 Manana Navy/Marine All-Stars, my father received orders to Kentucky. It's not every day a Navy man gets assigned to a state that's approximately 600 miles away from the nearest ocean. But this was a special case. Dad had been selected to take a one-year sabbatical from the Navy and pursue his Master's Degree. He elected to enroll at Asbury Theological Seminary in Wilmore, Kentucky, the institution from which he had graduated in 1966 when I was four.

I was happy for Dad but upset that the Navy had disregarded what effect such a move would have on my future baseball prospects. I knew the military was very busy untangling itself from Vietnam, but for goodness sake, wasn't there *someone* at the Pentagon keeping an eye out on the home front? It was enough to make a young Republican throw away his "Nixon '72" buttons and join the McGovern camp.

So there would be no All-Stars for me, or for Eric, who was eligible for the first time. We were crushed. No potential trip to the glorious stadium at Williamsport, Pennsylvania, for the Little League World Series.

Some of the coaches felt bad for us and tried to ease our disappointment. Mr. Redelman said Eric and I could practice with the team until we moved, and even arranged for an exhibition game just so we could get some all-star competition under our belts. Another coach who I barely knew offered to let me stay and live with his family until All-Stars was over, but that didn't work out.

At the last Little League All-Stars practice in which I participated, Duane McGregor and I met on the mound to alternate pitching batting practice. True to form, after pitching practice was over, I hurried over to consult with the catcher. Nonchalantly I whispered to him, "Who was faster, Duane or me?" I guess bad habits die hard.

A week later our family moved out of our temporary lodgings at the luxurious Hale Kalani Hotel and boarded a 0630 AM flight back to the mainland. It was a sad morning for me. Despite the occasional harassment for being a haole, I loved Hawaii. Overall, the local kids I knew in school were wonderful, Manana was a great place to live, and what could be better for a budding baseball player than year-round tropical weather?

For the first time in my young life, I was old enough to know what I was leaving and to worry about what lay ahead at our new home. Would I make friends in Kentucky? What would happen with my baseball there? Would I ever see Hawaii again?

As the plane rose up over Honolulu, it hit me that I was flying all the way across the ocean. A song kept playing in my head—one that had played on the local radio a lot lately even though the track first came out in 1966. It was The Rascal's, "My Hawaii," and the heart-achingly sung lyrics kept filling my mind: "… I'll return… and spend my life… in… Ha-wa-ii…!" At this, the singer's voice trailed off in almost a choked cry.

But who knew when we would ever return to Hawaii? Let's face it, it's not the kind of place you stop by to visit while you're driving someplace else. Also what were the odds of … "Hey kids, since we're taking the sailboat to Japan, what do you say we stop over in Oahu and do some visiting?" And even if we did make it back in a few years, it would never be the same. All my military friends would have moved, scattered to a dozen other bases across the globe. Returning to an old military base is like coming back to your hometown and seeing all the houses are occupied by strangers.

As the 747 banked left, I could see Honolulu shrinking below, the ocean glistening as the sun began to rise. The island looked so small. It was hard to believe I had lived and experienced so many things on that small patch of green in the middle of the ocean for over three years. For the second time, I had a strong feeling that I was sitting in a front row seat to a turning point in my life, that I was witnessing a scene which would play over and over in my mind for years to come.

The next few weeks were jarring. We landed in Los Angeles, picked up our camper van which we had sent over by ship and took a long meandering trip across the country. Many of our stops were exciting: the 1974 World's Fair in Spokane; my Uncle Wes and Aunt Susan's house in Idaho; taking in a jaw-dropping canyon in Utah; camping by a river in the Ozarks with my grandparents and cousins. But the physical environment was unsettling. The majestic mountains, vast expansive deserts, large cities, and even the turbulent summer weather struck me like the foreign environments of a different planet. And where were they hiding all the Asians and Islanders? I was also very much aware that each turn of the wheel took me further and further away from Hawaii, from my cherished memories of school and baseball and strangely enough, from Cindy Medlock. I began to sense a new feeling, a kind of sad longing which seemed to hang over me like a heavy coat.

Postscript

As we settled into our new Kentucky home that fall, my brothers and I tried to recreate our Hawaii baseball practice routine. There was no nearby baseball park, so we used an open field a block from the house. Since it was just an uncultivated field, the conditions were very frustrating. Apparently, the grass was only mowed at the beginning of a new Presidential administration. I heard it was a particularly bad time for kid baseball players when FDR didn't give up the White House for twelve years. The ball was constantly getting lost in the tall grass and weeds. On one occasion, after nearly twenty minutes of searching, we not only found our ball but also discovered seven old washing machines and a rusted 1965 Ford Mustang.

Even when balls were batted into very short grass not far from where we stood, they would still sometimes mysteriously disappear. This was a phenomenon which we had also experienced in Hawaii. If one was a conspiracy theorist it would be easy to imagine there was some loosely-organized worldwide confederation of ground hogs who snatched baseballs, retreated into their underground tunnels, and sold these prizes for a hefty profit in the black markets of Hong Kong. I just know that there is some kingpin's kid overseas that has a dozen baseballs in his closet with "Cook" scrawled on them.

Besides the thieving ground hogs and tall grass, our field was pockmarked by rodent and snake holes, large rocks, various wildlife creatures, and just general uneven terrain, making baseball competition more than a little tedious. I was beginning to see why *basketball* was so popular in this state—there were no decent flat fields on which to play baseball!

Even the local high school's baseball field sloped ridiculously down the right field line. Standing at home plate, it appeared the right-fielder had nothing but an upper torso. The last straw came when the weather turned cold and our aluminum bat turned into a tuning fork whenever we hit a pitch. The sensation was that of a jolt of electricity being sent through your hands and forearms. So one day, I announced, "Boys, it's time to play basketball." And so we did—every day.

Maybe our eventual move over from baseball to the world of basketball wasn't that cut and dried, but it's not too much of a stretch. The fact is, though we still retained a fondness for baseball and we never truly abandoned it, by high school all of us boys spent far more time on the hardwood than on a diamond. Of the four of us boys, Kevin most retained his baseball passion and all-star caliber talent, the longest.

The Homecoming

My first return to Manana since leaving in 1974, took place in 2004. To my surprise, the old 1950s style housing units were still there. But they were abandoned. All were soon due for the wrecking ball. New, two-story units with red tile roofs were to replace these old familiar, but beloved, warhorses that held so many memories. I must admit, it was eerie and more than a little sad to drive and walk around the wide Manana streets. Where once they had been a beehive activity with children playing in yards and in the roadways, now there was hardly a soul in sight. The few people to be seen were mostly government or construction people.

Our house at Birch Circle still stood, and I knew I was looking at it for the last time. Like the other units in Manana, our house was empty. I wanted so much to walk up to it, peek in all the windows. But there were official-looking people walking around and I didn't want to come off as suspicious. I'm not sure how my pleas of, "I happen to be an upstanding officer in the Air Force," would be digested under these circumstances. So I simply stood in the yard and stared, swimming in a flood of memories.

The big empty grass field towards the back of our housing unit was still there, but much overgrown. The rusted chain link fence at the edge of the field was also still there, and by its aged appearance, I wondered if it was the same fence Redbone and we boys climbed over on many an occasion.

Lastly I wandered to the far edge of the housing area, to the back street cul de sac where the "SLA Safe House" once stood. It was gone. In fact, you couldn't even tell a house had ever stood there at all. This did not come as a complete surprise. In the ensuring years since we left Hawaii, we had heard that the house had indeed been torn down. What family would want to be stationed in a house with such a terrible history?

Naturally, I made my way down to the old Manana ballfield. It was still there but was run down to a dismaying degree. The dugouts looked rickety and rusted. The once neat dirt base paths were now just uneven patches of grass and dirt. The outfield fence was gone. Once the true tangible measuring stick of our hitting prowess, a vacant stretch of grass only now marked where that fence once stood. Just beyond that vacant stretch of grass was the familiar tarp-covered fence behind which, now, was an empty, abandoned swimming pool.

That night, in my Honolulu hotel room, I decided to record my thoughts on revisiting all the happy and not-so-happy haunts of my Manana years. At the time I was working on my Master's, and these observations would be the genesis of a course paper. I still have a hard copy of what I wrote at that time:

"They were revolutionaries. Terrorists. They were determined to topple the U.S. establishment by violent means. At the same time they intended to create a utopia for the 'people,' the poor, the oppressed—but it had to be by their definition. In that climate of early 1974 they were no joke. Were they dangerous? Certainly, any hot-headed young adult carrying armed weapons is dangerous, so yes. Still, with the benefit of some 30 years hindsight, they hardly seem to have been legitimate 'revolutionaries' or 'urban guerillas.' Now, in 2004, young radicals of that makeup seem to be relics of a bygone era. They simply don't exist anymore. Perhaps in the end, my tormentors were something more common and universal: simply, just a bunch of 'dumb kids.'"

As it turned out, that 2004 observation was premature... and quite wrong. The Symbionese Liberation Army—the genuine article out in California, as well as the would-be Hawaii SLA I encountered—had offspring. They lay dormant for decades, but they started to awaken around the mid-2010s, and by 2020, they had exploded coast to coast. Youth who wanted "revolution" and were willing to go to violent ends to achieve it, were suddenly everywhere. And they turned out to be every bit as militant as the Yippies of the late 60s and early 70s.

I can't help but wonder if the Medlocks ever came back to Manana. Though such a pilgrimage might seem unimaginable, people do revisit sites of tragedy, if only to leave a wreath or flowers in memoriam. It's not like our family lost track of the Medlocks—after they left Hawaii (just a little later than us in 1974), they settled in Illinois where they still live today. Every year, they still send my parents a Christmas card and Christmas letter. Though they would often write a personal note of thanks to Dad and Mom for how they ministered to and supported them after the tragedy, I could not help but notice how Cindy Medlock was nowhere to be found in those official, yearly Christmas family bulletins. As sad as I found this to be, how could I blame them?

As for the families of Eddie Tangen and Keith Turner, I know less. There is no way of knowing if they dwell on that terrible spring of 1974, or if they've tried to move on with their lives by bringing their lost loved ones to mind as little as possible. I don't know—grief and loss works in different ways for different people. As Willie Nelson once sang, "It's not something you get over. It's something you get through."

Amazingly, I did actually hear from Keith Turner's daughter back in 2002. Yes, Keith was actually the father of a little girl at the time of my kidnapping. She was only a toddler at the time. When she tracked me down and wrote to me, she was a 28-year-old woman living in Florida and working as a school teacher. She asked me what I remembered about her father. I tried to be as gracious as possible, but it was a struggle to remember anything about Keith that I considered to be redeemable qualities. To my surprise, she told me that her father actually had aspirations to be a professional musician and was allegedly a talented bass player. So it would appear there was more to Keith than the terrifying individual I knew.

On these memories, on these questions, my musings will never allow me to find my way to fully satisfying answers as to why, as to what did it all mean? Nor would I say it's healthy to continually dwell on the past. But every now and again, it can't be helped. I supposed you could say I'm nostalgic by nature.

Earlier I talked in length about the dark labyrinth that Redbone and others like him never escaped. Simply by indulging the dark memories of what happened that late spring of 1974, I could also have found myself trapped there. The cost could have been an ongoing decay of my mental and spiritual health. But at some point I had to grab onto something that wouldn't deteriorate—and that turned out to be the very truths my parents strived to instill in us boys at home, in church, in those simple Sunday School lessons. The dark world is very real. But one lived on this planet who took every ounce of horror (even up to death) that this dark world had to throw at him. When he unexpectantly rose and walked out of the tomb, he not only found his captors cowering in fear, he trampled them underfoot and took any hope of permanent power away from them for good. That's the Good News.

It's that time of year again. It's spring again and baseball is again in the air. In fact, tomorrow night I'll be going down to the local municipal park to watch my son's first Little League game. No, he's not playing—his Little League years are long over. It will, however, be his first game as head coach of the Cubs. What's more, he'll be carrying on a highly worthy tradition. You see, my stocky son showed up at the first practice he called, wearing a white polo shirt and a white ball cap (okay, the bill was blue). He told his newly-gathered team, "When you arrive at the park for practice or games, I won't be hard to find. Just look for the big white blob."

Acknowledgements

This book would absolutely not have been possible without our parents, Dean and Ruth Cook, to whom we not only owe our mutual happy childhoods, but who are also the very reasons we were able to experience a portion of our youth in the Hawaiian Islands. Granted, my brothers and I all went more than a little baseball batty while we lived on Oahu, nevertheless, Dad and Mom took time out from their busy schedules to take us to ball practices, attend our Little League games and on top of all that, drive us deep into Honolulu to attend Hawaii Islander baseball games. We thought we would repay their time and efforts by becoming All Star Major League baseball players, but... came up a bit short in that quest.

We are also in debt to the very first baseball coaches we ever had—those who taught us the fundamentals of the game as well as the decorum of sportsmanship. The world definitely needs more Coach Snyders and Coach Redelmans today! However, we would also be remiss if we did not acknowledge those boys we played with *and* against—our buddies who contended (sometimes heatedly) with us on the ball field as we sharpened each other's skills.

Scott and I are also fortunate to have wives and families who stood by us, supporting our writing efforts (as opposed to subjecting us to comments along the lines of "pipe dream" or "Why don't you just write a short story?").

Lastly, there were those Major League heroes of the early 70's whose exploits inspired us and whose cards we coveted. Sadly, three of those mentioned prominently in this book passed away just this past year: Vida Blue, Brooks Robinson and Willie "Say Hey" Mays. We loved watching you play (even if it was on delayed, black and white television).

About the Authors

Delmer T and Scott Cook are brothers who grew up with the shared experience of not only having lived in Hawaii for three years as military dependents back in the early 70's, but also shared a passion for all things baseball at the time. Hence, the inspiration for this novel.

Both Delmer T and Scott have authored books in recent years. Most recent was Delmer T's 2022 work, DeShazer: Greatest Story from the Greatest Generation. The year prior, Scott Cook's book, Rehearsing for Doomsday was published by McFarland Books. In addition, Delmer T has published the following books: Pirates & Rogues of Monterey Bay (2019), Nueva California (2018) and Madame (2011).

Delmer T and Scott currently live in Kentucky and Florida respectively, though their youngest brother, Jonathan, and his family, live in Honolulu, thus keeping the Cook Hawaiian tradition alive.